Elizabeth Wilson is Professor in the Faculty of Environmental and Social Studies at the University of North London. She has long been involved in the women's movement, the lesbian and gay movement and in left politics. She is the author of a number of books, including *Adorned in Dreams* (Virago, 1985) and *The Sphinx in the City* (Virago, 1991), and contributes to the *Guardian* and *New Statesman and Society*. She lives in London with her partner and daughter.

Elizabeth Wilson

The Lost Time Café

Published by VIRAGO PRESS Limited, 1993
20–23 Mandela Street, Camden Town, London NW1 OHQ

*A CIP catalogue record for this book is
available from the British Library*

Typeset by The Electronic Book Factory, Fife, Scotland
Printed in Britain by Cox & Wyman Ltd., Reading, Berks.

Acknowledgements

I should like to thank Ruthie Petrie and Faith Evans for all their help and support; also Angie, for saying that it was not as bad as she had thought it would be.

I am indebted to David Cesarini's *Justice Delayed: How Britain Became a Refuge for Nazi War Criminals*, London, Heinemann, 1992. Acknowledgements are due to the following: Romuald Misiunas and Rein Taagepera, *The Baltic States: Years of Dependence: 1940–1980*, London, C Hurst and Co., 1983; Milda Danys, *D.P.: Lithuanian immigration to Canada after the Second World War*; Toronto Ontario: Multicultural History Society, 1986; *The New Statesman*, 1945–1947; and *The Daily Worker*, 1945–1948.

In memory of David Widgery

A sense of irony
did not vitiate your indignation
nor your compassion

' "I learned that one can never go back, that one should not ever try to go back – that the essence of life is going forward. Life is really a One Way Street, isn't it?" '

Agatha Christie,
At Bertram's Hotel

'A perpetual stream of strangers and provincials flowed into the capacious bosom of Rome. Whatever was strange or odious, whoever was guilty or suspected, might hope in the obscurity of that immense capital to elude the vigilance of the law.'

Edward Gibbon,
The Decline and Fall of the Roman Empire

Prologue

Her hand hung down towards the floor. Exquisite nails, redcurrant nails; nails like red poison berries – their redness was absolute with no trace of orange or blue, just dulled, darkened and shiny, like drops of blood. Those perfect nails, they were the point at which flesh became art.

All else was a wave of black hair and a blue robe, a tumbled body on an unmade bed. The orange curtains, drawn together, suffused the room in a hot half-light. A fly fizzed against the windowpane. The air smelled of stale biscuits, but there was an undertow of something worse, of something beginning to be sweet and rotten.

I bent forward to shake her by the shoulder, to touch her hand. How could a hand be cold in that hot room? The clammy coldness, like an electric shock, jerked me back against the wall. I edged towards the door, still looking, afraid to turn away. I moved slowly at first, then faster, faster – till I was running down the stairs, running through the shadowed house in a whirling eddy of panic and horror, running, running away. Behind me, the dusty air settled back on itself once more, in layers and sheets of silence, which draped and stifled the empty rooms, so deathly, so waiting, so still.

Chapter
One

The motorway was never empty. Day and night fellow travellers hummed along like beads threaded on wires of speed, pulsing together, suspended molecules zizzing through space, each locked up alone in the capsule of a time machine: loneliness without solitude.

At three in the morning I'd been one of a group of travellers straggling into the empty airport out of a last, late plane, final drops of the daily gush of humanity washed across the planet. I'd skated along the moving floor as if with winged heels. At each barrier stood one uniformed official – but no-one had tried to stop me, no-one had asked for reasons – although I could have told them: it was all because my father died.

An airport was neither heaven nor hell, just the twentieth century version of Limbo, a nowhere, a place where anything goes and nothing could happen. Not until I broke cover into the hot, acrid darkness outside the terminal did I return to an earthly world of pollution, viruses and murder.

I braved the hopeless monotony and loneliness of the long-term carpark and as usual it was a surprise to find my car, still there where I'd parked it three months earlier, my Murasaki, a silver car like a bomb in its silo, as if nothing had happened, as if time had stood still, as if I'd never been away.

As I coasted the curve of the roundabout I met up with the others – my companions. In a shoal we swept the camber, accelerated down the sliproad and roared into liftoff on the motorway, speeding towards an unnatural floodlit night. My fingers barely touched the wheel as I burned forward unreeling down the endless road like one of the scarves of mist that floated above the metal surface. Time capsules moved past and dropped behind on their parallel lines, each metal bubble encased the anonymous head and shoulders of a robotic traveller, tranquil and motionless yet flowing along in a stream of moving time.

Two drew level with me and as they hovered alongside, I saw that they were driving Murasakis too. Identical triplets, we drove together for the length of the highway, now one, now another driving ahead, then falling back – a trio of strangers riding together. When we came to the struts of concrete bolted into the knot that marks the end of the motorway, each of us spontaneously lifted a hand in greeting and farewell as we peeled off under the overpass and splintered into our separate ways.

I came round a bend onto the ring road, and then, while I was still in the shadow of the high wall, there was a tremendous jolt. I braked, screeching up against the wall, and came to a halt as a flashing light and a high pitched siren wail came round the bend and a motorbike bumped to a stop just in front. The figure who walked towards me was armoured in black leather from ear to toe and wore a helmet that hid the face.

'You know you ran over a dog just back there.'

I got stiffly out and looked back to where a body as large as a panther's lay in the road, a stream of blood trickling away from its head.

'You were coming too fast round the bend.'

I felt dizzy. I leant against the car, might be sick. The cop – if that's what he was – pushed back his visor and I glimpsed his unfriendly eyes, black pools in their sockets. The sodium lights pulsated brightly and little caterpillars of red and purple throbbed across my field of vision. There was a violent pain in my head.

I lay in a white room. The walls were white. The bed was white. Through the window I could see the white, white sky. Against the sky was a building like a flying saucer.

I could see myself lying on the bed. My face was a mask of perfection, the brows and lashes skilfully darkened and drawn in fine black lines, the lips a perfect ogee painted red. My hair was tucked away off my brow and out of sight beneath a headband made of crêpe bandage.

I seemed to be floating above the bed, I clung like a dove to a corner of the ceiling, gripped with admiration of my perfected self. The gauzy curtains floated in the breeze.

I opened my eyes. A man in a white coat smiled down at me.

'Feeling better now?'

I opened my mouth to speak, but my throat was parched.

'We'll soon have you back on your feet again.'

Then I noticed the plastic tube that linked me to a bottle of transparent liquid suspended above the bed. At the sight of it I seemed to disintegrate, my perfection was shattered, and I became no more than a bag of bits and pieces held together by that plastic umbilical cord, an assortment of unconnected functions, malfunctioning circuits, detached wires.

I was pierced by needles, invaded by rays, they took specimens of my bodily fluids to be deconstructed in some distant anonymous laboratory.

How long did this go on? If I disintegrated, so did time. I didn't count the days. And no one knew I was there. With my father dead, my husband left behind, there was no one *to* know.

And then one day, the plastic lifeline and the plastic bottle had gone. I could sit up. I felt hungry. I was alive.

4

The daylight was very bright. They brought me a meal they called lunch, and after I'd eaten it I swung my legs to the floor and stood up. It was hard at first. I was stiff. But I made it. I walked to the window. I was high up. I looked out over the city, Kakania. It stretched away to the horizon in every direction, a little hazy in the hot, late sun. I had come home.

I looked round the room. There was a cupboard in the corner. I opened it. In it was a white coat and a pair of trainers, nothing else. I'd expected my own clothes. Nothing – I found nothing but my bag in the bedside locker, and a niggling shadow crossed my mind, a frisson of paranoia. They took away my clothes – as if they'd wanted to keep me a prisoner.

I dressed myself in the white drill overall – quite smart, a kind of coat dress – and tied on the gym shoes, which were a touch too large. In my bag I found my make-up, that was the main thing. With lipstick and mascara I could pass for, well, for sane. When I'd made myself look as normal as possible I opened the door of the room. A corridor stretched ahead of me. I walked to its end, and found a stairwell lit by a wall of glass bricks. I held on to the flat, black painted metal bannister rail and started down the stairs. I was so stiff. I counted ten flights before I came to a door like the exit doors you find in cinemas; I pushed on the horizontal rail and found myself in a residential side street.

I walked down the road, turned a corner, and hit the expressway, which roared above my head. I walked along the road which ran alongside and beneath it until I reached a bus stop. There I waited. It seemed like a long time – already I was wilting in the late afternoon heat. I began to feel afraid. What if I were still ill? My stomach churned, my heart jumped – were these symptoms of the illness, the accident, or . . . something else?

A bus finally cruised into sight. I climbed upstairs and sat at the front with the city opening out before me.

This city was wonderful. Built on hills it glittered in the sunlight. From the air it seemed so small, but as you drew near it swelled and swelled and as you dived in it engulfed you.

The bus rolled slowly down towards the centre. The city seethed like a maggoty sponge, yet its surface sparkled. It presented its oleander bushes of pink and cream flowers like bouquets. Here children played by lakes where parrots and bluebirds tumbled out of the trees; there, in the silver towers of the moneymarket, machines clicked and chattered to send money flying around the world, enlaced with the airwaves sending words and images that also circled the globe.

I was sucked right into this great sponge. I looked down and saw streets choked with traffic. At each curb the crowd massed and waited; the individual atoms of which it was composed spread out round obstacles – road works, street vendors; they hurried singly or pressed forward in pairs, loitered or stopped, turned and zigzagged, and the sum of their individual movements wove into a great web the life of the city. I felt removed from it all. I looked down as if from a great height, but this was an illusion. I was about to plunge in, I had a destination too; I was going back to my father's house, I was going home again.

In my father's house she waited for me. Her hand hung down towards the floor. So deathly, so waiting, so still.

Chapter Two

Bulky and exposed, my father's house reared darkly up, casting a shadow across the space that opened out where three streets converged at the top of the hill. They were deserted, but I felt as if unseen eyes watched me – from the house, from all the houses staring blankly, blindly at me.

Someone was waiting for me. My father had died in strange circumstances. Now there'd been a second death – so someone had come back. That must be right, mustn't it; two deaths in the same house must be connected. Yet who could have wanted to kill Anna?

So perhaps they'd come for me. Perhaps they'd made a mistake, thought Anna was his daughter. Was me.

Or maybe I was going absolutely crazy. I'd gone mad, that was it. That cop had cracked me on the head and stamped all over me, damaged my brain.

To get away as quickly as possible, that was the idea. It would be a long walk back down the hill. I was still weak. But I mustn't hesitate – someone might still be hidden in the shadows, at the turn of the stair, behind a half-closed door.

Then I remembered. I went round to the garage at the side of the house. I unlocked it, and there in the shadows my father's car was waiting, shabby and familiar, an old cream Lada Riva. I had its keys. I had all my father's keys. I got in. I sat in the sagging seat. It was so shabby, but it reminded me of my father – old-fashioned, from another era, like him. I rested my head against the steering wheel and began to cry.

I soon stopped, though. I had to. I was on my own now. No father, no husband, a woman alone. I had to get moving. Only – where? Where should I go? I thought about it.

After a while I drove away from the quiet street, down the hilly turnings of the old town, past the squat palm trees in the square, and up on to the expressway. I cruised past blocks of flats, past rundown residential districts, past the Botanical Gardens and past the shattered factories until I joined the traffic gliding towards the bars and cafés that had spread out around the bay.

'Adam.' I made it warm and intimate, but casual, as if I'd seen him yesterday.

It *was* Adam, wasn't it? He turned – blank for a split second, before a look of panic disturbed the smooth arrangement of his face.

'It's me. I've come back. Don't look so upset. I thought you'd be pleased to see me.'

'I'm not – I am. *Of course* I'm pleased to see you.'

He leant forward and kissed my cheek. He smelled different – richer, with a tang of citrus fruits: Dior *Eau Sauvage*. I didn't like it – not on him at any rate. Also, he'd had his teeth capped. Before, they'd been rather unpleasant. Now they were smooth and white.

'You've changed,' he said. 'Your hair – you've cut off all your hair. Still look great, of course.' And then he looked away, as if he wished he hadn't said that. 'I heard you were in town,' he said.

'Who told you? *Who told you?* No one knows I'm here. I haven't *seen* anyone –'

'No one. Honest. Why are you so upset? I just said it, don't ask me why. I dunno, I just had a feeling. Intuition

8

– I was thinking of you.' He laughed nervously. 'Only joking.'

'What's the matter with you? I come in and you look like you've seen a ghost, you knew I was here, you didn't know I was here – what is this?'

'Hey . . . don't get upset. I was just surprised, that's all. Have a drink.'

Yet it hadn't been exactly surprise . . . or rather, it had been more than surprise.

'I haven't any money. I need a cash machine.'

'On the house, of course.'

'In that case – I'll have a margarita.'

While he made it I looked around. Most of the Café was in shadow, but at the far end of the front salon light glittered through the venetian blinds and cast stripes of shadow across the terracotta floor. That was new – the blinds. Bit of a cliché. Otherwise the place hadn't changed. Large mirrors doubled the size of the rooms, and they were furnished with a haphazard selection of second-hand chairs, sofas and tables: little round antique tables, square marble-topped tables, tables with formica tops grained like black granite, painted tables – and the chairs arranged round them were various as well, bentwood, Italian matt black, squiggly metal with absurdly high backs. And the sofas – a Victorian *chaise-longue* with its guts hanging out, overstuffed art deco monsters, 1960s modern . . . The jumble of styles made for an atmosphere almost like it was someone's sitting room. The walls were painted in cheap pastel shades of flesh colour, *eau de nil* and peach. Rickety shelves held postcards, old books, little vases. A staircase to one side wound up and round to a balcony decorated with plaster swags painted in gold, pale pink and pastel blue. Up there, or so I remembered, was one big table piled with old magazines, and plastic wall vases filled with artificial flowers.

The Café – this was the Café Des Temps Perdus – the

Lost Time Café, the place you came to if you wanted to lose yourself, to become whatever, whoever you chose, the place you came to if you wanted to escape the reality principle, to be in a world outside time. It was shabby, it was casual, but that was the point – it was a home for the homeless, a refuge for the poseur who might be a genius, for the broken-down star, for all the rebels, with or without a cause.

Only it wasn't quite as shabby as it used to be. Nor was the clientele. Some Japanese tourists sat near the front, by the door, some slightly-pissed businessmen were propping up the bar, the chic set – still wearing black after all these years – sat on the sofas, which were set the length of the walls on the raised parterre at the back of the back room. In darker corners couples sat discreetly murmuring or, less discreetly, kissing.

A few of the old dissidents still clung on, I noticed. They had commandeered a large round table in the centre of the room. A noisy crowd, they laughed and smoked. Someone spilt a cup of coffee, and there was a burst of laughter. They were enjoying themselves. Or having an argument. Or both. I knew a couple of them, but they hadn't seen me yet. I had to deal with Adam first. I'd talk to them later.

He placed the triangular glass on the bar and peered at me; an attempt at an intimate look. I raised my glass to him, but I was thinking I wasn't going to like this subtly new and different Adam. He looked smoother, his face had filled out, was almost puffy, the skin was tougher, darker, no longer a young man's skin. His hair was beautifully waved, and I loved his dark blue silk shirt, but –

'You've changed too,' I said.

Now, he shook his head. His smile was rueful, apologetic, shifty.

I said, larding it on, 'You've made such a tremendous success of this place. It's wonderful, the atmosphere.' I had to butter him up. For the moment at least.

He liked it. A slightly fatuous smile twitched his – chiselled, would you call them – lips. 'How white of you to say so.'

It surprised me to hear him say that, to use that expression. He went on, 'Mostly luck, you know. Luck, and hard work. I've worked hard. When I – we – first got here it was just a moribund bar by the docks. A dockers' pub. That's what it was. Not exactly promising. But I gambled on someone realising that you could clean up. I talked to the owners, persuaded them you could do things. So they put in a bit of money, and of course when they saw it could turn into a prime location they put in some more – and then we bought them out . . . Yes, it's been a mixture of luck, graft and flair,' said Adam. 'You have to take risks – everything was pirated. We used to show old movies on the walls, never cleared copyright. The music was demo tapes, stuff they'd made in somebody's garage. Unknown bands. Great sounds. Wonderful music. And then – the way it was decorated – a lot of the stuff came off tips – and the mirrors came from a nineteenth-century restaurant in Prague – got 'em for practically nothing, they were turning it into a hamburger joint – and a friend in the Ministry cleared them through customs.

'When we were first here there were a few raids – drugs – well, that was the excuse – but then they were told to leave us alone – and the Ministry's been very helpful over migrant workers.' He laughed. 'I work them like slaves, of course, but then I pay them higher than the odds. I drive a hard bargain, you know. You wouldn't *know* me – I've reduced Italian wine merchants to tears, had Polish patissiers on their knees, eaten health inspectors for breakfast. I'm hoping to open another Café soon, right in the centre of town. And then, well, maybe Paris, Tokyo, Manhattan.'

So Adam was going places. I was surprised. He'd been a bit of a groupie to the old crowd we used to hang out with, Occam and I.

None of what he said explained the Café's success, of course. Who can account for an ambience, an atmosphere? Well, part of it – ironically – was due to Adam's radical connections. That had made the Café seem a daring and exciting place to go. That group of dissidents in the centre of the room – they'd been his first customers, that was for sure, he'd be the first to admit it, in fact his only customers. The place had been a centre for the alternative radical scene. Now, that hint of radicalism was giving the place tremendous cachet. Customers loved it. It was like a new kind of slumming, a little whiff of danger.

And maybe it salved his conscience to have them sitting there, sitting all evening over one cup of coffee, one glass of wine.

But there was something Adam hadn't mentioned, talking as if the whole thing had been all his idea, all down to him. And that was his partner, Khan. It had been Khan's idea in the first place. I hadn't known Khan, or hardly. He wasn't one of the old crowd, he turned up shortly before I left for the States with Occam. The recession was really bad – everyone losing their jobs. But Khan had this idea for a Café and he had a bit of money to invest. They ran it together. Adam was the business brain but it was Khan who'd given the place its special feel. Khan was always the frontman, who sat by the cash desk, looked out over the huge room, made sure that everyone was enjoying themselves, and he turned the place into a party. Or he held court in the back room, at his own particular table, and everyone came to talk to him about their troubles or their hopes. Total dedication – he lived, breathed and slept the Café.

I didn't think Adam had that kind of gift.

'Where's Khan?'

Adam was looking round the room as he replied, 'He was ill – hadn't you heard?'

'I've been away, remember?'

'Well, he was ill – and –'

I didn't even want to ask the next question. 'And now – how is he now?'

'He died.'

'Was it –'

'Yes, it was.'

I took a gulp of my sour, salt, sharp, icy drink. The silence was awkward. Adam looked down at the counter, pressed his lips together and nodded his head up and down. 'Mmm, mmm, it was terrible.'

'I'm so sorry.' And I was. I was sorry for Adam. 'Hard for you. To fill the gap.'

Adam shrugged, shook his head. 'I've tried, but – oh – don't let's talk about it now.'

Silence . . . silence. Masked by the hum and buzz of the Café, of course, but thick between us. After a while, he said, 'How's Occam?'

'Occam! Oh, I've left him.'

This produced a change in his mood. His hand stole out and wrapped itself over mine. 'I'm sorry.'

The hypocrite!

'I'm not.'

'What happened? Tell me. I always thought you and Occam were kind of civilised about that sort of thing.'

I looked across the room. 'Oh Adam, don't pretend you didn't know it was a marriage of convenience. Occam and I were friends. You know that. Only, well – I fell in love with someone – and – I suppose . . . everything seemed different . . . for a while.'

Another lie, of course. You call that love! Well – yes, you do; a gut-wrenching obsession, a dark, awful feeling, a deep, secret current that sucks you into the undertow of things, swills you down a whirlpool and spits you out with the rest of the sewage.

I'd rather dance on the surface of life, the way I always used to. And it was going to be that way in future. Definitely. 'We used to stay at a place called the Hotel

Louisiana,' I said. 'It was just a sleazy downtown motel in LA. The room was always hot, there was a fan but it didn't work, the neighbourhood was dangerous at night, we were just holed up in that room, just fucking.'

Adam didn't like it. His face tightened, very very slightly. 'You sound upset,' was all he said.

I shook my head. 'I just don't want to talk about it. Boring. I'm not interested in the past. Who needs all that?'

Yet I was playing on the past like mad. Cashing in past credits. That was my main reason for this visit. Seemed like a brainwave at the time, when I sat in the Lada and thought of what to do. Adam: he'd always carried a torch for me, hadn't he? I could ask him to do anything, he'd never refuse. The problem was, I began to sense those credits had passed their cash-in date. Better not annoy him . . . stupid to have mentioned my great affair.

Yet that wasn't the source of the unease. It was just that from the minute I'd walked in there'd been that little edge to his manner, making me feel I wasn't as welcome as I'd once have been.

Understandable, really. Hadn't I always used him, in all sorts of ways, and wasn't I planning to use him again? Our friendship wasn't exactly built on mutual respect and liking, blah, blah, blah, but on exploitation. Me exploiting him. Me despising the wimp for doing anything I asked him. Could it be that the worm was turning? I felt outraged, offended. I needed him to be the same for ever: pathetic, soppy, humbly bringing up the rear, carrying my parcels. So to speak.

Then he said, as if he'd read my mind, 'I haven't changed, you know.'

But he wasn't referring to his devotion to me, for he continued, 'I still believe . . . all those ideals we used to have. But – well, *things* have changed, haven't they? You have to roll with the punches. And we were all a bit naive, weren't we? As if our meetings and our marches and our protests could ever change the world.'

Then he said, 'I'll be back.' And I was left leaning against the bar. I clicked my fingers at the waitress, and she poured me another margarita.

So Adam, the groupie, the hanger-on, had done better than anyone.

Better than me, for a start. And now where was I in this strange new world? 'Your problem,' Occam always used to say, 'is you've got too much money. No incentive. You're . . . cushioned.'

Yes, indeed. Wasn't that why I married him, for want of anything else to do – a marriage of convenience so I could go and live on the West Coast, and while away the time having lesbian affairs.

Mrs Occam Unwin. What a name. I liked it. Perhaps I married him for the name. Occam's parents were philosophers, and they named him after a philosopher from the Dark Ages, or perhaps it was the Middle Ages. Some dark, oppressive time, at any rate. 'Christ knows why,' said Occam. He was born in a time of boom and progress after all, and nobody guessed we were starting a slow, slithery descent towards a new Dark Ages of our own, lurching onwards through history in the direction of chaos.

I thought of going over to the big round table, and saying hello to Myra. It had to be done at some point – the return of the prodigal dyke. But I hesitated. I wasn't fit to talk to anyone just yet. I even felt shy – and a little strange in my stiff white coat, and my hair they'd chopped off at the hospital. And no one seemed to have recognised me. That made me feel weirder still. Who was I? What was I any more?

'Doing okay?' It was Adam again. 'You look a bit pale. Need something to eat?'

I had to take the plunge. I had to tell him.

'Something's happened, something horrible. I've got

to talk to you. It's too noisy here – can we go somewhere?'

'I can't leave the bar.'

'Adam! Please! It won't take long, a few minutes.'

He looked at me. 'We're so busy, I mean – later on . . .'

'*Please*, Adam.'

'What's the problem? You do look white. Well, just a few minutes then. I live over the shop, you know, we can nip upstairs. But I can't stay long. Still, I suppose Gennady can keep things going. And there's Jeannie, of course.'

He went over and spoke to a blond waiter, who turned and looked at me, and nodded.

Upstairs was this bare room. A piece of white calico, secured with drawing pins, was stretched across the lower half of the window. A clapped-out three-piece suite stood in for furniture. No carpet, just bare boards. A dump, a lumber room. My heart sank. This wasn't good for my plans. I'd thought he'd have had a bigger place than this. He astonished me. But then, no. He'd always been a puritan, the sort of man who has just the one set of clothes; or two, identical. A workaholic, and anyway, his life was the bar. That was where he lived, I imagined. This was just a place to sleep, to be in the wings for a while.

'Is this all?'

He laughed uneasily. 'What's wrong with it? There's a shower, and a kitchen on the landing and another small room.'

'I need somewhere to stay – just for a day or two.' A mistake to blurt it out like that. A shifty, hunted look flickered across his face.

'Tell me what's happened. What's the matter?' he said.

His hand on my shoulder, he steered me to the couch. He was all concern. Yet there was a cold, dead space between us.

'I'm still jet-lagged,' I said. And in a strange way, I was. In spite of those days in the hospital (how long *had* I been there?) perhaps even because of them, I hadn't got back properly yet; mentally I was still walking beneath the eucalyptus trees in a flat sun-drenched landscape, a suburb whose endless sameness made it like a dream.

'My father died earlier this year you know . . . three months ago –'

He made the usual murmurs of embarrassed regret.

'I came over for the funeral, but I didn't stay to sort things out. I needed to go back – everything happened at once, I had all this unfinished business with Occam. At the time – it seemed like I had to do that first, to end one thing before I . . .'

Not true. Hadn't I just run away because I couldn't contemplate what I thought had happened? And of course I was desperate to get back to *that*. The Hotel Louisiana. That was the business I hoped was unfinished. I'd have sold my father for a few more nights at the Hotel Louisiana. Nothing to do with Occam. That was cool, everything was cool so far as he was concerned. But the Hotel Louisiana affair; that was something different.

Well, forget that, I wasn't going to get into anything like that again.

'My father died in very strange circumstances. The police were called in, of course, but they said there were no suspicious circumstances. They said he must have had a seizure; or maybe he'd tripped and fallen down the stairs. I never believed them. Something just seemed – all wrong. He'd been burning papers . . .'

He was a tall man, a big man. I hated to think of him lying crumpled up at the bottom of the stairs.

'He wouldn't do a stupid thing like that. Someone must have pushed him.' The more I thought about it, the more certain I became. 'That huge house – he'd rented out a room to a student. Anna. I didn't know her – only met her when I came over for the funeral – I didn't like her all that much, very quiet and reserved. But there seemed no reason not to let her stay on. Caretaker, sort of thing. Until I could come back again. And now . . . I came back to the house, my father's house, and she –'

My throat went very dry. It was hard to get the words out. Almost like a confession. I couldn't look at him as I spoke the words.

I felt his hand tighten on my knee. I looked up then – the expression on his face was hard to read. Disbelief? Humouring me? Pity? Concern? There was something else as well.

'Are you *sure*?'

'Sure! Are you mad? You can't not be sure about a dead body, for Christ's sake.'

'Love, you're in shock . . .' His hand moved up and down my thigh. 'You've . . . have you told the police? Have you reported it?' His voice was low, strained.

I shook my head. 'I know – I know I should have, but – I just wanted to get away. And then, I – I think they might have been after *me*. Whoever did it.'

'After *you*?'

'It might have even *been* the police.'

'Look, you're overwrought.'

'They might have thought Anna was me.'

His arm went round my shoulders. '*You*? But that's ridiculous. Why should anyone – I mean – well, people like your father – they're not relevant any more. I don't mean to be rude, but, well, your father was just an old, well-known ex-Communist. And that simply doesn't matter any more, if it ever did. Why on earth should anyone want to off him?'

Adam stood up, went and looked out of the window. With his back to me he said, 'You musn't let your imagination run away with you, you know. It sounds hideous, finding this body, but you musn't – I mean I'm sure there's a simpler explanation – burglary – I don't know –'

Even running over the dog, and that weird policeman (if that's what he was), and ending up in the hospital, that might all be part of some plot against me. But I didn't feel like telling Adam about all that. He clearly didn't believe what I'd told him already. That was it, he was *humouring* me.

'Love, I have to get back to the bar. We'll talk more later.'

I stayed upstairs in his flat for a while, re-did my face, and wondered what to do. I'd stay here tonight at any rate, whether Adam wanted me to or not, but it was no long-term solution.

I had no long-term solution.

I went back downstairs to the café. The place was jammed. Adam was looking harassed.

'Gennady's buggered off somewhere,' he muttered as he passed me. 'What the fuck's he up to? Not like him. Jeannie said he said he'd had a phone call. I'll bloody *mince* him when he comes back.'

I was left sitting on my own by the bar. This then was Adam's new life. I was part of his old life, the way things used to be. Not surprising if I made him feel uneasy.

I even felt a little jealous of the Lost Time Café. For I could see he'd fallen in love with his bar. I liked it, too. The steady engine of noise, the voices and throbbing music, propelled us all forward in time. The Café expanded in a golden glow. The noise rose, pumped to a steady roar. There began to be a clash of plates and clang of cutlery as the waitresses whirled the meals through the swing doors from the kitchen with a swoop and a rush of air.

'I'll have another margarita,' I said.

There was a slight lull around nine in the evening after the early, pre-theatre diners had left. Later, said Adam, the cinema crowd and the club-bound ravers would start to pour in. In the meantime it was once more possible to see from one end of the room to the other.

The door was flung open. A young man stood poised,

his hand gripping its slanting chromium handle. He remained on the threshhold, looked all around.

The group at the big round table looked up, and Myra stood up, held out her arms theatrically. 'Lennox!'

Voices hushed, heads turned to look. His face was striking, with its wide, pale forehead, its high cheekbones and slanting, deep-lidded eyes. He raised his hand in a slight, deprecating gesture of recognition and the buzz of talk resumed as he walked over to the round table. There was something self-contained, controlled, held in, about the way he moved. His shoulders were broad, and although he wasn't especially tall, he looked quite powerful. He bent to kiss Myra's cheek, and his black hair, long, thick and curly, fell forward, momentarily hiding his face. Then he took an empty seat.

'Aren't you going to say hello to them?' nudged Adam. 'The old crowd . . . well, some of the old crowd. You haven't forgotten them, have you?'

'I've never seen *him* before.'

'Oh . . . no.' Adam frowned slightly. 'Lennox. You wouldn't know him. He's a bit – well, *louche*, a bit of a jailbird, to be quite honest.' (What a funny old-fashioned term to use, I thought.) 'Radical gay – direct action, all that shit. Was it GBH on a policeman, this time – no, something worse, I think, affray, there was a riot . . . I can't remember. You know the sort of thing. I thought he was still inside.'

'Gay, is he?'

''S'right. Only he'd say queer or bent or something. Gay's too mimsy for them these days.'

'He looks like a fallen angel.'

Adam laughed. 'Nice way of putting it, I always liked your sarcastic wit. He certainly fancies himself – God, he's even wearing a combat jacket; how pretentious can you get?'

Well – I'd meant it for real, but it *was* a bit naff. Just

as well Adam thought it was a joke. I went over. 'Myra – remember me?'

She looked up, stared at me in mimed amazement. 'Justine! Well, this is extraordinary. First Lennox, and now – a real blast from the past.'

'Mind if I join you?'

She pushed back her curtain of white hair and gestured towards an empty seat. 'You remember André and Leonard?' I smiled and nodded, although really I didn't. I did remember Vlad, though, a wispy, sandy-haired man of about forty, who looked insignificant but made successful cult films. 'And this is Jade.' Jade, a crop-haired blonde, was wearing a white vest, and had 'I love Marilyn' tattooed on her shoulder.

'I thought you were in California.'

'I was.'

'It's wonderful to see you, darling. Isn't this marvellous – two unexpected visits in one evening! How lucky can we get? Lennox just got out of prison. Sit down, sit down, there's room.'

They were drawn to Lennox. For a while he held the floor. There was violence and cruelty and even death in his stories – like that of the screw who OD'd on drugs he'd stolen from a prisoner, and tried to fly off the roof – but his audience fell about laughing as he transformed the prison system into black farce. Lennox didn't laugh, though, he let the others laugh, as he told his stories in this deadpan way: oh, by the way, I've been to the end of the night and back, type of thing, our man from the frontline, our messenger from hell, his *sang froid* unblemished while bullets whistled past on every side.

Then he stopped talking, and listened instead. He drew them out, and took it all in, silent and still while the voices rose, and the others guffawed and gestured and punched one another on the arm. He just watched them with a half smile, cat-like, contained, yet intent.

I forgot about Adam's shifty manner, the weird little

off-colour vibes I was getting from him. This was the scene. For the first time in months I began to enjoy myself. I felt as if I'd been here forever. As if I hadn't a care in the world.

As if there were no corpse in a shadowy house in another part of town.

Chapter
Three

The Lost Time Café closed soon after three. By that time even Myra and her satellites had drifted away.

The waiter called Gennady had reappeared eventually, and I watched him as he went round straightening a few chairs and collecting the ashtrays. The waitresses, Jeannie and Julie, and Mikhail the cook, had departed with the last of the punters.

Balding slightly, Gennady had pulled his hair into an oiled-back blond pigtail. Like Jeannie and Julie he wore a dark green waistcoat, white shirt, dress trousers, and even at this late hour he chatted as he danced between the tables.

'So – you liking the beautiful Café?' He flicked his duster across the bar.

'It's great.' I yawned.

Adam was counting the takings. 'You should have gone to bed.'

I registered the point – he wouldn't even try to persuade me not to stay. Yet, perversely, as soon as he said it, I began to get a second wind. What was I doing here? This was crazy. I should never have left the house in the first place, should have called the police right away.

'No, I can't do that. I have to go back.'

'Oh, love! Look. You've waited this long . . . I'll take you over there first thing in the morning.'

'You needn't come. I have the car. I'm going on my

own. I'm okay.' I was fed up with him for no special reason. He just had that effect on me, always had. I straightened up, slid off the bar stool. 'I kind of forgot about things for a while. The Café's terrific, great atmosphere. Made me feel so much better. I panicked back there, up at the house. Stupid of me – I'm okay now, I'll be fine.'

Adam slowly pushed the till drawer shut, stared downwards, seemed to be making some sort of calculation. Then he looked at me, slowly drew his hand down over the slackness of his cheeks, mouth and jaw as if peeling off a mask or a scarf.

'I'd better come with you.'

'No – you stay here.'

I didn't want him with me – and yet, of course, I did.

He sighed. 'Come on, let's go, I'll take you. You'll lock up, Gennady. And don't bloody bugger off like that again.'

Gennady was poised, resting for a moment, and had lit a cigarette. He looked at us both. He seemed untouched by Adam's rebuke, he remained amused, quizzical – until abruptly a serious, almost mournful look indicated some unexplained change of mood as he said, 'Sure, I lock up. Take care.'

We walked out on to the pavement. Even now it was hot. No wind came off the bay. The warm air clung to me like cobwebs, and breathed a warm, stale, suggestive sigh against my cheek, an unwanted caress.

I walked over to where I'd parked the car. 'I'll drive you.'

He looked at it. 'In this? Are you mad? This car's not even legal, hardly. For Christ's sake, it's falling apart! You really been driving this around the place?' He laughed. 'No kidding.'

'Okay, you follow me in your car, then. Which is it?'

'This one.'

He indicated an enormous, smooth monster. It was incredible. 'What is it?'

'An Alvis.'

It was old, but in perfect condition. It shone a lustrous ice-blue in the floodlights, a huge 1950s convertible, massive, yet simplicity itself.

'Oh – that is really *sublime*,' I breathed, 'that is *beautiful*' – forgetting everything in admiration of the sheer excess of this ocean liner of a car. 'How can you bear to drive it? Aren't you terrified?'

He laughed. Evidently not.

Sticking close to each other, we back-tracked from the harbour, up a network of dark, narrow streets until we hit the motorway bridge that rose above the low houses back from the shoreline. We drove back past the Botanical Gardens. Moonlight silhouetted the palms and thick flowering bushes, and bleached the branches and hanging leaves, as if with strokes of whitewash. Later the freeway carved through scenes of disaster and blitzed dereliction. A mechanical digger was parked in a wasteland of rubble, a dinosaur on a prehistoric landscape. We drove on, the city spread open unravelling before us, many cities in one, all cities in one. A whole city sleeping. I liked that. I liked to be alone, driving through the night.

Then we drew near the old town and the university quarter. Up, up we climbed, disappeared into the grey stone streets, the banana trees and dwarfish palms in the square, and on up to where the three streets converged in front of that dark cliff, my father's house. The slamming of our car doors shattered the utter silence.

'You have been here, haven't you?'

'Been here? Of course not. What are you talking about?' He sounded annoyed, or as if he thought I was mad.

'I didn't mean recently. In the old days. With me.'

'Oh – oh, yeah, years ago, mmm, not sure, I think maybe you brought me here one time,' he said. 'Yes, I think you did.'

We crossed the cobbles, I turned the key in the heavy, carved wooden door, and we stepped inside. Rooms opened off from the square hall, and wide stairs of polished wood led up and divided to create a gallery at first-floor level. Beneath, a passage led to kitchens. Unplanned extensions at back and side had created unexpected lobbies, spare rooms and what my mother called 'glory holes'.

For a child those box rooms, coat cupboards and maids' attics had been exciting, too exciting. Hiding in the dusk, playing murder or sardines, you could suddenly feel lost, cut-off, cornered, walled up for ever, immured. One day they would find the skeleton – and then a fear unbidden crept out of the walls, like damp. Rising damp, rising fear, rising to choke you, panic fear . . .

'It's a beautiful house,' said Adam.

Yes – and it was my mother's house much more than it was my father's. On the surface, the house had everything to create an atmosphere of reassuring comfort: the Persian rugs on the parquet of the hall, the smell of lavender polish, and the eighteenth-century furniture. And yet –

'Hard to believe they were Communists, isn't it?' I said.

Adam laughed uneasily.

As I grew up, I blamed them for their hypocrisy. How dared they hang on to all this when they wanted to revolutionise society.

We stood in the hall. There was a peculiar little pause. Then 'Where – where is – it?' said Adam.

'You mean the body,' I said coldly. I led him upstairs. Anna's had been one of the unexpected back rooms, opening off a lobby which you reached via a corridor that kinked away from the landing and down a couple of steps.

'In here.' I forced myself to go ahead of him. Somehow I couldn't show him too much of my fear. I pushed open the door and switched on the light.

'Aaah.' It came out as halfway between a little sigh and a stifled scream, and I put my hand to my lips, staring at the crumpled bed and the – but what *was* it – like an animal crouched there, a scalp, a mess of hair. There was no body, nothing, just an untidy bed where someone had lain not long ago.

'It's a wig,' said Adam, as he stepped forward, snatched it up, and twirled it round on his finger with a peculiar little nervous laugh.

'Oh – this is –' Was I going to laugh or cry? My heart pounded. I leant against the wall – just as I had done hours ago. Perhaps I'd been here all along in this nightmare, perhaps the Café had been only a dream.

Adam looked round the messed-up room. 'We should have a look around, I suppose,' he said. He stared at me a moment. 'You are sure there really was someone? You didn't just imagine – I mean, seeing the wig . . .'

I shook my head, but I wasn't sure. Had there been a body? Perhaps I had imagined the whole thing. I drew my hand over the limp mauve cotton, repelled yet under some compulsion.

Of course there had been a body. I'd seen it, hadn't I?

I sat down on the chair by the desk, and looked round. Untidy, but not especially revealing. There were the usual items of furniture, a wardrobe, desk and dressing table, relatively solid stuff, made in the thirties – I recognised some of it, in fact the desk had once belonged to me.

Adam opened the cupboard door. An old suede jacket, a pair of jeans, a long tweed skirt, a black coat, a little heap of shoes at the bottom of the cupboard.

'Not many clothes.' He went through the pockets and I watched dully.

'Nothing here but screwed up tissues and bus tickets,' he said.

The chest of drawers was stuffed with garments. He

rifled through it desultorily. I watched him, feeling wooden and inert.

In the bottom drawer Adam found an envelope, which contained a passport. He leafed through it: 'Alison Fotiriou,' he read, 'date of birth –'

'Alison Fotiriou?' Now I was slightly revived. 'That's not the name she used.'

'Fotiriou,' he repeated.

'Her name was Anna Musgrove.'

'Odd.' He rummaged about in the drawers. 'Look at this.' Now he'd pulled from a paper carrier bag a squashy black thing like a dead animal. 'It's another wig,' he said.

There was a slight, mild horror in this dead, detached hair.

'But it's the same as her hair,' I protested, stupidly. 'I mean – she had long black hair.'

He laughed then. 'That could be because she always wore a wig, love, you always saw her wearing a wig.'

'Yes . . . yes, of course.' I roused myself and started to look through the stuff with him. There was something indecent about plunging your hands in the limp, drab heaps of much-washed cotton. The garments were both impersonal – unrevealing – and suffused with the intimacy of the underneath, the disregarded. Drawers full of crumpled socks and knickers and slightly-soiled bras were the opposite of display, like a depressed child, curled up, taking refuge under the bedclothes, guarding a dull, a banal secret, a secret everyone knows, the not-bothering of the private space, the lonely bedroom.

'So what do we know about Anna?' Adam squatted on his heels, a straw sunhat in one hand.

'Not much. My father got her from the University. She was a student. That's all I know. I don't know anything about her, I only met her when I came back, after my father . . . I knew nothing about her. Now I'll never know.'

'You know she had two names, and a wig. Looks like she had something to hide.'

I took a deep breath. 'Whoever killed her,' I said, 'don't you think – don't you think they might have been after me?'

'No, no!' He sounded horrified. 'Why on earth should you think that? Oh, you mustn't – Oh, Justine, please.'

He seemed really upset. His protectiveness had always irked me, his solicitude seemed insincere, for it was all an excuse to paw me, to create a false intimacy – but I was stuck with it now: I'd chosen to turn to him, after all. Christ knows why.

Grey light began to seep round the edge of the curtains, and glow through the orange material, while the yellow glare of the electric light was losing its harsh clarity.

'Let's go downstairs. I can't stand it in here. I need some coffee,' I said.

'Look – I don't want to harp on. But you are sure there was a body, aren't you?'

'You don't believe me!'

'I do, I do, love, but how could it disappear?'

'I've thought about that. Someone came back.'

'Well, obviously someone came back!' His mood seemed to change and he snapped, 'Corpses don't move by themselves. That's the whole point of a corpse. It's lost the power of movement. But – *how*, for Christ's sake, the whole thing's crazy.'

The smell was still there. I pushed the curtain aside and opened a window. 'I'm going downstairs.'

The kitchen was very old-fashioned, with worn terra-cotta tiling on the floor, a cracked butler sink and wooden furniture, and it hadn't even any built-in cupboards, just a huge old chest of drawers in which cutlery and saucepans were – eccentrically – kept. I put on the kettle and searched around for some coffee or tea.

Adam hovered, looking at me – and now he seemed more anxious and jumpy than I was. He rubbed his hands together and shifted from foot to foot. 'I'll look round the house – they must have got in somehow.'

That didn't help. It made me more nervous, made the house more frightening, reinforced the way in which it had never quite seemed safe, there'd always been that little undercurrent of mystery, of shadows, of ghosts.

Adam began by looking round the kitchen. Everything was secure. The door was bolted, the window locked.

'Dad was always careful – he went round every night, to make sure.'

'You say that like the old man had done the rounds yesterday evening.'

'It feels a bit like that.'

I found a jar of coffee granules. There was also milk in the fridge – mysteriously, until I realised that it must have been Anna's. That was creepy too. I sipped my coffee. It wasn't nice. I carried the mugs and followed Adam, and together we wandered through the ground-floor rooms. He tested the windows as we progressed.

The house had changed since I'd been here three months ago. Anna, who'd seemed so tidy and prim, had really let it go downhill. That annoyed me. Although I hadn't spelt it out, that had been part of the deal – she'd look after the place.

How different it had looked when my mother was alive. Then each room had served a different function, but now they all looked more or less the same. Veiled in dust, they housed shelf after shelf of books, out-of-date hardbacks and paperbacks; it was like being in a junk shop, the more so because there was too much furniture everywhere, a sofa in the dining room at right angles to the table, odd tables in the drawing room, also piled with books and papers, while the study itself seemed to be literally overflowing with written and printed material of all kinds, with boxes of newspapers and boxfiles of stencilled and Roneod communications, two old typewriters and – how anachronistically it sat there – the latest in computers.

Also, my father must have vacated the upstairs bedroom and used the study to sleep in, for alongside the easy chairs and round one-legged table was a narrow divan, with a plaid travelling blanket folded across it, while on a hook behind the door hung a shabby camelhair dressing-gown edged with twisted silk cord. That brought him back to me vividly, but I swallowed the lump in my throat. I didn't want Adam to see I was close to tears. I pretended to be looking at the books.

'I'll check upstairs,' said Adam. I heard him plodding through the rooms above, and then his steps came softly down the stairs again. 'You've got a huge job of clearing out to do.' The comment irritated me; as if I didn't know. 'All that heavy furniture, those great wardrobes of clothes in the bedrooms. But it's the papers and the books, isn't it? No wonder you couldn't face it straight after he died.'

He pulled up a chair and sat down close to me. 'What are you going to do now? There's no sign of forced entry. That means, well, whoever got in had a key – or an invitation.'

I still had the idea of it having been the police. Or of someone having been after me. I knew it was irrational but the feeling haunted me.

'I'll have to go to the police. I ought to call them now. Don't know if I can face it. They were useless about my father . . .'

I thought he'd tell me that of course I had to call them. But he said, 'Is that really what you want? Won't they think you're being a bit, well, melodramatic? I mean, there isn't actually a body, is there?'

'You think I'm crazy, don't you?'

'No, of course I don't, love, but it's just that none of it makes sense, love, does it?'

But then nothing made sense.

'So what's your explanation?' I asked him crossly.

'Mmm.' He looked hard at me. He really didn't believe

there'd been a body. I could tell that he didn't. I wanted to scream.

'You have to believe me, you *have* to!'

'Okay, okay – calm down. I know you're upset, I understand, believe me I do, but you're making it worse. Just trust me. I'll take care of it.'

How could he? More empty words. 'Oh, for Christ's sake!' I twisted away from him, didn't want even to look at him.

'Don't let's quarrel. You can't stay here. You'd better come back with me.'

Yes, I'd better go back with him – but I didn't want to. I hated this house, it frightened me now, but at the same time it drew me closer and closer into its old familiar embrace. I couldn't stay. And yet I couldn't leave either. I took a deep breath, trying to stay calm.

'It's sweet of you, Adam. I'll come back to your place later – I'd really appreciate that. I can't see myself sleeping here – but if it's a nuisance, I can always go to a hotel.'

'You're better coming back with me. You need to get some rest. Then in the morning you can start sorting things out. Get the locks changed. That sort of thing.' Very soothing, very gentle, humouring a child.

'It's morning already,' I replied sullenly.

'Let's go now,' he said.

'But what about the police?' I said.

'Forget it – we'll talk about it later.'

I didn't want to go with him, but I didn't want to stay. I was desperate to wrench myself free of the python squeeze of the house, with its memories, its sadness, its reminders of loss, and above all, its guilt.

Guilt? Why had that word come to mind? But I suppose we all feel guilty about the past, about our parents.

Much as I wanted to flee the house, though, I'd become more and more certain I didn't want to fling myself into Adam's arms either, couldn't stand his suffocating attentiveness, for it was tinged with that something – an emotion I couldn't name.

He'd shifted his chair round closer. He had his hand on my arm. I shook myself free of the nightmare, stood up. Made a decision.

'Okay, I'll come back with you now. You're right. I must get some rest. I'll sort things out later.'

Chapter
Four

I lay in a white room. The walls were white. The bed was white. Light poured in through the uncurtained windows.

I was back in the hospital. I shut my eyes and rolled over, burying my face in the pillow, hoping I would drift back into sleep, but the light was piercing. I opened my eyes again.

This was not the hospital. The bed was narrower and closer to the floor. A camp bed. My hand groped for my watch, and touched bare boards. I looked at my watch. It said eleven. I propped myself on one elbow. I had that indescribably terrible feeling you get after only four hours sleep. That's when we'd got back to Adam's place – seven; not even the early hours.

Adam had started work straight away. Said he'd get some sleep later. I was desperate for a shower, but I didn't want to encounter him when I had no clothes on. I listened – but I was sure he wasn't in the flat now.

It had been a mistake in one way to come looking for him. Some people would say it's not important and you're making too much of it, but it definitely wouldn't do for him to get the wrong idea. I wrapped the sheet round me, and looked into the next room, just to make sure. It was empty. I crept into the shower, which produced a pitiful trickle by my standards, which require that a shower should be more of a sand-blasting experience. Then I dressed in the white coat and the sweaty trainers again. One thing I'd have to do soon was get some proper clothes.

I slipped down the stairs. The Café seemed only just to have opened. Adam wasn't there. A few coffee drinkers were scattered through the rooms. Gennady was behind the bar.

'Ah! It's you.' He seemed delighted to see me. 'I make you wonderful French breakfast.'

When he brought it, he sat down beside me. 'You don't mind?'

'Of course not.'

'White of you . . . as they say.'

'Yes – why do they? It's so racist.'

Gennady smiled. 'Well, yes – but then don't you think people have to have a sense of humour? It's only a joke, you know. It was this cult TV serial that started it, *The Return of Bulldog Drummond*.'

'*Bulldog Drummond*!'

'Oh, the Bulldog Drummond series is the great thing this year. Everyone loves it, even the intellectuals – oh yes, well it is racist, they say, but then it's so camp. And totally period anyway.'

'Jesus!' I spooned up the steamed milk, thick like whipped egg-white, from the top of my cappucino.

Gennady watched me, and he wasn't smiling now. 'I think your father's death is making you sad,' he said.

'What do you know about my father?' I was so startled I sounded brusque.

'Oh, I hear you talking, and you're looking sad all the time, you know.'

I frowned. It didn't please me to hear this; I hadn't known my feelings showed that much. Why, I hadn't even known I *was* that sad.

'Or maybe it's that you're a little worried, a little scared,' he said.

I liked that even less.

'It's all rather difficult – complicated,' I said coldly.

'When you come back after being away . . . I've been away a long time – and now – you know, it's like – I guess when you go back to Russia it'll all seem pretty strange.'

But now I must have said the wrong thing, for he stopped smiling, and stood up. 'It was pretty strange before I left,' he said, 'and I don't think I'll be going back very soon.'

'I'm sorry if I –'

'No, no. It's okay. I have work to do, that's all.'

I read a newspaper that was lying around. The front page was covered with the usual political and foreign stuff. Civil wars abroad and nothing much at home except a few bombs and scandals. Less than civil war. Or civil war by other means. A government scandal was rumbling along, and threatening to unseat the Prime Minister, and even threatening the National Coalition. On an inside page a thinkpiece profiled the politicans considered most likely to take his place. There was the Chancellor, Vera Dance, a horse-faced woman, but she was thought to be too much of a moral traditionalist, indeed very right-wing all round; there was Roland Rodgers, the Social Democrat Foreign Secretary, *bon vivant*, said the article, but, by contrast with Vera Dance, a little too laid-back and high-living for the job; there were a couple of rising stars, one an intellectual-looking type in spectacles, the other a glamour boy – these were outsiders, as was Alex Kingdom, Minister of the Interior, distinguished, but surely too old at seventy. The author of the article backed the glamorous one, Peter Grand. His recent negotiations in Europe had been a great success, and . . . but I hadn't followed politics in California, and in any case, one party politics appeared inherently tedious, so I turned to the fashion page and ate my brioche selection.

I wasn't anxious to hang around until Adam came back. I found my father's car where I'd left it, and set off for the house once more. I opted this time for the route through the centre. Which turned out to be a big mistake. Soon I was caught up in a terminal traffic jam. A mains had burst and water was cascading down a flight of steps between two levels of the city. We crawled through thoroughfares stuffed with boutiques and tourists and taxis and restaurants. Soon the line of traffic went off into a huge diversion. The heat was intense, so I wound the windows down, although the fumes were pretty terrible too – the Lada was too old-fashioned to have air conditioning. It did have a radio cassette, so I clicked in a tape, and a sound waterfall of exquisite despair poured out all over the jammed ranks of stationary drivers, as I treated them to *Madame Butterfly*. Strange how cheap great music is.

High above me in his cab a lorry driver bellowed into his phone. After a while he shouted down to me, 'It's bombs again – two in the city centre. Central station's closed, terrorists, they think – major disruption, bloody marvellous, innit – "it's predicted to last throughout the day",' he mimicked a posh radio announcer's voice. 'My boss phoned through. Be here the whole bleeding day.'

Slowly, slowly, we were winding round an industrial estate in some far distant outlying area of the city, a no-man's land of hangars and hedgerows and electricity generating stations sending out invisible waves of carcinogenic energy. The traffic inched forward in soft-focus haze.

I thought about what I had to do. It was a way of trying to control my fear. Anna: tell the police; inform her next of kin, whoever they were – I knew nothing about the girl. I'd never met her until my father died. It was she who'd rung long-distance. Her voice had whispered down the line with constipated formality, 'I am so sorry to have to tell you this, Mrs Unwin, but your father –' I hadn't known my father even had a lodger.

So the flying visit. Just to see to the funeral – and to let Anna know she could stay on. And all the while I was desperate to get back to California and the Hotel Louisiana.

Then as I gently melted in the heat of this traffic jam, I wasn't even thinking about my father's effects, or even about Anna – I was thinking about *that* again. Somehow I had to burn it out of my brain. Exorcise it from my body. I wondered if the lorry driver could see me, see my thigh where the white coat fell away. But I'd slipped a little forward from him now. Every few minutes we moved forward by a metre or so.

The traffic jam idled in the heat as far as you could see along the three-lane carriageway. I thought about the Hotel Louisiana. And then I found myself thinking about another time.

The apartment was messy, clothes all over the bedroom, the sheets weren't very clean. As I was undressing he made a slight noise, and I turned to see he had a big erection. My indifference to him personally – that was the turn-on, that was the point of it. Because of that I wanted to kneel down slavishly, to lick him, to have him shove it in my mouth, to satisfy him, to pleasure him and to receive no pleasure in return myself. I wanted him to say, 'Do as I tell you,' and to discipline me when I didn't do it well enough. Instead, I lay back on the bed and we went through the motions as usual, and he took a long time to come and didn't seem to enjoy it much, and I came thinking about what I hadn't done to him, hadn't done because . . . because he was Adam, I suppose.

Afterwards, we lay in the unwashed sheets and a sudden movement of my feet precipitated something squashy and unidentifiable directly on to my crotch. In a silent panic of disgust I felt for what turned out to be a screwed-up sock – sexual ennui and repulsion condensed into that one dirty sock.

Madame Butterfly poured out from the speakers. Then I became aware of angry hooting and came to, realising that I'd failed to move forward in the rhythm of the lines of cars. There was a gap in front of me at least ten metres long, and the driver behind was going crazy.

My father's presence suffused the empty house. Just beyond my field of vision, he might be in the next room, and this sensation of his closeness, although it was eerie, didn't frighten me. I stepped into his study, the room he must really have lived in during the last years of his life.

My father wouldn't have liked me to go through his papers and start throwing them away. They were important to him; his life's work consisted of the boxes and drawers and files and cupboards of papers that surrounded me now. In dismantling these I would be destroying him. It was as if his death was not really complete, that some part of him was still around so long as all this stuff was here. And yet, as I sat there, it was not his presence that I sensed just beyond the doorway, just out of sight, but his absence that seemed almost palpable, a strange, soft absence that gathered in the corners of rooms behind doors or on the bend of the stairs or beyond the turning in the corridor.

I couldn't face the papers yet. Instead I went upstairs to my own old room to see if any of the clothes I'd stored there were fit to wear. I knew there was a little cache of discarded favourites, things I'd once liked too much to throw away when they went out of fashion or began to wear out.

I opened the wardrobe. Some of the stuff was not too bad. There was a pair of loose, pale trousers, a blouse or two, a red, flowered jacket, a couple of dresses. Because it was so hot I put on one of these, made from pale, purple-sprigged viscose, with puffed sleeves and a little crochet collar. I tried to think back, to remember times I'd worn it, must have been centuries ago. I picked out a pair of red sandals, wrong with the dress, but an improvement on the sweaty trainers. I looked at myself in the large wardrobe glass and loathed the effect – it was all so feminine, so pallid, the dress exuded sexless femininity, and was all wrong with short hair. I was costumed as a former self, a self who hadn't met those California lesbians, or ever been to the Hotel Louisiana.

I went downstairs again, and telephoned for someone to change the locks. While I waited for the locksmith, I went out into the garden at the back. Everything was neglected and parched. The lawn and shrubs were overgrown and the flowerbeds so weedy they'd almost disappeared. The lawn sloped downwards towards a stream which ran beneath the trees that separated our garden from the gardens of the houses beyond. The stream was dried out now, it was no more than a deep ditch. I looked up and down it. Perhaps Anna . . . Anna's body could have been brought down here, carried or dragged along to where the stream ran under the bridge that led into the cathedral close and the heart of the University. But . . . Why? I thought of walking along the gully, but I was afraid of snakes. Instead I wandered back up towards the house, looking closely at the ground for any signs of something having been dragged along. The ground was too dry, however. Here and there the whitish grass was flattened, but the only interesting thing I found was a thread of blue caught in the spikes of a rose bush. I picked it off and looked at it carefully, but I found I couldn't remember what sort of material her blue robe had been made of, or even exactly what colour it had been. The more I rolled the thread between my fingers, the more I peered at it, the less conclusive it became.

The locksmith came and changed the locks. Adam had promised to join me in the house at four o'clock, so that we could start going through some of my father's papers together. It wasn't yet three.

I decided not to wait for him. I locked up the house, and drove the car the few hundred yards to the University. In the heat of the day the air was leaden, the sky brassy. I parked, and walked across the first courtyard. The buildings, meant to look old, were constructed from pinkish grey, rusticated stone, and had pitched roofs, Arts and Crafts style. They had been built around 1900 when the University was moved up onto the hill, or rather the cliff. Dignified but chintzy and so conservative, they were covered now with creeping vines and ivy.

It was quiet up here. Through the open french windows of a refectory the sound of cutlery being cleared rang out, but punctuated the quietness rather than disturbing it. I walked into the entrance hall.

It was much more American than when I'd been a student. Now, the hall was more of a hotel lounge, with soft carpets, deep sofas and a kind of obsequious feel about it. Was this the result of the private funding against which my father had campaigned? Private funding or not, such old-fashioned notions as porters – permanently employed men who belonged to a trade union – had gone by the board, and the enquiry desk was serviced by students.

The atmosphere of obsequiousness didn't come from them. The long-haired blonde glowered at me and went on biting her nails. Her companion had short, curly dark hair and very light eyes in a slanty feline face. There was also a male student in the background, seated at a computer. His shoulders bulged out of his T-shirt.

The dark one looked me over. The other two were tanned, but she looked pale, her skin white and heavy, like camellias, her pale neck emerging from a black T-shirt. There was a heaviness about her altogether, about her powerful shoulders and arms, her thick eyebrows. I wished I were dressed differently.

'Can I help you?'

I'd come up here on an impulse. Hadn't planned what

I was going to say. I explained my dilemma as best I could, and asked to see the Registrar.

'It's only us here at the moment. And the Registrar doesn't deal with casual enquiries.'

Perhaps there was no harm in telling the truth. 'This student – she's been staying in my house. I'm a bit worried about her. I've been away. And now I'm back, she doesn't seem to be around.'

The blonde went on biting her nails, and the bulging shoulders stared at his screen, but the dark student moved to a second VDU and said, 'Name?' I gave it. She keyed it in. 'Address? Mmm. That's what it has here. She's on the Social Adjustment Programme. Know where the Department is?'

I shook my head. 'I wonder, could you –'

The student began to issue me with elaborate but unhelpful directions. Then she said: 'Oh, shove it, I'll take you over myself, I'm due to finish here. And this place is a maze.' She turned to her companions. 'Okay if I go now, you guys?'

The blonde started to whine about how she'd wanted to get off early.

'You went early yesterday.'

'See you later, Star,' said the man.

Star came round from behind the curved counter. She was wearing scout-type shorts of beige drill, and collapsing espadrilles. She was taller than me, and I felt slight and wispy beside her as we walked out of the foyer.

She led me across a grassy square and into another peaceful quad, landscaped with lawn, massed shrubs, and eucalyptus trees. Beyond this, we walked behind some laboratories and into a dingy hinterland, and the buildings deteriorated from Ivy League to stained concrete. Eventually we reached a neglected tower block in a distant corner of the campus. This certainly hadn't been part of the University as I remembered it.

'The campus just swallowed up what used to be the old Tech.,' said my guide. 'There's a plan to replace the buildings soon.'

On this side the whole district beyond the campus was a slum, from one street to the next you'd left the quiet garden city precincts, the old-fashioned streets (remnants of their cathedral close days) and had crossed a boundary into an inner-city region of multi-occupation, corrugated-iron fencing and boarded-up shops. The building we now entered seemed more of a piece with this landscape than with the main campus, or at least to mark an intermediate zone between the two. It was a mean edifice and its exterior was defaced with ancient graffiti.

Inside we found worn linoleum and chipped furniture. It reminded me of a hospital. A shabby concourse was furnished with a few chairs and a small coffee counter.

'You okay now?' said my guide.

'Sure, but wouldn't you like a coffee? I've taken you out of your way.'

She looked at me, then at her watch. 'Okay.'

The waitress spoke in a rapid, jerky West African accent. 'I've never had any customers all afternoon, you know that.' She poured the coffee into polystyrene cups. 'I sure they'll close this place down soon, and I lose my job then, you know.' She smiled, but sadly. 'They are always trying to cut down on the catering.'

'Food's hideous in the main canteen,' agreed Star.

'But I thought the University was rich.'

Star shrugged. 'Yeah, but I think they're trying to close down Soc. Adj. altogether.' We took our cups to the plastic table and chairs. 'So what's the problem? Why are you looking for this student? It said on the file that she was living with Professor Hillyard – well, in his house. So how come . . .'

'He was my father – he died recently.'

'Oh. I'm sorry.'

An awkward silence. I wished I hadn't told her. I blundered on, 'I just need to know why she doesn't seem to be around.'

'Probably away or something.'

'Well, but I've been back a while, and there's no sign of her, she didn't leave a note or anything. I thought if I talked to her tutor – there must be someone who knows where she is. I need to sort things out in the house, you see.'

'Maybe you should talk to the secretary – she's in that room down there, I think, just at the end.'

While we drank our coffee Star told me she was doing postgraduate studies in film. But I almost wasn't listening to what she was saying, because I was hooked on a fugitive resemblance I couldn't place, just wanting her to talk, didn't care what she said. At one point I told her I'd lived in California, LA and Hollywood, that sort of thing.

'Oh – it's European film that interests me –'

She didn't seem in a hurry to depart, and in the end it was I who made a move.

She smiled and lingered for a moment. 'If . . . if you need more information, I'm always on the desk on Thursdays. And Tuesday afternoons.' And she sauntered away.

A plump, pink-faced secretary with a cloud of grey curls sat by herself behind a desk and a keyboard. I explained the problem as casually as I could, and, telling this story for the second time, I even began to believe it myself.

'Anna Musgrove . . .' She ran her pink nail down a list on the wall. 'Jon Smith, that's her tutor, I'll see if he's in his room –'

She dialled a number. He was. She explained my enquiry.

'Room 142. Just down the corridor.'

I'd begun to wonder if Anna even existed. Now it seemed as if she did – on campus at any rate. Everything seemed so normal up here. No one was worried or alarmed. Maybe Adam was right and I had just imagined her, lying on the bed. After all, when I got back to my father's house I'd been ill, I'd just come from the hospital.

Jon Smith was a tall Afro-Caribbean. He motioned me to a plastic easy chair, and listened gravely to what I had to say.

'Anna should be on her residential placement,' he said. 'She should have started yesterday. We haven't heard that she didn't. I'll check up with them tomorrow, just to make sure, but I shouldn't worry. Mind you,' he continued, looking through the file in front of him, 'Anna had been . . . she wasn't doing as well this year as last. She seemed preoccupied. We were even beginning to feel, well, that possibly her commitment was rather in question, if she had the survival skills. Burn out's such a problem in this job.'

'Perhaps my father's death upset her.'

'Could be . . . could be.' He looked at me. 'This must have all been very difficult for you.' He paused and now he was looking at me with a hundred per cent attention. 'You've had a bereavement. During the grieving process, one can get things out of perspective.'

So he, like Adam, didn't believe me. I was hysterical, unbalanced by death. Anna was in her residential placement, whatever that was. Everything was fine. It was all my imagination.

Then I remembered the blue thread. Where was it now – lost, vanished, a speck of fluff, nowhere. I started to sweat. I wanted to get out of here. The unreality of it all was getting nightmarish again. I stood up.

'I needed to check it out, that's all. If you say everything's all right, that's fine. I just wanted to be sure.'

He stood up too. 'You were right to come and see us,'

he reassured me, 'but if by any chance there should be anything wrong, I'll let you know at once. I don't think there's anything to worry about, though,' he repeated.

He seemed to be about to escort me out, but I didn't want that. 'I can find my own way.'

I didn't want him escorting me out of the department. I wanted to see the secretary again.

Chapter
Five

Instead of returning to the house to wait for Adam, I drove down to the Waterfront.

Myra sat hunched over her Tarot cards in the opening of a pink-lit tent, among the other small-time entrepreneurs. Clowns, painters, portrait artists, musicians and contortionists squatted, stood or posed against the railings above the beach, along with over-priced 'antiques', racks of second-hand clothes, batik T-shirts, old photographs and boxes of used postcards.

Myra was deep in consultation with an anxious-looking middle-aged woman. I waited until the client had left, and when Myra saw me, she stood up, pulled the flaps of the tent together, and pinned to the tent flap a notice which said, 'Back in ten minutes'.

'I've been going since eleven o'clock, I deserve a break.'

She took my arm and led me to a café further along. We sat in the window. The woman behind the counter, a smiling Italian with a dark, fierce face, greeted Myra as though she were a princess, and brought us a plate of Italian cheesecake, some peaches and mugs of strong tea.

'So – you're back. How are things? You come back alone?' She didn't mean Occam.

'Yeah. I'm alone.' I didn't want to talk about that.

'You're in some kind of trouble or something?'

'I'm in all kinds of trouble.'

Myra stared at me, looking me over closely. I felt she could scoop me up, take me over, sort me out. Her face seemed huge, magnified. There were a few broken veins on her imposing nose. Her eyebrows had been rather savagely plucked. However, all she said was, 'Perhaps you'd like a reading?'

I laughed. That was a mistake; she looked offended. The fortune telling was meant to be taken seriously then. 'How much d'you charge?'

'To you – fifty écus.' I must have gaped, for she added, a little defensively, 'Well, a girl has to live, darling.'

'Does it make a lot of money?'

She shrugged. 'I'm getting to be known – there's talk of a TV programme. But we're meant to be talking about you – aren't we?'

The idea of emotional intimacy with someone as overpowering as Myra always daunted me. Even now, when she was sitting down, she towered over the table, her thick, white, slightly-waving hair centre-parted and hanging over her face – a face which looked out on the world like a Georgian portrait, ruddy, blue-eyed, in command, an embodiment of the Enlightenment. It was the white hair, especially, that gave her this air of an eighteenth-century country gentleman; which, for all I knew, her ancestors had been. It was the face of Reason, of Authority.

The words I needed to say stuck in my throat, and so – for she abhorred a silence – she did, in fact, talk about herself. She'd only recently discovered her vocation for the Tarot. Its occult tradition seemed at odds with her public school accent, which transformed it all into theory and intellect: the origins of the Tarot, the symbolism of the cards, the reasons why clients might prefer it to psychoanalysis. As I listened, I almost forgot that the other side of it was superstition and credulity, and that we were talking not about scientific learning, but about a sleazy little tent along the waterfront, with punters forking out more than they could afford for a few tips on their love life.

Myra, clearly, didn't see it like that. She gave every client an hour at least, she said, it was more therapy than magic. 'Not that I've *anything* against witchcraft, you know, as a matter of fact I've got rather a soft spot for the Old Religion.' But it was draining, like therapy, too. 'I feel absolutely wrung out at the end of the day.' At one level, she said, you could look on the cards as a way of framing your thoughts, setting an agenda, asking the right questions. At a deeper level the symbols and pictures could trigger off associations in the unconscious. These things went very deep. 'In a way it's a visualisation of Jungian archetypes.' There was a mythic level, a reaching back to an earlier, more spiritual civilisation –

Myra was almost two persons in one – the high-powered intellect and the eighteenth-century face represented rational thought; the heavy body clad in pale grey clothes of indeterminate shape, the purple nail varnish, the amethyst and topaz rings, spoke of a more disruptive, wilder self. Long ago, when I'd first known her, she'd been a classical scholar, but that period of her life now seemed remote.

I took the plunge. 'I am in trouble, Myra.' But I could only bear to say it as a sort of joke, self-parody, and she laughed. Then she scanned my face more closely.

'Seriously . . .'

I nodded.

'Come back to my place. We can talk better there.'

We returned to her pitch. She closed the tent flaps, and took down the notice saying she'd be back in ten minutes.

I drove, Myra directing me along a route which snaked away from the sea and through the margins of the city until it abandoned us near a motorway.

'You better park here,' she said.

We walked down a ramp underneath the road. The

tunnel stank of piss. At its end light gleamed, a white square which almost blinded me to the graffiti on the mosaic walls. In the dim light I saw a shuffling surly beggar. Passing a dark heap against the wall I hardly realised that it too was an indigent, a tramp, one of the army of the young and old, who in a perkier moment might hold out a piece of cardboard with written on it the words 'Young, hungry and homeless'. The older ones just coughed, spluttered, cursed and lurched.

At night, Myra told me, it was lonelier and more fearful. Not for nothing was it known as knife alley or razor road. 'Most people don't leave the estate at night,' said Myra, 'some of the women won't even venture through by day.'

Yet the inhabitants of the estate were other vagrants, squatters, dissidents, ex-prisoners, men on the run. 'You'd have thought they'd help each other,' said Myra. But no.

We came out onto a concrete deck, an open plaza; on all sides the long vista of tall blocks. At weekends, said Myra, there was a different kind of market. Arabs, Asians and Africans set up stalls, a whole culture of barter and bargaining around the exchange of secondhand car parts, tyres, radios, pulp fiction, tapes, magazines and clapped-out domestic machines. Today there were only a few stalls and no customers.

Even on such a hot day a breath of wind was funnelled between the towers. The ground floors were boarded up. The blocks, said Myra, were under some vague sentence of demolition, the original tenants had long since been moved out. The flats were given over to various licensed, semi-legal and squatting residents. All sorts of scams went on. Even those who paid no rent – to the official landlord at least – were tolerated; the days of bailiffs and mass evictions a thing of the past, for it had dawned on the owners that it caused less trouble and was also much cheaper to let things be. The residents could fight one another and the homeless troglodytes of the underpass.

'The government,' said Myra, 'has found that *laissez faire* meant fewer demonstrations, occupations – the natives weren't so restless. The dissidents became sleeping dogs. Police grumbled of course – they've always seen the slabs as boltholes for criminals and agitators. They didn't like the change of policy and they do still make raids, unpredictable sorties – they claim it's to flush out drug pushers, fences, prostitutes, escaped convicts, terrorists. But it has been better, at least till recently.' Myra paused and frowned. 'It's odd . . . just lately the government's beginning to clamp down again,' she said. 'Not sure why. Maybe it's because of these new bombers . . . Anyway, a lot of the people who used to live here have gone into the Tunnels.'

The Tunnels? The sun sent piercing bars of light between the towers. The plaza was white with heat, and empty, so empty. 'The old underground system, the subway, miles and miles of disused tunnels,' Myra explained. 'You know, after that huge bomb – were you here for that, let's see it was in . . . when was it? Anyway, there was such a panic about safety and what with one thing and another, and there was a big accident. They just decided it wasn't profitable, they just closed it down. There was a huge outcry, of course, but what do outcries matter any more?' She laughed. I followed her as she strode across the plaza. 'Not many of us left here, now,' said Myra. 'Thank god I'm making a bit of money at last, I shall definitely have to find somewhere more salubrious quite soon.'

'You mean there are people living down there?'

'Yeah, like they did during the Second World War, I believe.'

We walked on past the towers to where an older part of the estate had been built in municipal cottage style.

'When this was built,' said Myra, 'around 1910,

they called it the Garden City by the Sea. Look at it now.'

The gardens were patches of chickweed littered with twisted prams and abandoned car tyres. A savage-looking mongrel, chained to an iron pole, was howling. Rubbish was bursting from bags piled alongside the roadway. There were more boarded-up windows and a couple of front doors broken down to reveal empty rooms scattered with broken bits of furniture, disembowelled mattresses and heaps of rags.

Myra had painted her front door bright green. Inside, someone was playing Country and Western. Myra unlocked the three locks and called 'Hello!' There was no reply.

The houses had been well built. The floor, though blotched and worn, was woodblock, the walls solid, the fireplaces marked with cast iron surrounds. What was extraordinary was that Myra, or someone, had opened the main room upwards to create a double-height room, with a sleeping deck around the top. A typewriter stood on a flimsy card table. This, apart from a wicker chair and some piles of cushions and a mattress, was the only furniture.

The music ceased, and a voice called, 'There's no water.' A lanky child came in from a back room.

'This is Emma,' said Myra.

I looked at Emma. A sickly angel, with bright hair and transparent skin, the sort that bruises even at a look. On drugs, I should think.

'There's no water left,' she repeated.

'Yes there is. I put new bottles in the fridge.'

'To wash with, I mean.'

The girl bit at the side of her thumb.

Myra turned to me. 'There's been no running water for weeks. We drink bottled water – but we have to queue for water to wash by, bring it up in buckets, cans, anything.'

'I need to wash before I go out.'

She looked okay to me – except that her sort of pallor gives the skin a perpetually greyish look. Myra turned to me.

'I wonder if you'd mind, Justine, helping me,' said Myra.

I didn't believe this: we were going to get the water for this brat to wash in?

'Are you serious?' I muttered.

'I'm tired, I only just woke up, and I gotta go to work,' whined the child.

Myra gave her a big hug. 'Of course, darling.' She fetched two buckets and gave one to me. She took a watering can as well. Outside she explained, in lieu of an apology, 'Emma's had a hard time.'

I remained silent.

'When's she gone, we can talk.'

The standpipe was one block further on. A white man and two black women were waiting their turn. Myra greeted them.

'Is Emma working tonight?' one of the women asked. She too looked very young. When Myra nodded, she said, 'Tell her I'll call for her then.'

They talked about the bomb in the city centre. The second woman, who was older, laughed. 'Guess there's a lotta people like us today. No water. They said pipes burst, it hit the mains or something.'

We toiled back down the road with our buckets of water for Emma to wash in. While the two of them were in the bathroom – it sounded as if Myra was actually bathing her – I sat on one of the huge cushions and wondered what I was doing here. Then I remembered something.

When I'd seen the secretary again, in the department of Social Adjustment, whatever that was, up at the University, I'd got her to give me the telephone number of the establishment at which Anna was supposed to be completing her training. Now I looked it out, and dialled. A man answered.

'Can I speak to Anna Musgrove, please.'

'We keep getting phone calls about her. Yesterday her boyfriend rang to say she was ill and she'd be starting late, but she hasn't turned up yet.'

'Her boyfriend? He rang yesterday?' The day I'd left the hospital, the day she was murdered. 'What time of day did he ring?'

'I don't know, I didn't take the call. Look, who are you anyway? Are you from the University?'

'Just a friend,' I muttered, 'it doesn't matter.' And hung up quick.

Emma appeared. She was transformed. Hair, a shining curtain, fell in a waterfall over her shoulders. She wore a black lycra bathing dress with long legs that stopped above the knee, and a long chiffon overskirt. Her legs, silkily shaved, ended in red high-heeled sandals. Make-up flushed her cheeks. There was a knock on the door.

'That must be Darienne.' Emma lit a cigarette.

'Be careful, Emma, won't you. Remember –'

'Yes, yes, yes.'

Together the two teenagers clattered off down the road.

Myra sighed, raised her arms in a huge shrug. The worried, yet somehow proud mother – only Emma wasn't her daughter. 'She works at a gambling joint. I'd like her to stop, really – it's dangerous in a way. It's not exactly prostitution, but it's – ambiguous, shall we say. Gangland, drugs, hostessing. I want her to leave, really. But she makes such a lot of money, she's sought after. The men go mad about her. And she's safer with me than with some pimp who'd beat her up and use her takings to finance his drug habit. Then she *would* be on the game. I look after her. And she goes to college during the day. She's studying for a domestic science degree.'

I wanted someone to look after me, too – someone big

and reassuring, with a hug like a bear and a huge bosom. Unfortunately they didn't fall for me, that type. I didn't fall for them either. It was just that it would've been so deeply comforting.

I wondered if they were lovers. I could have asked, but I preferred not to.

'She won't be back till late,' said Myra. 'I often go to the Café in the evenings – I'll be going there later – you too maybe?'

'I'm staying there,' I said.

Myra raised her eyebrows.

'Oh, don't get the wrong idea.'

Myra smiled, her lips curled with the malice of the dedicated gossip fiend. 'What idea? You *are* jumpy.'

'I'm scared.'

'Yes, I can see that.'

'Does it show so much then?' I wasn't even conscious of it myself all the time – it came in waves and then receded. Recurring nausea. I was feeling worse, of course, since the phone call.

'Yes – it shows.' She placed her large hands on my shoulders and looked down at my face. 'You don't look well. You don't look well at all. Sit down. I'll make you a tisane. And then we'll have a reading.'

I sipped the herbal tea. At least it wasn't rosehip, but all those teas are awful, and what I really needed was some high-octane caffeine.

'Now tell me . . .' she began as she drew the cards from their worn purple suede case. Her face remained expressionless as I blurted out my tale of Anna's death and disappearance, my spell in hospital, my accident, my departure from California, Occam and me, all leading back to my father, that other unexplained death haunting his house and my consciousness. The one thing I left out was my lost romance, the ashes of lost hopes, the diamonds of my tears, etcetera. Not yet, anyway. Myra's attitude to such things had always been: so it ended, so what's new. No drama, no fatal passions, it's sick to feel nostalgia for past pain. She relished the gossip, of course.

In any case, the Hotel Louisiana episode was beginning to recede, displaced by an unexpected new obsession that was seeping through my brain and insidiously taking over the centres that produce the love chemicals. This, more than the deaths that frightened me so much, was what I really wanted to talk about with Myra. Yet I'd have died sooner than mention it.

'Cut the cards.'

They looked sinister, the cards, with their decadent, arty little drawings full of signs and symbols. I watched apprehensively as she dealt in silence. There was something vaguely disreputable and seedy about it all. I could never have said so to Myra, but Tarot cards seemed somehow like the porn of the spiritual world. I've nothing against porn, mind you, it's probably healthier than fortune telling. Both are aids to fantasy, but fantasies about the future, about love, money and success aren't extinguished as quickly as pure lust. There was definitely something illicit about the cards.

She began to turn the cards face upwards, one by one. 'This is the key card,' and she tapped the card at the top of the pyramid with her purple nails. 'The lovers – but it's reversed . . . Mmm . . . Next to the hermit . . .'

Her fingers moved to another of the images. 'It's not just what's happened now . . . not just some immediate thing, it's more something – things – that haunt you from the past . . . your whole way of coping with – it's more to do with sexuality that card, the lovers . . . but the hermit suggests you're trying to understand . . . it's very blocked, you know. There seem to be two themes – separate, yet they connect . . . now, down here, this is significant. Two knights together, swords and wands, and the wands reversed . . .'

'Doesn't it say anything about my father – or . . . anything?'

'Wait – wait – all in good time.' Her finger hovered over another card before she turned it up. 'Pentacles, pentacles – plenty of money, *comme toujours*, Justine. But isn't that part of the problem? I think it is. It means you never *have* to do anything, there's always money to fall back on.' She looked at me. 'Only now you've hit something that money can't solve. Right?'

'Money never solved any of my problems.' As she so rightly said, it created them. 'But what does it say about Anna?'

'Patience, patience.' She turned up another card, and another. But she was talking about my character, not events. Of course, it was all true, what she said. I don't know how she did it. She didn't know me that well – hadn't seen me for years. How had I managed to give away so much? Things about myself I'd never dream of mentioning to an outsider. Things I didn't even know I knew. This was not just the greasy card routine. I had to retract that judgment.

In between she did slip in the more traditional stuff, though, and in a way that was the worst. 'Mmm . . . I guess it's possible you could be in some danger – just look at all those swords . . . You need to rest, you need to think, you need recuperation. You haven't time though, there is a threat . . . the eight and nine of swords together – bondage, nightmares, powerlessness – a lot of this is related to the past,' she said.

There in the past, it seemed, was my father and a card with a Beelzebub figure on it. That could mean evil, Myra told me, or it could mean the unconscious: my unconscious, 'or – you know – the unconscious of history.'

That's what I was right in the middle of, the unconscious of history. All those stacks and boxes of papers and books in my father's library were part of that unconscious. As if I didn't know.

She went over the cards again, adding new meanings, new resonance, fresh layers of interpretation. She hadn't exaggerated in saying it was exhausting. I felt exhausted, at any rate.

'But what about the lovers?' I asked her. 'Can you tell me more about that?'

She looked at me. 'You tell me. I can see you're dying to talk about that. The card itself, of course, has a more extended meaning. As I was saying one can see it as indicating a time of choice, or an inability to choose –'

How did she know? But yes – I was tripping over dead bodies every way I turned and paranoia reigned, but the thing that was really eating me up was well, not the Hotel Louisiana now, but something in the same line – in the same line, but with a fatal difference: the romance of the Lost Time Café, you could say.

'Yes . . . No – I don't know. There's nothing to talk about. I had a rather tortured affair with a woman in LA. Well, not rather tortured. *Desperate*. I never felt like that about anyone ever before. I mean, of course I've always been a lesbian, but –'

'You *have* felt like that. Have you forgotten Barrie? Come on! That was supposed to be the biggest romance in history.'

'Oh, for Christ's sake!' The last thing I wanted to be reminded of was the appalling Barrie. 'I was *never* like that for Barrie. Barrie was an idiot, she was thick as two planks.'

'That was the whole point, wasn't it? Your bit of rough trade. Wouldn't have been any point if she'd had a PhD.'

'Myra! How can you?'

'You've always had a tendency to mistake sex for grand opera. But you must try and remember that an orgasm is not the same thing as an aria.'

I thought perhaps it was, but I wasn't going to argue about it now.

'It was all very relaxed in California, up until then, you'd have approved,' I continued, 'but somehow I didn't really like the person I was meant to be. Lesbianism over there – it was all so cheery, so normal, so – almost a bit like being in the Guides you know. All safe sex and softball. I wore shorts all the time. It wasn't, you know, very deviant, radical, transgressive –'

'Oh, *please*. Oh God. Just because you got in with the wrong set,' said Myra sarcastically. 'Until you met Miss Grand Opera of Southern California, that is. I suppose.'

I thought of my lover, wearing shades, as she walked down the street, I'd forgotten its name, through a hispanic section to the Hotel Louisiana. For the first time I felt a milder, a bearable emotion, a kind of affection, almost a saying goodbye.

'Actually,' I said, oh so casually, 'it was changing towards the end. One or two of them were getting into gay men, almost like it was fashionable.'

Myra refused to be impressed. 'Are you saying you're shocked? I don't see why. *You* always played it both ways for a start,' she said. 'You *are* Mrs Unwin after all.'

'You know that was an arrangement – we were friends, we still are. It was just to get residence in the States.'

Myra raised her eyebrows. 'That's what they all say. But no one gets married for nothing.'

'I've slept with the odd bloke, yes, that's true, but –'

Myra stared hard at me. 'Why should you be bothered, anyway? In any case, darling, what I always say is there's a fag hag deep down in every woman. *And* in a lot of straight men as well. You just don't want to take it too seriously, that's all. And as you say, seeing a gay man is a *very* lesbian thing to do these days. Lesbians and queers, what could be more transgressive?'

'It's interesting, isn't it,' I said carelessly, 'when a sexual identity doesn't necessarily coincide with sexual desire.'

Myra gave me a very old-fashioned look. But all she

said was. 'Darling! I've had more identity crises than you've had hot dinners.'

Which was true. Except that, 'You always knew you wanted to be a woman, Myra.'

She had to concede that. She threw another spread, and told me more about myself, a lot of which I didn't want to hear. The cards, though, always seemed to carry the same message: the threat from the past, but linked in an as yet mysterious way with something in the present.

Afterwards we drank more herbal tea, though I'd have preferred a stiff gin by that time. The Tarot had been like I was back in the hospital, the cards like those samples they extracted from your body, to be analysed in some distant lab. What they showed could not be altered, you couldn't pretend it was otherwise. Things you didn't know were there, but full of sinister portent; unalterable: a diagnosis. Malignant cells. The hand you were dealt was the hand you were dealt. Nothing you could do to change it.

That was paradoxical, for Myra rejected traditional medicine, alternative healing only for her. Which in turn was paradoxical in another way, since she'd had to submit herself to the most traditional of traditional medicine in order to be made surgically a woman.

Chapter
Six

Back in my father's house, the faded smell of dust and old books stole over me. I was confronting a houseful of dead matter, the cultural accumulations of a lifetime. The stuff was dead, but it lived on, inert and malignant, as if my father's ghost had returned to haunt me.

I wished it was as in ancient Egypt, where the most cherished belongings of the deceased, along with whatever it was thought they'd need for the journey to the afterlife, were placed in the tomb, to comfort the soul and make it feel at home in death. My task of clearing out would accomplish the very opposite. As I parcelled up books for the library and folded suits for the charity shop, as I dismantled the papers and threw them on the bonfire, I'd be destroying the routines of his life and all his projects. This was a non-ritual signifying unbelief. For my father and those like him, the only afterlife could be in this life. It was this life that he'd believed in, and the only immortality was in the afterlife of ideas.

'We have a choice,' he used to say. 'Socialism or barbarism; there's no third way.'

Well, we'd got barbarism. Maybe that was what really had killed him. He simply couldn't bear the way things had turned out.

As I steeled myself to dismantle it all, I knew it would be like destroying not just my parents' life, but my own past as well. From now on there'd be only the lies of memory, my memories. His had gone.

He'd been disappointed in me, politically that is. We'd been a Communist Party family, I'd been a Communist Party child, but I'd left the fold. I'd become a bohemian and then a lesbian. I'd rebelled. It was all a bit much for my dad – although I have to say he took it pretty well.

I had to start somewhere and a row of boxes stacked with folders seemed as good a place as any. I began to look through them. It was depressing. The politics, the issues, the language, came from a forgotten time.

This whole house was a museum of political activism, a monument to the memory of Communism, to the death of a huge collective hope. The mountain of words and paper sucked me into their empty labyrinth, but there was no longer a thread of meaning to lead me safely through. I almost felt as if my father had expended a lifetime's effort in vain, like the medieval Alchemists in their search for gold.

Yet the labyrinth also testified to a great vision, and I knew that at the end of his life my father in his last work had been excavating its history in order to uncover the reasons for defeat, indeed it had been more than that, it had been intended as the rediscovery of a lost past, a kind of resurrection, at least a reassertion of its value.

For me there was all too little meaning in the dusty files, and I'd no idea what I was looking for, so I left them and went over to his desk. I let down the flap to reveal pigeon holes and little drawers, in which I found a leather box of small, polished Victorian cairngorm stones, which had belonged to my grandmother, some unused stationery, and a sealing wax set, some old coins, a pair of scissors and a paper knife. These objects had once annoyed me, they were old-fashioned and irritating in the way a parent's mannerisms can be. They had always been part of my mother's non-Communist past, the relics of her family background. Now they reminded me of her.

I was about to close the flap again, when I noticed a little leather notebook in one of the pigeonholes. I took it out and with a quickening of mood saw that it was a diary – presumably my father's – for the current year. I turned the pages with a surge of hope. Surely a diary was going to tell me something.

Most of the pages were empty. On April 4, however, he'd written the initials U.F., and on April 6, which was the day before he'd died, there was an entry: Jack, 7.30.

Jack – Jack – I tried to remember, to think back over the names my father used to mention, in letters or on my visits from the States. I thought back further, to the years of the demise of the Party. He'd been so troubled by it all, he'd talked obsessively, written me letters, telephoned. I wished now that I'd listened more patiently, instead of which I'd brushed his distress aside, impatient and embarrassed. I'd known his world was collapsing around him, but what could I do – it was finished after all. He just had to get used to it. That's what I'd felt.

They always referred to it as 'the Party' – as if no other political party existed. The very term was shorthand for something which those on the outside could never really understand, for it was smothered in cliché and stereotype. Everyone on the outside had believed the Party was malignant, a drab yet sinister nightmare, with members like my father in the unsavoury role of middle class intellectual, privileged fanatic, cravenly toeing the Party line, yet at the same time duping and manipulating the workers – a fool, a fraud or a villain; more likely all three.

Of course I remembered it differently. It had been boring, it had been fun as well, but above all to me it had been ordinary. It was my life after all, as a child, it was what I was used to: the visits to the Moscow State Circus, the Red Army Band and Eisenstein films, and the times we went camping in the summer.

Then, of course, I'd known that We Were Right, and

that it was unfair that we were the ones who were seen as wrong and wicked, but by the time I was in my teens, I disliked it all. My father spent years battling against comrades with whom he disagreed as the Party tried to deal with succeeding decades of decline. And, with the collapse of the Soviet Union everything crumbled to dust. The Party was no longer wicked, sinister or fanatical after 1989. It became quite simply meaningless. All along, it now seemed, the comrades had been locked in error. They had been blind, crazy, the victims of irrationality and foolish belief – just like the medieval Alchemists, in fact, trying to create gold out of dust. Now, there was not even a language in which to talk about socialism, much less something as insane as revolution.

Yet the comrades had never been mad. They weren't just another religious sect, or a new kind of flat earth society. They were the very opposite of irrational. In fact, they were *too* rational, believing as they did in 'scientific' socialism. That 'scientific' set it apart from religion. For if, at one level, communism's appeal was to the emotions, to the longings of the hungry, the exploited, the wrecked, if, at another, it appealed to self-interest, asserting the right of each and everyone to a slice of the great cake, yet it also appealed to reason; it was logical, it was just. So, above all, my parents were right, so utterly, and sometimes self-righteously *right*.

They campaigned and wrote and raised funds. It was their life, a struggle that was both mundane and vastly abstract. It was a struggle for better wages, for a hospital ward, for lower rents, but at the same time it was a metaphysical struggle which challenged the apocalyptic, almost medieval figures of the Ruling Class, Big Business or Capitalist Ideology.

Yes, my parents and their friends were decent and sincere, they were right. All the same, there were things that didn't add up – intangibles of social resentment and unease. My friend Janet Morris, for example, who lived on a council estate, and whose father was an engineer until he got blacklisted because of his work for the union: years afterwards Janet had said to me once, 'Coming to your house, it was like a different world, you know – you had cheese with blue mould in it, and when the salad came it was covered with oil' – unlike the salad at her house, which had dark green lettuce leaves with maroon circles of beetroot and clammy tongues of ham arranged in lifeless inedibility.

At the heart of 'the Party' lurked something sadder and subtler than hypocrisy, and certainly than evil. Those class differences shouldn't have existed inside the Party – and yet they did. My parents never referred to them, yet everything in our house re-emphasised them – and of course, it was part of their marriage: he, the working class boy made good, she the rich girl who rebelled against her background. For them, it must have been deeply romantic – and later possibly just an embarrassment.

And then I thought – but of course, Jack, Jack Morris – Janet's father. He could be the Jack of the diary. Jack Morris, the blacklisted engineer, they'd never ceased to be friends. I had to find him.

I began to look hurriedly through the desk drawers, hoping for an address book, some letters, anything. In my haste, I wasn't looking carefully, but it didn't matter, because I knew the Morris address. It was familiar from my childhood, and came back to me right away. 6 Meadow Road, Porthill. It was up on what had been a pleasant council estate behind the Port. Of course, they might have moved, but it was a lead at least.

So that was Jack – but who was U.F? The only name that came up was Urban Foster. Foster, a well-known journalist, had, like me, grown up in the Party, but he'd long ago left all that behind him and was well into the mainstream, a successful media pundit. Unlikely my father would have been in contact with him – except that what if my father had wanted to give him some information, suppose he had a story, suppose he'd found something out.

In that case I should be looking for the work he'd been doing. I went back to the boxes. The stuff was filed in chronological order, but there was nothing from recent times, nothing to suggest information to interest a journalist. It was all from decades ago.

Yet – someone had wanted something, something my father had or knew. On the face of it that was absurd. What could my father have known that would be of interest to anyone, that would make someone so desperate they'd *kill* him for it?

On the other hand, if he'd been murdered, why should whoever did it have hung around for three months and then returned? Anna's body might have disappeared, but I still *knew* I'd seen it. I was sure she was dead. But why? The more I thought about it, the more convinced I became that they must have thought Anna was me. That was why they'd waited: if my father was dead, then I was the person who had whatever it was they wanted. So they waited until I came back. Someone somehow knew I was back and so they came . . .

Only I wasn't back. I was lying in the hospital with a drip coming out of my arm.

But they thought I was there. They thought I had something, knew something, the same thing my father knew.

Then I realised that didn't make sense either. The place wasn't ransacked. Nothing was taken. Everything was just as it had been. The only thing was: he'd been writing a book, but there wasn't a manuscript; and so far I hadn't found any word processor disks either.

The estate where Jack Morris lived had gone downhill. Grass grew between the paving stones. The houses, built in a plain, Swedish 1960s style, with clapboard along the top, were looking shabby now, the clapboard buckled, the paint peeling. I walked along the road, looking for number 6.

I remembered him at once. He was slightly stooped, his hair was white and he'd gone bald on top, but the smooth face, like a brown egg, was still unwrinkled, the eyes still clear grey. He stared at me, not hostile, but puzzled, not remembering me, yet knowing he ought to.

'I'm Justine – Janet's friend, Charles Hillyard's daughter – you don't remember –'

He held out his hand. 'I couldn't put a name to the face. Well, it's a long time since we've seen *you*! Come in – good to see you.'

Like his house he was mildly shabby, but shipshape and in good order.

'Marion's out at a meeting – I'll make some tea.'

'Still going to meetings then.'

'Oh, we battle on. Our big thing these days is the Port development.' He carried on talking from the kitchen, which, in conformity with the open-plan of 1960s design, was separated from the living room only by a counter.

'We were very sorry about Charles, you know.' He was waiting for the kettle to boil. 'We had our disagreements, but I always respected his views. And he always listened. He wasn't ever a dogmatic man. And in broad terms our analysis of the situation was similar. Of course the Party needed to change, but the baby got thrown out with the bathwater, that's how we always saw it. In spite of all that had happened, how are things ever to improve if there's no organisation, no Party to give a lead? He and I wanted to go on as Communists, you know – we wanted a restatement of what it really stood for, what we still believe in, what I'm sure many people still believe in. I'm sure you do. And many young people: an end to injustice, racism, the savage exploitation that capitalism brings, the threat to the environment . . . But people went mad, you know, had to throw everything out. Destructive. And of course things have got worse and worse since then.

Still – optimism of the will. Sanity will prevail. We just have to work to rebuild from the bottom. There's no alternative.'

The kettle began to give forth a warbling shriek. He poured water into the teapot.

'It was the same in the socialist countries. People started off with this tremendous pent-up anger and resentment against the dead hand of Brezhnev, bureaucratisation, the stifling of debate, but once it got started the whole thing unravelled and you ended up with the destruction of things that were worthwhile, the very idea of socialism, even the possibility of a better society. But of course we know that a better society *is* still possible, that the basic idea that we call socialism is right.'

It was years since I'd heard anyone talk like that. It was like the old times.

He brought two mugs of tea. 'D'you take sugar? I haven't put any in.'

I didn't take milk either, but what the hell.

He sat down opposite me, and smoothed the thin filaments of hair across his bald crown. 'What do you see today, when people aren't offered any alternative to this rotten capitalist society of ours? There's only cynicism, selfishness, disillusionment – or a rage that has no legitimate means of expression. That's when it gets dangerous. There *is* an alternative: a different kind of alternative – bombs, riots, destruction, disorder. The road that leads to fascism. Charles knew that too, of course.

'At the end, he got very frustrated. As you know, he was fairly familiar with the Soviet Union, he couldn't bear to see what was happening there, and the way the West descended like vultures on the corpse. It angered him beyond belief.

'He and I were different, you know. I mean, we agreed in essence, but I just got on with local things, he – it undermined the whole basis of his work. How could he write, how was he to make sense of it all? He'd always been an intellectual Marxist, and now, well, nobody wanted to know. In a way he was more or less silenced. You know what his publisher said to him? This was a number of years ago now. "The bottom's dropped out of the Marxism market, old chap." Can you believe it! Well, he simply did not know which way to turn. And he let it get to him in the wrong sort of way. Destructive. He got angry in meetings, even abusive at the finish, when the Party was disbanded. It wasn't helpful. And then afterwards – you've been away, you probably didn't realise just how badly it took him.'

'No.' I'd neglected him in other words. 'That was really what I came to see you about –'

Jack Morris was more than willing to talk about their last meeting.

'Oh yes, he *was* agitated. I even began to feel he was verging on the unbalanced. In the first place he was talking about people we knew years ago – people who were dead, who'd disappeared, it didn't make a lot of sense. And then he said – he was sitting there, where you're sitting – he started to talk about how he'd been approached. "They've *approached* me," he said, "they want me to do some work for them." "Who?" I said, "what the hell are you talking about?" But he wouldn't really tell me, it was all hints and winks type of thing. But of course I knew he meant the Russian Opposition. Couldn't be anything else, really, could it? The question is, what in hell would they need Charles for?'

Jack Morris nursed his mug of tea, leaning forward against the table, and stared into the pinkish liquid as though it were a crystal ball.

'In the end I said, "Charles, either you tell me what all this is about or let's drop the subject. If you've got something to tell me, if you need my help – out with it. Otherwise, let's talk about something else." "I can't tell you," he said then, "not at the moment. Later on you'll see. I believe it's the right thing to do. Politically. But although I can't really talk about it now I want you to know that I'm doing something. Just in case anything happens. Of course it won't. But just in case."'

Jack got up to fetch the teapot, and I sat there, trying to take it in. It didn't prove anything, of course. It seemed to make it awfully plausible, though, that his death hadn't been an accident. And in that case, Anna . . .

'He had a lodger,' I said. 'She's disappeared.'

Jack disregarded this piece of information. 'Frankly, your father was always a bit of a romantic. I mean he was a good comrade in his own way, but there was always that – he wanted things to be more dramatic somehow. I've noticed over the years, some of the intellectual comrades were a bit that way inclined. No offence, but – I tried to get him interested in the campaign around the Port, but he never really got involved.

'There's a big new development, you see, land reclamation. They're pulling down that part of the expressway and re-siting it underground. That way they'll get rid of the no-man's land underneath – it became a total no-go area, drug dealing, murders, gangs, you name it. The land'll be worth a fortune, the big boys have been fighting over it for years. Couple of them have put forward plans. We've been trying to get an opposing scheme off the ground, housing for ordinary people – large sections of the East Beach'll go, the scavengers, the homeless down there, shovelled out, God knows where. But there's some very high-powered financial deals involved. It's an uphill battle but we fight on. And we're getting people on our side. Chap who runs that trendy café down there, what's his name, Adam Motion, he's got involved – his joint'd be wrecked if this plan goes through.'

'Adam! *Really*? No kidding.'

'Friend of yours, is he?'

'Yes, but –' It wasn't just Adam's involvement I found

surprising. It was hard to understand how the sort of community opposition Jack was describing could still continue at all in the general atmosphere of collapse, apathy and intimidation.

When friends had visited us in California they used to bang on about how awful it all was, how the country was falling apart in a mixture of chaos, apathy, violence and repression. The reality was so much less melodramatic. I saw now that there was never going to be a coup, a *putsch*, that wasn't the Kakanian way, just a long, slow, incompetent slide to a state of things that, though worse, it would always be an overstatement to label as fascism. No one was shooting protesters or muzzling the press. It was all much subtler than that.

Jack put his hands on his knees preparatory to standing up. 'Got to get down there now,' he said.

I offered him a lift, but he said he had his bicycle. He wheeled it out into the road and leaned against it as he said to me, 'I hope you won't mind me saying this, but it was a pity you couldn't arrange a proper Party funeral for your Dad. Well, I suppose you can't say *Party* funeral now. Political funeral anyway, a proper memorial meeting. Comrades would have liked to speak, you know. No hard feelings – I don't want to have a go at you, but a lot of comrades felt – cheated, you might say, not having a chance to pay their last respects in the way they would have wanted. And I can't help feeling it's what *he* would have liked.'

'I know. I'm sorry too.'

I *was* sorry. I should have given him a proper Party funeral, I should have done it properly. Instead I'd just bundled him off to the crematorium, as though he were like anyone else.

He patted me on the arm. 'Never mind.'

'How's Janet?' I asked.

'She's living in the country – up North,' he said. 'She and her partner work on the Ecological Reserve – they're

71

very dedicated Greens. The going's getting pretty tough there too, she tells me. Did you know there are fascist greens? Stone me! Fascist greens, right-wing communists, fundamentalist anarchists. Talk about the world turned upside-down.' He laughed with a kind of exasperated disgust.

We shook hands. 'Come and see us again,' he said. 'You're always welcome. Marion'd like to see you.'

'Thanks, I will.'

As I turned away, I remembered there was one more thing. The initials: U.F. He was wheeling his bike into the road.

'Oh, Foster – you can find him at the *Daily Post*. Though I don't know why you'd want to talk to him. I doubt if Charles . . . shouldn't think they were on speaking terms. Charles couldn't stand all those trendies. Of course he's done okay. Big time journalism now, TV and all that.'

'Well – is there anyone else you could think of? Anyone else with those initials, I mean.'

'U.F . . . U. –' He considered it. Then he shook his head. 'I'll keep it in mind, though,' he promised. 'Keep in touch anyway – you know where to find us –' and he gave me another pat on the arm. 'No use dwelling on the past. There's so much to do in the present.'

'I wish I'd talked to him more.'

'No good thinking that way. Things are as they are. You have what he gave you, you take it on from there.'

I watched him ride away, and then I went and sat in the Lada again.

Chapter
Seven

The sun through the curtainless windows woke me at six. I didn't remember too much about the night before, except that things somehow hadn't panned out.

It had started with Adam sulking. He'd ignored me at first, but eventually, as I'd known he would, he came over to Myra's table.

'Where *were* you? I went to the house. You weren't there. I was worried.'

What could I say to him. I'd had nothing to say, no excuses for my rudeness. In fact I'd been rude again. I'd pulled my chair round, so that I was sitting almost with my back to him, leaving him isolated beyond the edge of the circle. It hadn't deterred him.

He'd started to tell me more about his plans for raising money to start another café. He had some backers, but things weren't quite sewn up and anyway he needed someone he could trust. Even to run one joint like the Lost Time Café required a partner. He couldn't go on indefinitely without someone like Khan.

As he'd talked it had dawned on me that he had me shortlisted for the job. He didn't say so in quite so many words, but he kept asking if I'd started to think about selling the house, my father's house, that is. 'You'll get a packet from that,' he let slip. As if he didn't know I was loaded with the stuff already.

The money wasn't the main thing, though. He wanted

a . . . mate. 'Gennady's okay,' he said, 'but . . .' But what? But of course I'd be more to him than Gennady ever could be, wouldn't I? Gennady was Adam's employee, not a friend, not a partner – and anyway they all despised the Russians. I'd already noticed that in Kakania hatred of Russians surpassed even hatred of blacks.

So – it was there if I wanted it. I could be high priestess of the Lost Time Café. What a wonderful idea.

If only it wasn't for Adam. I could just see the scenario. It didn't appeal.

The weird moment of the evening had been when Lennox had walked in with a girl. I'd had this feeling of horrible disappointment, then with a disorienting double take I'd recognised her – the student up at the University, the one who'd taken me over to Anna's department, the one who'd shown an interest in me, or so I thought at the time, the one called Star, the one who'd reminded me of someone. Of Lennox, of course.

The music had been louder than usual: Stone Cold Junkies playing 'Steel Tampon'. It was exciting. Lennox had put a hand on my shoulder. As he leaned down close to me, his dark curls had fallen forward and brushed my cheek before he pushed them back.

'What are you drinking – it's going on Myra's tab?'

'I'll have a margarita.'

It was later that things had gone wrong. Vlad, the sandy-haired film director, had pinned me in a corner for hours to tell me all about his latest movie. A red-headed beach boy had turned up for Lennox and the two of them had gone by the time I resurfaced. Later, Myra had become quarrelsome. Finally, Adam had come on rather strong, hadn't he – nothing I couldn't handle, of course, but that almost made it worse. I shuddered at the memory of the cringing, whipped spaniel look. I couldn't believe he'd still be moping about over me after all these years. That'd be so stupid it wasn't flattering. It was sick. Surely he must have a girlfriend somewhere. I'd have to ask Myra about that.

The trouble was, who else had I to rely on? Who cared about me? Well, there was Myra. Of all of them she was the only one I trusted. And even she went over the top at times.

I dressed and tiptoed downstairs. The Café, empty, stank of drink and stale cigarettes. I let myself out, and walked across the open space in front of the Café to the water's edge. I looked out to sea. The morning light was transparent, and at this hour the heat was bearable.

A few years ago there'd been floods, and the quay had been built up and reinforced. To my left cranes and a bulldozer, a huge crater, and out in the water a structure of wooden piles all testified to the reclamation of the dock. Above, an expressway arched over the long stretch of derelict land before curving left and shearing down towards the coast road leading to Angel Point. That must be the motorway they were going to demolish. To my right were the beaches and the front stretching as far as the eye could see before curving round towards Snake Beach.

I needed some breakfast, but I didn't want an early-morning encounter with Adam, so, with all the windows of the Lada open, I floated through the empty streets. Nothing open yet. No one about.

Up beyond the hilly side-streets, though, the city was waking. I reached a wide boulevard in the centre, left the Lada beneath the plane trees, and looked for a café, buying a paper on the way. They'd washed down the pavements, and rivulets of water ran in the gutter. It smelled clean and fresh and it was even chilly in the shadow of tall buildings. I chose a bar, sat down inside, and began to read my paper.

Yesterday's bombing was still the front-page story. A large photograph showed the Minister of the Interior inspecting the scene. The tall figure in languid linen suit was vaguely familiar from my pre-Californian past. With his thin, pinched, but good-looking features – good-looking in that special upper-class way – and his foppish hair falling over his forehead and giving him the air of an ageing schoolboy, he was part of my mental furniture, jumbled in the lumber room of useless information ingested all day and every day. A dislikeable man, arrogant and authoritarian, I seemed to remember that he was also strangely frivolous, absolutely shrivelled with irony and cynicism.

A revolutionary group called Albion had claimed the bomb. The paper carried a long centre-page thinkpiece speculating as to their identity: radical Nazis? An exotic import? Or an old group, up to new tricks – Irish, Libyan, German?

The article surveyed urban guerrilla groups all over the world – the Balkans, Malaysia, Finland, everywhere had them these days – but concluded that Albion, as the name implied, was a genuine home-grown product, formed by a group that had broken away from the Patriotic Party.

The Patriotic Party in its turn was a recent development. It had all happened while I was away. The New Democrats had split between the pro- and anti-Federal-Europeans; hence the need for the current coalition with the bulk of the Social Democrats, but with the New Democrats still in the driving seat. It was a sick situation; it had finally destroyed the Left, for once the bulk of the Social Democrats had decided to form a coalition with the Right – well, there were just forty or so socialists to form an opposition. They called themselves the Socialist Democrats now. Everyone had to be a democrat, whatever else they were, even the Patriotic Party, in fact they most of all, since they claimed that Europe was destroying democracy.

Probably even Albion would claim to be democratically fascist. Albion – or so the article claimed – had been formed by elements from the Patriotic Party (mostly from their youth group, I guessed) who were fed up with the PP's impotence in Parliament, and had embraced direct action, campaigning for a separate state now: 'Home rule for the Albion Nation'. The mainstream PPs looked respectable by comparison.

The article conceded that there was an alternative view, that Albion was not one but several groups, and that they could not be seen as simply right-wing, as straightforward fascists. 'It is no longer so easy to say what we mean by those worn-out terms, "left-wing" or "right-wing". We need a new vocabulary,' the article's author concluded. Only then did I notice that the article had been written by Urban Foster. I could guess what Jack Morris would have to say about that.

The bomb story was also flickering on the TV screen inside the café. The screen filled with a long, pink face, with pinched nose, and two flakes of blue for eyes; the Minister of the Interior again, this time addressing the nation.

'. . . This appalling outrage . . . cowardly . . . innocent people . . . no hiding place . . . rest assured . . . Yes, we take pride in our national heritage, but . . . the destruction of our way of life . . . My friends, let me say this to you . . .'

Yet I couldn't help feeling that it suited them well to have crazy bombers acting the part of the bad guys. That made it easier for them as they tried to mend fences with the 'respectable' far right, the Patriots, as a little insurance policy just in case some life still stirred in the Social Democrats, and they attempted to assert their independence.

One thing I'd noticed already: although when friends came over to California they'd done nothing but moan about Kakania, now that I was back everyone looked appalled when they heard I'd been living in L.A. But weren't you terrified? Did you carry a gun? Yet they didn't turn a hair at the bombs. They'd grown used to it. It happened. That was all. It had crept up on them so slowly. People couldn't remember a time when there hadn't been bombs. It was all part of the slow slow slide to . . . what? To the general decay that wasn't quite fascism but had ceased to be democracy, I supposed.

I was out in the streets again. I had to buy some clothes.

I made for the Galleria, a former department store now reconstructed as a mall of boutiques, with fake Art Nouveau stairways and glass lifts. I roamed from shop to shop, in search of a new personality, or at least a different regimental uniform, one that'd tell me my new identity. Black jeans, white t-shirt, black leather jacket were no longer enough. Maybe I would be a dandy now, and flaunt my psychic masculinity at Lennox, dressed in black leather, yes, but also in cream linen, dark green silk, aubergine jacket, chocolate trousers, turquoise eyes – or psychic androgyny more like, with sleazy satin camisoles and knickers underneath, and high-heeled shoes made of soft red suede.

Much better than California, where no one wore black and everyone looked so bloody healthy.

The *Daily Post* offices rose like a cliff of black glass. I pushed through the doors and found myself in an airy atrium. There were the usual fountain, palms and weeping figs, and open escalators flowing up and down through space, all a bit old hat now.

I decided to pretend I had a story for Foster. Perhaps he'd remember my name, we'd been Party children together after all. I framed my request to see him in a way I hoped was intriguing, and the receptionist spoke into the phone.

I waited on a leather sofa that was too low and too squashy. The receptionist read a book. Every little while a biker surged through the doors, moving like Cro-Magnon man. Otherwise the place was deserted.

Then a figure appeared at the top of the escalator. I watched him. As he came down, I realised it was Urban Foster, but I couldn't say I recognised him. He was still short, of course, but he was no longer skinny. He'd barrelled out, although a very smart white linen suit was cunningly cut to disguise this. He still had the same mop of curly blond hair and had added big, round red glasses. He didn't exactly look older, he just looked like an elderly toddler.

'Justine! What brings you here?' He held my hand in both his, but I didn't think he was pleased to see me. 'I'd heard you were on the West Coast.'

'The West Coast of what?' I said coldly.

He ignored this attempt at a put-down. 'Shame about your father. Look – why don't we have a drink – place I know round the corner from here – have to be back in twenty minutes, expecting a call from Alex Kingdom's office – he's Minister of the Interior now, you know.'

I was amazed he'd give me even twenty minutes, but I wasn't going to show I was impressed. He smiled slightly, he was coming on like he expected me to kiss his feet or something. I gave him a tiny, enigmatic smile. I was developing a whole new range of smiles now I was back in Kakania – the bland, all-purpose Californian smile was totally inadequate.

The bar was light and everything was made of glass. In fact it was like a fish tank, and evidently passers-by were meant to stare in and catch a glimpse of the famous. Unfortunately at this time of day it was almost empty. We had no trouble getting a window seat.

I hadn't thought it out at all, but I think I'd half assumed that I'd tell him the whole story. Now I realised it might not be so clever to spill the beans to some journalist about how I thought my father had been murdered. I decided to approach it from a different angle.

'My father had a lot of documents – he was working on an account of the Party, semi-autobiographical. It just occurred to me that you might be interested. I wondered if he'd been in touch with you – you see there's an entry in his diary –'

But I saw from the elderly toddler's face that this wasn't anything he'd ever want to hear about. A shutter came down behind the outsize glasses. Why did he dress as though he were the anchor-man on a kids' TV show?

'Justine – you've been away, so I'll forgive you, but don't waste my time. The Party – I mean, how could that be news? That's *years* ago. Someone with your father's views, he's *history*, Justine. We've had the postmortems – just as we've had the postmoderns –' and he giggled. Was that supposed to be a joke? 'Yes, all that's over, I'm afraid. Your're lucky you missed them. I'm glad it's all over. Such a big, big handicap to New Thought. I know – I was in the Party myself, for years, you know that – too many years, and I can tell you, that sort of thinking went out with – with Galileo. The Communist Party was the political equivalent of the flat-earth society. Its demise was the best thing that happened to the forces of radicalism since –'

But this time he couldn't find a colourful enough comparison and his half-finished sentence drifted away over our mineral water. I must have looked shocked or something, for he added, 'Your father was way out of time, Justine. I mean we've had to look at the really *new* ideas. Even, well – not Albion of course, no definitely not Albion, but for instance, the Patriotic Party. I know some people call them fascists, too, but that sort of label game doesn't interest me any more. So sectarian, that was one of the crimes of the Left, wasn't it, that dreadful sectarianism: the stigma of weakness, the sign of impotence. In my opinion some of what the PP say really does make sense, you know – Labour camps for the unemployed, for example. I mean, did you know that was a serious Fabian Society demand at one time – before the First World War? Well, Sidney and Beatrice Webb believed in it, anyway.'

'So you didn't go and see Dad, he didn't visit you –'

'Good Heavens, no!' He laughed and then stared hard at me. 'Is that why you wanted to see me – to see if I'd interviewed your father?'

He looked incredulous.

'Yes, I thought . . .'

'Look, I absolutely have to go now, Justine – Alex Kingdom, they may have phoned by now . . .'

He was clearly put out. Perhaps he'd been hoping that I'd ask him to do me some favour, that he could be patronising and important, and flirt with me a bit, lead me on and then say no. As it was I was just some has-been, a crazy woman who thought the world might still be interested in her dinosaur of a father.

We parted at the door, and then he looked at me with just a flicker of mystification, as if he thought there might after all have been some story there that he'd missed. But no – he waddled away, feeling famous and important while I, the discarded supplicant, drifted back to my shabby Lada and all my unanswered questions.

Chapter
Eight

In the morning, I drove down to Camden Bay. I took Myra with me. Two heads were better than one for the sort of mess I had got into.

This part of the city backed up from a bathing cove. The small front with its open-air lido, cafés and shopping parade had an air of the 1930s about it. There were many bleached white bungalows set in leafy roads; further up, blocks of flats like ocean liners had been built to look out over the ocean. The dwellings seemed to inhabit a distant yet 'modern' time: modern in a period way, yesterday's futurism become tomorrow's retro chic. It was a neighbourhood to which elderly couples and widows tended to retire.

I'd come to Camden Bay in search of Violet Frankenberg. Since Urban Foster had turned out not to be the U.F. of my father's diary, I'd gone back to the house and looked again, and in the desk I'd found a sheet of paper. On it was written 'Violet Frankenberg' and a telephone number. When I'd looked at my father's diary again it was obvious that the 'U' could be a 'V'.

'Violet Frankenberg didn't really want to see me,' I told Myra. 'She was quite unfriendly on the phone.'

We parked the car outside Arcadian Mansions, and walked out of the heat into the dank lobby. There was a lift, the open kind with clanking iron-grille doors, but it wasn't working, so we climbed the tiled steps to the second floor, and rang the bell of flat number nine.

The woman who opened the door was sixtyish. Her skin was pale and polished like bone, and she wore no make-up; the straight nose, large blue eyes in deep sockets, and high cheekbones were set in an oval face: past beauty gave her a forbidding, haggard look. Her straight grey hair was cut in a fringed page-boy – probably she'd worn the same style for forty years or so. Once it must have been smart as it swung round her face, but now it looked faintly witchlike. She was dressed in drab beige trousers and shirt. Perhaps she'd once been so beautiful that clothes hadn't mattered – not that that ever stopped anyone liking clothes. Now, anyway, she had the bleached look of dried leaves and grasses.

'I rang you – I'm Charles Hillyard's daughter. This is a friend of mine – I hope you don't mind . . .' I blenched at her cold stare.

'Come in.' Her reserved, ungiving manner didn't change.

She led us through a tiny hall and into a living room. The functional light oak furniture dated from the 1940s or 1950s as did the colour scheme of cream and celadon green. The paint was sallow and couldn't have been retouched for years. One wall was lined with books from floor to ceiling, and newspapers and periodicals were scattered on the coffee table, the floor and the hard little sofa on which she gestured us to sit down.

'So how can I help you?' It wasn't that she was rude; on the contrary, she was perfectly polite. It was just that her lack of enthusiasm was forbidding.

I found it hard to begin. I had no idea how to breach that impenetrable indifference. I tried to choose my words carefully as I wilted under the stare, and was it my imagination, or did she freeze a few degrees more when I mentioned my father? 'You see . . . well it's the circumstances of his death. There's something I find a bit odd about the way he died,' I blundered. 'I mean, he was perfectly all right, and then suddenly –'

'People do die suddenly, you know.' Then she added, more kindly, 'I expect it was a shock.'

'Apart from that – well, there's all his papers – masses and masses of stuff there, you know, it's so hard to know what to do with it all, whether it's even all intact. I wondered if you – or anyone – would be interested in . . . well, seeing it, perhaps –'

'Taking it off your hands?' She raised her eyebrows by a hair's breadth. 'The Communist Party archive was sold abroad – to the Hoover Institute, I believe. And then I suppose you'd have to consider whether it's all worth preserving. Charles's every utterance.' Her lips flickered with the ghost of a contemptuous smile.

It was getting worse by the minute. I hurried on, to get it over with as soon as possible.

'The main reason I wanted to talk with you was I found his diary, and you were probably one of the last people he saw before he died – and – well, I just wondered whether you remembered – whether he'd said anything – and, you know, just generally how he seemed –'

She looked away then, out of the window, as if considering.

'He did come and see you, didn't he?'

'Oh, yes – yes, he came. I hadn't seen him for quite a long time, we hadn't been in touch for – oh, a number of years, we were – well, before the Party disintegrated there were disagreements and divisions – I'm sure you know all about that; although you weren't Party yourself, were you?' This last remark was spoken with inquisitorial disapproval. 'We didn't see eye to eye about what was happening,' she added in a flat voice – and stopped.

We waited for her to continue. She didn't.

Eventually Myra said, 'This must all seem very intrusive, but you can understand that Justine is anxious to know how he was before he died.'

'He appeared perfectly well – physically well, if that's what you mean. His visit was rather unexpected, and we didn't resolve our differences – I don't think there's much more I can say.'

'You mean you quarrelled?'

'It was more that there was no common ground.'

'I know this sounds melodramatic, but I just have this feeling – I'm quite worried about how my father died . . . I'm even wondering if it was – a natural death,' I said.

Her expression seemed slightly to rigidify as if the skin had been pulled more tautly over the skull, and her leaden, unrelenting gaze seemed almost accusing. There was a horrible silence, and then she said, 'It is hard to come to terms with sudden death.'

Silence again.

'Well,' said Violet and waited. I went on sitting there, failing to take the obvious hint. After a further pause she stood up, and said, 'Well, if there's nothing else –'

Myra stood up too. 'We must go. I'm sorry we've taken up your time.'

'Oh! My time! I have plenty of that, I can assure you.' But she didn't sit down again.

I wasn't wanting to leave, I'd got nothing of what I'd come for, but I couldn't think of anything else to say. Myra had to nudge me towards the door.

Once she'd shut it behind us, however, I burst out, 'Oh why did you say that? Why did you let her push us out? She knew something, didn't she? Why did you let her bully us into creeping off, as if we'd done something wrong?'

Myra gave me a bracing look. 'It wasn't my fault. What could we do? She'd had enough of us. Anyway, I don't think she was holding anything back. Nothing sinister. If you want to know what I think, I think she was just shy.'

'Shy or not, I'm sure there *was* something. She completely clammed up.'

We were walking back to the Lada. A man was leaning against the bonnet.

'Oh Christ, it's Adam. What on earth's he doing here?'

'I'll make myself scarce.'

'No don't, Myra, stay with me.'

When we came abreast of him, he smiled in that apologetic way of his, 'I wondered what had happened to you, love.'

'What are you talking about, Adam? I can look after myself you know. How did you know I was down here, anyway?'

'I must be off, darlings,' said Myra in her plummiest voice.

'But Myra, how will you get back without a car?' I asked, panicking. I was desperate to mull it over with her. Adam was the last person I wanted to see.

'There is still a bus service, angel.' And she billowed determinedly away.

'Let's have a coffee somewhere,' said Adam.

There was a Polish patisserie in the little parade of shops. We sat inside and ordered cheesecake and cappucinos. They were playing an old Ella Fitzgerald tape.

Adam said, 'So tell me what you've been up to down in little old Camden Bay.'

He was annoying me so much I could hardly speak. Then I caught him looking at me in that sad, ingratiating way of his and I suddenly felt sorry for him. Perhaps it was because Violet Frankenberg had been so ungiving, but it all at once seemed mean and pointless to be quite so rejecting. I told him about the visit.

'It was probably only about some dreary old Party squabble. I mean, that's most likely why he visited her,' said Adam.

That was the way I thought about the Party, but it annoyed me when he said it like that.

'You don't know that – how d'you know *what* it was about.'

'It sounds as though they must have been friends once.'

'Well, I suppose they worked together in the Party,' I said, 'but I don't remember her ever coming to the house – I don't remember her at all.'

I wondered what she was doing now. Looking through old documents, old diaries. Or dismissing me as full of bourgeois hysteria. Or sitting there, rigid with shock.

'You think I'm mad, don't you?'

He smiled. 'Of course I don't think you're mad,' he soothed, 'it's just that –' He shrugged. 'It's just that, well, just because he went to see her – I mean, I don't suppose it has anything to do with anything. Not really. He tried to make it up with an old friend.'

'And then right after that he was –'

'I know you think something happened to him. But nothing supports that. Where's the evidence?' His voice was sounding strained now, as if he were losing patience. 'It's all getting out of proportion, love.'

'Well then, so what about Anna? There's no *evidence* for that either I suppose.'

'Justine – are you *sure* you saw, I mean couldn't it just have been the wig – you know, when we went back and there was the wig?'

'You keep saying that. And I keep telling you that of course I'm sure.' I'd raised my voice and the waitress and the other coffee drinkers looked up for a moment to stare at us.

'Okay, okay, I know you're feeling stressed and over-wrought, but *don't shout*. Please.'

'*I am not overwrought.*'

He was looking tense and upset, one of those men that can't stand scenes. 'Ease up, give it a break. I care what happens to you, you know. I just think you should have a rest, forget the whole thing, go away, turn your father's estate over to the lawyers, let them deal with it all, have a holiday, do something sensible with your life.

You don't want to go meddling in things that won't get you anywhere, some wild goose chase, you could get into trouble –'

I stared at him. Now *he* wasn't making sense. 'If it's a wild goose chase, why should I get into trouble?' I asked. 'I can't believe you – you're saying forget it, forget I found a corpse in the house –' Again my voice was rising. He looked anguished, and gestured with his hands.

'If there *was* a corpse,' he muttered.

'Oh Christ! We're not getting anywhere, are we?'

Then I remembered what Jack Morris had told me. I'd intended to mention it the other evening, but then Lennox had turned up and I forgot.

'I hear you're still politically involved,' I said slyly. 'Why were you keeping it such a dark secret?'

He looked at me sharply. 'What? What are you talking about?'

'You know – the port development. The campaign. I keep meaning to tell you, I saw this old friend of my father – well, Jack Morris, you know him, don't you? He's running this campaign against the developers, he said you were part of it all. He said the whole plan was a threat to the Café.'

'Oh – that's right. Couldn't think what you were talking about for a minute.'

'So why didn't you tell me?'

'Well . . . I wasn't sure you'd be interested – you're all caught up with this other thing.' He looked down and stirred the dregs of his cappucino with the teaspoon. 'You didn't tell me you'd been to see Jack.'

Outside the Café, Gennady was lowering the dark-cream sunblinds which stuck out over the pavement tables, shading them from the sun. It was nearly midday.

I sat with Adam at his own special table – and Adam, once he'd brought me another coffee, which as it happened I didn't want, held court. A stream of media types and newshounds took their turn at the seat beside him. A telephone on the table rang every few minutes.

So he had managed to take Khan's place, after all. The Café was the pivot and meeting ground for many different social scenes, and Adam was the pivot of the Café. He was making out fine without Khan. After a while, though, I thought it wasn't quite the same as it would have been in Khan's day. These weren't radicals; they weren't local types either. There were none of the supplicants, cranks and politicos who used to come to Khan for help. Khan used to deal with friends and friends of friends, who needed money, drugs, social contacts, connections, legal advice or therapy, he'd been a one-man alternative advice bureau. Adam was running a very different scene. This was high-class hustling. These guys were out to do deals. The talk was all of contracts, treatments and putting packages together. It wasn't that much different from any other little media hack scene. Any minute I'd see Urban Foster waddling through the door.

When Myra turned up, she was red in the face.

'Wish I had come back with you,' she puffed. 'Waited hours for a bus. Get me a mineral water with lime, will you, darling.' When I returned with it I had my reward. 'Emma thought you were wonderful,' said Myra graciously.

'Oh *good*,' I said, but she didn't notice my sarcasm.

'Aren't you working today?'

She shook her head as Star and Lennox came through the door.

'Do they always go about together?'

Myra smiled at me. 'No – but he *is* just out of prison. I suppose she feels she has to look after her little brother. She doesn't usually show up so early in the day.'

'Where do they come from? Who are they?'

Myra looked at me. 'Oh dear,' she said, 'we're going to have to talk about this. *Some other time*, though.'

Lennox sat down. 'This place just isn't the same any

more. Adam's changed it. Since he's been on his own. For the worse.' Then he looked at me and smiled faintly. 'I shouldn't have said that. Adam's a friend of yours.'

I waved the very idea away. 'Not really,' I said, 'not exactly.'

'It's just the bunch of posers you get here. I suppose *he's* okay, but –'

He's not, actually, I thought, but it seemed disloyal to say it. Anyway, he was all right, really, it was just the misfit of our relationship, if you could call it that. I felt riven with guilt. Adam had been kind to me, he cared about me, while all I could do was –

I put one foot on the rung of Lennox's chair. 'Don't you like the Lost Time Café then?' I said. 'I think it's great.'

'That's because you're into seduction, and it's a seductive kind of place.'

Before I'd had time to stop being stunned and work that one out, he said, 'Adam seems to want to do me a favour.'

The three of us looked at him, Myra, Star and me.

'The man asks me if I need money. Stupid question. Ex-cons aren't usually known for their affluence and I won't be able to sign on, right? More sensible question – what's he offering? "Just think about it," he said. But he didn't tell me *what* I was supposed to think about. Doesn't matter anyway, I've got a job as a biker. Zooming round delivering parcels to people who can't wait for the post.'

'Where did you get the bike?' said Star sharply.

He treated her to his slow smile. 'That would be telling.'

'Oh, come on Lennox, you don't want to get mixed up –'

'It's okay, it's cool, on the level.'

'But why should Adam – ?' I couldn't understand it.

Lennox shrugged. 'Who knows. What is Adam – a philanthropist? A crook? An opportunist?'

'I can lend you some money,' I said casually.

He stared at me with his strange, light eyes, and treated me to his Mona Lisa smile. 'And would *you* tell me what you wanted me to do in return?'

I knew I had to brazen it out. 'Ye-es, I would. But as it happens it's for free. No strings attached.'

'Generous.' He raised his eyebrows and turned it into a campy little flirtation. 'You should give it to the movement, darling,' he said.

'If only there was one,' said Myra.

'There is. Believe me.'

Star said, 'Oh, don't start on about that. Justine doesn't want to hear about all that. It's stupid. Shit, you talk about Adam posing.'

She faced round to me. 'I'm going to the movies in a while,' she said. 'D'you want to come? It's a wonderful film, Wilma Hecht's latest. It's on at the European Institute. Wilma will be there, and we're going to talk about a new project afterwards. I really want to work with her. Who wants to come?'

'Who's Wilma Hecht?' I asked. I thought of the boxes of papers in the house by the University. I thought of all the things I had to do to set my life in order. I thought of how I had to rent a flat, or take a room in a hotel, put the house on the market. I thought of the coldness of Violet Frankenberg.

'Okay,' I said.

Gennady waltzed over. 'Telephone. Is for you.'

I took the call by the bar. 'Hello?'

'This is Violet Frankenberg.' The cold dead voice came down the phone. 'I'd be most grateful if you could find time to call round again.'

'Of course – whenever's convenient.' Lennox had made me feel nervous, but this was worse.

'Oh –' a dry little laugh, 'I have very few demands on my time. I'm sure you're much busier than I am. I leave you to suggest when. Now, perhaps. Yes. The sooner the better, I think.'

I looked over at Lennox, who was lounging carelessly at the big round table and staring at its surface as though lost in thought. Star was standing up and ready to go.

'I'm not really free until . . . later.' I watched as Lennox, suddenly revivified, sprang to his feet, and started to talk to Star.

'This evening then? I should have preferred to see you sooner than that, but . . . well. Shall we say six o'clock?' The telephone clicked. She'd rung off.

I went back to the table. We seemed to be leaving.

Chapter
Nine

We'll go in your car,' said Star.

We dropped Myra off on the Waterfront. Then, keyed up and nervous, almost shivering with the novelty of them, the brother and sister, riding in the back, I took directions for the European Institute.

Suddenly, without any warning, Lennox said. 'Drop me off by the Botanical Gardens. I have to see someone. I'll come to the flat later.'

So he wasn't coming with us after all. He kissed his sister.

Star got out too, opened the front passenger door and sat next to me, just the two of us, on our way to the movies. It wasn't what I'd had in mind, but I was highly conscious of her next to me, in a strange, tense, yet flat sort of way.

I tried to think of ways I could get Star to help me find out more about Anna. I'd get her to ask around on campus . . .

She told me about her film course, she was on to her final project. As she talked, she sat sideways and stared at me. I drove too fast on the freeway, nearly missed the turn-off and swerved dangerously across another car.

'Don't stare.' I laughed, but I felt a bit shaky. 'You're making me nervous.'

She just laughed softly. 'Love your shirt.' And she reached over to feel it on the shoulder. 'Myra says you're rich and married, but a dyke.'

'You could say that,' I said. But could you? 'Isn't every-one just queer these days? Trying to redefine deviance, make it less predictable?'

'In a way that's what my project's about. It's a film version of *Skin*. Have you read it?'

I hadn't. I'd read about it, though – the autobiography of a beautiful woman fetishist, Saffron Queen.

'I've read *Slaves of Desire*,' I offered – her previous book. 'Quite a turn-on in its own way. Rather difficult to film, though.'

'It'll be a horror film.'

Sex as horror; Occam's academic friends used to talk about 'transgressive texts'. Those were the ones which gave their authors an opportunity to show off about what they did in bed, but Occam's friends took it all quite seriously. There is no last frontier of outlawry, they used to say. Transgression is an ever-upward-moving spiral, always new taboos to be broken.

'What's the point,' I said, 'of making more and more explicit films? Weren't those old films about frustration, longing, adultery, really more interesting?'

Star looked surprised. 'They were more romantic, I suppose.'

'Everyone says nothing's taboo, but there are taboos,' I said, 'repression's taboo. Fantasies are taboo. In those Saffron Queen books, everything always does happen, there's only reality. It's the new puritanism, sex as ugly, sex as torture, endless compulsory sex. All that blow by blow banality. Blow job banality.'

Star laughed, with a little catch in her throat. 'Well!' she said, 'an old-fashioned girl.'

The film venue was like the interior of a surrealist aero-plane. The jazz was loud. We strolled across the pink carpet and bought ice-creams to take into the movie. Star's friends were lounging up against the bar: Vlad, who today looked even shorter and more insignificant by comparison with his companions, with his thinning hair and sandy-coloured ancient clothes; a tall, thin ravaged-looking man called Derek; and Jade, the young woman with very short bleached hair.

'Where's Wilma?' Star asked.

'She can't come, got held up,' said Jade.

'Shit.' Star began to mutter in an undertone to Jade.

Then it was time for the film. The air conditioning was doing overtime – the auditorium was like a fridge.

The film was about four women who set off on a journey through Latin America on an immensely ancient train. After an hour or so they were kidnapped by revolutionary bandits and taken into the hills, to the guerrilla camp amidst the ruins of an ancient civilisation.

The film was a journey of self discovery and it was also a satire about the idea of self discovery and about different kinds of film genres. It went on a very long time. Eventually the women – except for one who stayed behind and became a votary of the ancient religion of the Incas – returned to the West and set up an Argentinian tango nightclub.

At around the time when the women were kidnapped Star took my hand and wove her fingers in mine. Perhaps she felt I would like it if she did old-fashioned things like holding hands in the cinema. It was nice to have someone caressing my palm, it was even exciting. And she did look like him, after all – only that just made the whole thing seem even more peculiar.

When it was finally over, and we came blinking out into the daylight, Star said, 'Could you drop me off?'

I looked at my watch. The film had been so long that it was now well after four, and I didn't want to be late for Violet Frankenberg. 'Where d'you have to get to?'

'Avenue West.'

I hesitated. Avenue West was in the opposite direction from Camden Bay, and to drive over there and get back by six would be pushing it.

'Oh well, never mind –' Star looked disappointed.

Then I remembered Lennox's parting words. He'd said he was going back to the flat. He might be there by now.

'It's okay, I'll take you,' I said.

I drove her over to the sprawling district through which Avenue West was cut like a canal. Once it had been Afro-Caribbeans and hippies in perpetual carnival, but now it had changed. The high stucco houses had been repainted – pale blue, almond pink, pistachio. Inside their rooms they'd hung valuable paintings. The oleander bushes were everywhere, thickly blooming in pink and cream. This district was big-M money. Then down towards the railway tracks we crossed a boundary. Now the tall stucco houses were peeling, not painted. The dusty plane trees rippled their shadows across roads full of garbage. Afro-Caribbean children played on the crumbling porches and steps. We drove under the motorway. On the far side a block of flats had been built, the side nearest the road a blank wall to protect the tenants from the sound of the traffic.

'This is it,' she said, as we cruised past more crumbling mansions.

The pavement was so hot I could feel it through the soles of my sandals. But inside the house the stairwell was cool. The ground-floor doors were boarded up. Some of the bannisters were broken, and bits of plaster scattered the beautiful curving steps.

Star's flat was in a time warp. Once or twice I'd been to squats like this in my early teens, with its posters and camp ornaments, culled from tips and junk shops, its orange crates covered with batik cheesecloth, mattresses on the floor and walls and doors painted in shades of petrol blue, crude yellow and dark red. In the cramped living room, the curtains were drawn together and the windows were shut, creating a zone of hot shadow. One thing was different from the seventies, though, for across two huge TV screens images flickered with the sound turned down. I watched. On one screen a film I soon recognised as *The Third Man* cast huge shadows, which reared up in empty cobbled streets and bomb craters in a devastated city of perpetual night. On the second screen pulsed hard-core pictures of men fucking men, men sucking men.

It was strange. As I watched the monotonous fucking I had to admit I felt aroused.

Star touched me on the arm. I turned towards her.

She put her hands on my thighs and moved them upwards between my legs.

'Star – I have to see someone.'

She pulled my shirt open. She laughed. 'Your nipples are quite hard,' she murmured.

'Look, I do really have to be somewhere.'

But she pressed her mouth against mine. We stood glued together, kissing. Her tongue felt big and hard. She held my buttocks, rubbed against me. I put my arms round her neck. I could see my watch. I reckoned about twenty minutes was the most I could stay. I thought of Lennox walking in on this and that made me feel really excited.

We stumbled down on to the floor and didn't wait to undress, although she was pulling at my shirt. The room was a tip. The sofa cover felt scratchy against my bare back. Her mouth was on my nipples and her hair felt coarse and dry as I pushed her head down, and her mouth moved over my stomach and into my cunt. I couldn't stop thinking about how I shouldn't be here, and about Lennox. Suppose he walked in now. It was only by dint of forcing myself into a monumentally violent fantasy about him that I managed to come. Oral sex was never my favourite thing anyway, but I was so relieved I did come that I started to laugh. At the same time I felt angry, as if it had been her fault. I pulled her up against me and bit her as I kissed her and pushed my fingers inside her in a rough kind of way which made me feel powerful, gripping her hot, wet fur. We rolled on the floor and I felt a great powerful sense of what she was, of a femaleness I hadn't expected, and she was gasping and groaning and struggling to let go of some huge force, a dammed-up torrent of sex. Slippery with sweat we lay there. It was a kind of angry struggle, but that made it exciting, and especially as all the time I was pretending it was Lennox.

She began to ride my buttocks. I could feel her nails in my shoulders. My nipples rubbed against the carpet. I could smell dust.

The telephone began to ring and she lurched to her feet.

'It's Wilma.'

Perhaps it was just as well that Wilma was more important than me. I could feel a little less guilty. She came right back. 'That was weird . . . For you – they said you're too late – for your rendezvous.'

The room was hot, but she hugged herself as if she were cold. So was I. 'How could anyone have phoned me – no one knows I'm here.'

I looked at my watch. It said six-thirty.

'Was it a man or a woman?'

'That was the creepy thing. I really couldn't tell. Oh shit. I'm sorry.'

'I will have to go.' Trying to be glacially calm.

My shirt was creased now. I was going to be late. And I was afraid.

'Can I come with you?'

'No.'

I parked my car near the seafront, and almost ran up the hill to the block of flats. Windows were open on the stairs, and as I climbed them I heard birdsong from outside and odd domestic noises from within – a snatch of television, the banging of a hammer, the clash of saucepans. No one was about, yet behind closed doors lives pulsed away, the building was a honeycomb of secrets.

I reached the second floor and rang Violet Frankenberg's bell. The tinny sound died. I stood and waited. Nothing happened. About to press the bell a second time I noticed that the door was not quite shut. I pushed it.

'Hello! Miss Frankenberg!'

Silence. My hand on the open door I thought of the phone call. Too late for your rendezvous. I made myself walk into the flat. 'Hello!' I called again. Only silence. I called a third time. I walked into the little sitting room.

Violet Frankenberg lay twisted and crumpled on the floor, her body like a bundle of sticks, her face a red, jellied mess.

I couldn't have believed there'd be so much blood. I looked away quickly, but the image was there forever.

All around her books and papers were scattered from ransacked drawers and shelves, a whirlwind of words like fallen leaves.

I had to get out of here. Whoever made the phone call would surely bank on my coming over. Perhaps someone was waiting now, somewhere in the flat. I listened.

The body on the floor uttered a faint moan.

Jesus. She was alive.

'Miss Frankenberg! Violet! What happened.'

I knelt down beside her. I felt her pulse – but I was useless. I had no idea what to do.

It was possible, though, to get used to looking at the bloodstained face, and it wasn't as bad as I'd thought. At least the face itself was intact, not crushed, and the blood seemed to have come from a blow on the skull. Yet there was more blood on her shirt and on the carpet than such a blow could have caused. There must be another wound somewhere.

I looked around for the telephone, and dialled the

emergency number. The number had been changed since I'd been away, and then it took ages to get through to the ambulance service.

'She's moaning,' I said, 'what on earth can I do?'

'Just try to make her comfortable,' they said, and had me transferred to the police.

The police also said they'd come right away. But what did that mean – it looked like I'd be here for hours. The police would question me. I was first on the scene of the crime. It looked suspicious, they'd want to know all about me, they'd –

She moaned again, and there was a movement behind me. I whirled around, but it was only Violet Frankenberg, still on the floor, but twisting as if in pain. As I stared her eyes fluttered open. They looked in a horrible way even bluer than before.

I crouched beside her again. I took her hand, wishing like hell that I'd done a first-aid course.

'What happened? Where did they hurt you?'

She was staring at me, but her eyes were glazed as if she were looking far beyond me, at something I couldn't see. Her mouth moved, but only a sort of gurgling croak came out. Now her hand tightened on mine, as she tried again.

'He . . .'

'He? Who?'

Her face looked suddenly agonised. 'Khi – khi –' The guttural sound made me think of blood bubbling in her throat. I squeezed her hand harder. 'Khigeon . . . khi . . . khee . . .'

'Kitchen?' I repeated doubtfully.

Her hand loosened its grip. I looked down at her. Her eyes were closed again. I put my hand over her heart. I couldn't feel anything, but I thought she was still alive.

I ought to call the neighbours, see if they were any better at this than I was, see if they knew whether you should put a pillow under her head, or knew if the blood was still seeping away, or –

I stood up and went into the kitchen. It was neat and calm, untouched. No one had been in here by the look of it. I began opening cupboards, but what was I looking for? Key? Was that it? Was that what she'd been trying to say?

I opened drawers and cupboards. Everything was sparse and tidy. There were no keys anywhere. I looked around, and tried to think of other places where keys might be. Perhaps they'd been hidden. I crouched down and looked at the floor, which was tiled in mottled grey vinyl.

What about her, though? What about Violet? I wondered if water would help.

There was a knock at the front door. Someone called out.

The policeman was in his shirtsleeves. He was red in the face, and mopped his forehead. I stood in the kitchen doorway and stared at him across the devastated sitting room.

'I was just getting a glass of water. I thought –'

'You're Mrs Unwin? You found the body?'

I looked down at Violet Frankenberg, twisted on the floor. 'She's – she was alive –'

'She ain't alive now, love.'

I pulled the front door shut after me, took my sunglasses from my bag and put them on. I crept down the stairs, and my legs seemed to have been turned to cotton wool for the second time in an afternoon, and this time it was a far from pleasant sensation.

I walked away from the flats in the wrong direction at first. To retrace my steps seemed like a gargantuan effort, like climbing Mount Everest. I knew I was in shock. The policeman had been kind, he'd told me to make a cup of tea, and he hadn't asked many questions, just the essentials. I'd assumed he'd suspect me, there I was on the scene of the crime, alone with a dead body, but that wasn't the way the stereotypes worked; as a well-spoken white woman who'd done her citizen's duty by reporting the deed, I seemed to be ruled out from the start.

Yet it was my fault she'd died. If I'd got there sooner, if I hadn't gone back with Star . . .

I sat at the wheel of my car for what seemed like a long time. Then I drove up the hill to the freeway, and soon I was speeding to the centre of the city, flying along the overpass with the brilliant view of the port, through the gentrified terraces, past the abandoned warehouses. I didn't know where I was going. I couldn't think of anywhere to go except the Café, but I had a strong resistance to that. If I told Adam I'd found another body he'd know for sure I was mad. You just don't go round falling over bodies like that. Unless you've murdered them yourself, of course.

I drove around for a while. Someone had known I was at Star's. One of her friends? That was just too unlikely. But someone had telephoned. Who, though? Star was the only person who'd absolutely known I was there. Of course Star herself could have got someone else to telephone me there. I felt as if cold ice was melting down my back. Star had left the auditorium during the film – to go to the toilet, I'd assumed, but maybe it was to telephone. Her contact could have phoned us at the flat when he – or she – had finished with Violet –

But that scenario was crazy too. Star was Lennox's sister, and Lennox was a dissident, he'd just come out of prison, it couldn't possibly be her. She had no connection with all this.

Waves of golden heat hung in the evening air. All the Lada windows were open to the limit. I coasted down towards the city centre through suburbs where lime trees stickied the pavements and buddleias scented the petrol-laden air with honey from their purple phalluses.

To whom could I go with this horrible secret, bursting with it? Who could I tell? Not Star, not Adam. I missed Occam – at least my ex had been reliable, at least he was a friend. What friends had I here?

Well, there was Myra. I could tell her.

I parked the Lada illegally and roamed off along the Waterfront. It seemed a long way to Myra's tent through the early-evening crowds, and anyway it was a waste of time, for when I reached the tent Myra wasn't there. I ran back in the opposite direction. Now I'd got the idea that I had to talk to her, I wanted to see her so badly, I couldn't stand the frustration of her not being there. Now that I needed her.

I'd collected a parking ticket, but I didn't care. I reversed the car in a screech of brakes and shrieking horns and set off on yet another traffic-clogged journey to her place beyond the slabs.

When I got there I ran along the deck between the tower blocks. My lungs were bursting by the time I reached her front door.

A tall Afro-Caribbean opened it. Huge, dreadlocks, tiny red shorts.

'Myra? Is Myra here?'

He laughed. 'Man, you're outta breath. That's the way to kill yourself, man. Come in, sit down. But Myra ain't here, she's gone –'

'Gone!'

'Out for the evening – don't panic. She'll be back.'

'Oh, *Christ*,' I screamed with frustration.

'Take it easy – name's Baz by the way.'

'I'm Justine.'

'Well, come on in, Justine, sit down and get your breath back. Like a cup of tea?'

When he came back with the mug of tea – it was
ordinary tea this time, not Myra's horrible herbal stuff
– he said, 'Looked like you'd seen a ghost when you
come through the door. You're the one whose old man
died, right?'

'How d'you know that?'

He laughed. 'Don't look so worried! News spreads
fast around here. Myra told me. Or Lennox. I forget.
The dyke with the dosh wings in from outer space and
everyone wants to know whose side she's on.'

'What's that supposed to mean?'

'Means whatever you think it means.'

'Lennox a friend of yours?'

'Met him inside – not this time around. The time before.
Me, I been keeping my nose clean. Or let's just say I been
careful.' He roared with laughter again. But what was
so funny?

'Lennox was in prison before?'

'Sure thing.'

'What for?'

'Ask him.'

'Why are you so suspicious?'

He laughed. 'Me! Suspicious! Whatever give you that
idea! Let's just say we all have to be careful. It don't go
down so good to go round asking questions.'

I felt angry and totally frustrated. I stood up to go.
'Thanks for the tea.' I'd hardly drunk any of it.

'You'll find Myra at the Café.'

'That's what I was afraid of.' The Café – all those chic
creatures with their coffees and cocktails and carefree
laughter; Myra, surrounded by acolytes; Lennox; Adam.
Adam was worst of all. I couldn't face Adam. I couldn't
face any of them.

Back in the car I sat thinking. What would my
father have done? I smoothed my hand along the
wheel and thought of him sitting there, where I was
sitting now.

My father was methodical. He was an old-style rationalist. None of that stuff about listening to your feelings. He was all for listening to your brain. Okay, so you'd like to tell someone, spilling it all all over Myra will make you feel better, but is it really going to help?

The trouble was, I didn't know what *was* going to help.

Chapter
Ten

The only light was the moonlight. I wandered through the house. Lennox was there. We opened a door, and found a whole wing of the house I'd never known existed, rooms and rooms panelled in dark-brown wood. In the attics was a circular domed room with a little balcony, and this room suffused me with warmth and happiness, as though something wonderful, I didn't know what, was about to happen. Violet Frankenberg sat waiting for us. She stood up, she smiled –

The knock on the door was quiet. And someone was playing a Mozart clarinet concerto, very soft, very discreet.

I opened my eyes and remembered that Violet Frankenberg was dead. The knock came again.

I was in another unfamiliar room. 'Come in.'

Room service was a young man in a jacket but no shirt. He wheeled the breakfast trolley forward, wafted over to the window and drew the cord that opened the curtains. 'Bon appetit,' he said.

Oh yes. I'd wanted to be nowhere, I'd wanted oblivion, I'd wanted anonymity, so I'd checked into the best hotel in town. I'd come to the Ocean View Hotel to sit alone and drink, and cry over Violet Frankenberg.

I lay in the sanctuary I'd paid for, a vacuum of Japanese minimalism, and ate the fruit and the rolls and drank the coffee. I had a shower. I dressed. I looked at myself in the wall of mirrors. Who was it once said it's the badly-dressed people that are the most interesting? I certainly qualified today. I was wearing my crumpled linen trousers. My maroon nail varnish was chipped. A camisole strap hung down. The chipped nail varnish aesthetic, the super chic of laddered stockings, of black mascara shadows under the eyes . . . well, yes. At least it was better than the haggard girl in the flower-sprigged frock.

The light off the sea was dazzling. I looked out at my five-star view. I had a headache and my eyes hurt, but I wasn't in shock any more.

I telephoned Myra, and this time she was there, this time she came. The Ocean View Hotel was close to her pitch, after all.

We had more room service. I told her what had happened.

'So,' said Myra. 'She knew your father – and she's been murdered. There's not much room for doubt any more, d'you think? Your father's death can't have been an accident.'

We sat and looked at each other.

'I almost half-believed Adam, I mean I really wanted to be wrong –'

'Of course you did,' said Myra.

'It's frightening, I mean it's really for real.'

'We must go back up to the house.'

There were some letters lying on the floor. Mailshots and circulars addressed to Professor Hillyard still arrived almost daily. Today, a large manila envelope, addressed to me, looked more interesting. The handwriting was unfamiliar.

I tore the envelope and pulled out some typed sheets. I scanned the first page, unable to take it in, then, bewildered, I turned to the signature.

'Oh, *God* – it's from Violet Frankenberg.'

I sat down on the stairs.

'What's the matter?'

I laughed hysterically. 'A voice from beyond the grave.' I laughed some more, and then I started to cry. Myra sat down beside me on the stairs and put an arm round my shoulders.

'Let's read what she says.'

The sheets of papers were typed with an old-fashioned manual typewriter. As I read each page I passed it to Myra.

Dear Justine,

We are due to meet later today, but I find I am unable to get what you said about Charles's death out of my mind. I have been thinking and thinking about it, and it has ended with my writing you this letter. You may not even receive it before we meet, but it seems helpful to set things down in black and white. Helpful for me, at least.

I was *very* taken aback by what you said about Charles's death – it seemed unbalanced – and quite unsubstantiated. Frankly, I felt you were dramatising things, but perhaps I was prejudiced because you reminded me of your mother. It may even be that seeing you reawakened bitter and jealous feelings that were never acknowledged at the time. You don't look like Joyce, of course – you're more like your father in appearance, something else that rather threw me, that flickering of a likeness in someone so different. But anyway, something about you this morning reminded me of Joyce – your manner of expecting one to do as you wanted without actually asking directly.

Your father and I had a love affair, you see. I met your parents through the Party, of course. It's such a lost world, that time. It seems a hundred years ago. That whole world we lived in has tumbled about our ears. Can you imagine what it has been like for those who devoted their whole life to a cause, and then at the end had to confront the possibility of having been mistaken?

I was just an innocent little fool, I suppose. I adored your father. I was twenty-six, but I was pretty inexperienced, and it all seemed so hopeful and brave to begin with.

But gradually I found – of course, what else should I have expected – that attitudes in the Party to love and marriage were inconsistent and contradictory. On the one hand adultery was 'bourgeois'. On the other we were *above* bourgeois morality. Men and women were supposed to be equal in the Party, and in some ways there was a kind of equality, but in so many ways life was carried on on men's terms. It was a small, marginalised organisation and, like any other institution or group, it was bound to reflect the society in which it existed, and in so many ways my situation was just the same as that of any 'mistress', although we would never have used that term.

It took me a long time to realise that Charles really was devoted to *her*, that she always came first for him. Much later I found out that she had been in love with another man, a friend of Charles's, long before he'd even met me. Something had gone wrong, I don't know what. Charles had never mentioned that to me. I used to wonder if I was Charles's revenge. But that's unworthy too. It was more than that.

Our affair went on for years, but it wore out, and ended in acrimony and disillusionment. I suppose it was your mother's illness that first began to separate us, but there were all the political disagreements as well.

Perhaps we used politics as a way of avoiding discussing our private feelings, but our disagreements were real. Many of us in the Party realised that so much was left out of Marxism. We had to face up to the fact that socialism meant *nothing* without democracy. The end of the Soviet Union and what happened in Eastern Europe came as a great relief to many of us – but not to Charles. He saw it as a huge betrayal of socialism. My final quarrel with him was about Poland. He loathed Solidarity right from the start.

And perhaps we were naive again, for what's happened since is as bad as the Brezhnev years – worse. But doesn't the blame for that lie in the past as well? I think so. The Soviet Union just sat on everything, it just repressed all that nationalism and ethnic prejudice and anti-semitism, it never dealt with it, never educated people. It can't have done. And real education is a fundamental part of democracy.

However, that's not the point of this letter. What is disturbing me is my last meeting with Charles. I hadn't seen him for a long time. And then one day he rang me up, out of the blue. Wanted to come and see me, needed to talk to me. I wasn't keen, to tell you the truth, but in the end of course I agreed, and so he came.

And the minute I saw him I knew something was going on. He was – *excited*, like he used to be when he'd got hold of some idea or other. That was always so attractive in the old days, this well of enthusiasm and energy. He said, 'I feel I've got a new lease of life, Violet, I feel I can contribute.' But he would only give me hints. It was all completely nebulous.

He said one or two rather strange things. For instance, he said, 'The past is never dead, you know, you never know when it will rise up again.' Something else he said, 'Our friend will have a hell of a shock,' and something about, 'The irony of it is that someone whose life seemed such a seedy failure should have his revenge at last. His last scoop. Though maybe he didn't deserve it. But then again, maybe he did.'

I remember it almost word for word, because it seemed so odd, so senseless. He also gave me a little envelope and a photograph, but when I asked him what they were, what they meant, he wouldn't tell me. He only laughed in a peculiar way. 'Just in case anything happens to me,' he said. I asked what on earth could happen to him. And he said nothing would happen to him, but just in case, I'd have the record. The record of what? And he said, 'Me and my good friend. And *Joyce's* good friend.'

It was intensely irritating. It seemed so melo-dramatic, and unfortunately we ended up quarrelling again. We parted angrily. That saddens me now, of course. It made it all the harder to talk about when you came along with another dose of melodrama.

I doubted at first if there was really anything sinister about Charles's death. A man of seventy-odd drops dead. It happens all the time. But he *did* behave strangely that day.

Well, there it is then. I enclose the photograph. And we will talk later.

'God!' said Myra.

I snatched the sheets back from her and read the letter again. There was a stoicism about it, but there was a sort of dryness of the spirit as well, a lack of sentimentality, but a lack of pity too.

I shook the manila envelope, held it open and drew out of it the photograph. It was an old black and white snapshot, cracked in places and bent at the corners.

Three young men in uniform leant against the only remaining wall in a street full of rubble, and smiled at the camera with cheerful arrogance. As if the war had been one great adventure. I wondered who'd taken the picture, whose hand had clicked the shutter before disappearing for ever down the wind tunnel of history. My father looked so young, so different, for a split second I had trouble recognising him. He stood on the left of the picture. He wore old-fashioned, round, horn-rimmed spectacles, and the same haircut he'd worn ever since, a no-nonsense short back and sides. Amazing – he'd been handsome. I'd never thought of him that way. Delicate features, straight nose, but it was the smile which gave him that 1930s Young Pioneer look – fresh, enthusiastic, so confident of a revolutionary future, so confident, period.

'Who are they?' said Myra.

'That's my father.'

'And the other two?'

'Haven't a clue – but I suppose that's what it is – a clue.'

'The letter's sad,' said Myra.

'The past's always sad.'

I held the photograph flat with my fingertips and stared at those three strangers: my father and – but who were the others? My father looked casual to the point of untidiness – but that was no surprise. By contrast the man in the middle wore his hat at a rakish angle, his tunic smartly done up. He was much shorter than my father, and his face was rounded and heavy beneath the peaked hat, he had a slightly bulbous forehead and thick eyebrows frilling over a roman nose and fleshy lips. Handsome – but you could see how middle age would coarsen him, he'd become gross, red, with beetling brows, heavy jowls.

A tall youngster completed the trio. He was extremely thin, and had a narrow gothic face. I had a feeling I might have seen him around in the Party long ago.

Myra and I sat side by side and looked at the letter once more. 'Well,' said Myra, 'the first thing is, what your father said about after the war – and what he was doing now, in the present. "His last scoop" – what does that mean? And "Joyce's good friend" – would that be her lover?'

'I don't know. And then there's the snapshot,' I said. Who were the other men in the photo? Standing there in the middle of war-torn Europe as if they hadn't a care in the world. And how would I ever find out more about them? 'One of these men might have been her lover. But so what? He surely wouldn't have come back nearly fifty years later and killed my father in a fit of jealous rage.'

Myra was silent for a bit. Then she said, 'You know, there must be clues in this house.'

'There are – hundreds – in amongst all his bloody papers.'

'I was thinking of more personal things – private papers, diaries, letters.'

'It's so hard to imagine him *having* love letters – keeping them,' I said doubtfully. 'My mother now – that's different, but . . .'

'But did you think he was the sort of man to have love affairs at all until you read this?'

'The photo albums,' I cried. 'They were kept in a drawer at the bottom of my parents' wardrobe. Let's look upstairs.'

The bare mattress with two neat piles of blankets, the dusty dressing table, the old, old photo of my grandparents, the portrait photo of me and my mother, the silver brush and mirror set – another room lost in time. I wondered why my father had never altered it. Perhaps it was because I'd never helped him. Perhaps it was because he'd never been able to cope with my mother's attachment to all her possessions, those badges of privilege. How badly matched they'd been.

'My mother always talked to me about injustice; it was colonialism then. And the Americans, the cold war, Vietnam. And peace, always peace, the peace movement. I always thought they were so *right*, I mean there was no chink in their armour, no moment of doubt. But now I see they were just a seething mass of contradictions too.'

Myra laughed. 'That's parents for you.'

I opened the wardrobe drawer, and yes, there was the familiar cardboard box with the name and logo of a long-defunct department store on its lid.

The photographs were grouped in envelopes. There were ancient ones of my parents as children, most of them of my mother. There was their marriage photograph. They stood outside the registry office. My mother wore a full, almost ankle-length dress in a dark colour, with a light, tightly-waisted jacket and a hat with a little veil. Beside my father could be seen half of another male figure, presumably the best man, but his face was out of the frame.

There were pictures of me as a baby, as a toddler

playing in a garden. There were holiday snaps. Some of them had obviously been taken in Eastern Europe – my parents posed with men in ugly suits, in one case under a statue of Lenin. There were photographs from marches and demonstrations.

We found what we were looking for when we'd given up hope, in an envelope tucked away at the bottom of the box, on which my mother had written in her neat hand 'University'. There were three little square photographs. In the first, my mother was standing between two men against one of the ivy-clad buildings in the front quad of the campus. All three were laughing, and carrying little piles of books. The men were my father and the stocky man. I turned it over. On the back my mother had written 'Self with Colin and Charles,' and the date.

'Look at this.'

'You see!' Myra triumphed. 'We've discovered something. I knew we would.'

'That his name was Colin. Not a lot to go on.'

The second photo was of 'Colin', my father and a young woman by a tent. The third was of Colin and another woman seated on some rocks at the seaside. On the back of this one my mother had written simply 'Brittany – Colin and Winifred'.

'Well, but it's something,' said Myra. I could have hugged her for that 'we'. 'We just need to do some research, that's all. And there don't seem to be *any* photos of the tall one. So maybe he's out of the picture altogether. But here's *this* guy – Colin – with your old man in the army, and then again at University. That's afterwards, isn't it? Is it?'

'Yes. That's right. He was one of the ones who went to College after he got out of the army, at least, I think so.' How little I knew about my parents' life when you came down to it.

Someone called Colin – I was looking over Violet

Frankenberg's letter again. Myra sat squarely planted on the bed.

'I was thinking,' she said, 'you see in the letter – see what it says your father said. "His last scoop." Now what does that suggest to you? Right? A journalist, of course. So what about looking through old newspapers?'

'Oh, *Myra*! Christ! That would take for ever – even longer than looking through Dad's stuff.'

Myra smirked. 'Not necessarily. What about the Party paper – what was it called?'

'*Workers World*?' Now that *was* a good idea. 'But he might not have worked for the Party,' I said.

'It's quite likely he did, though, isn't it. It's worth a try.'

'There might be old Party members who remember him too.'

'It'll take a while. But not *that* long.'

'If only we knew his surname.'

'"A seedy failure" – people might remember that.'

The shock of Violet Frankenberg's letter was seeping through me more and more. My parents in this late and unexpected light of passion and adultery and estrangement – it was hard to believe. Had they been unhappy? Had my mother's life especially been sad, unfulfilled? She'd been ill for so long, died so early. It was so hard to remember, to know – but maybe that was where the secret lay.

'We'll go and see Aunt Susan,' I said.

Chapter
Eleven

I told myself that I wasn't in shock any more, that I'd recovered from Violet Frankenberg's death, from finding her, but it wasn't true. Shock veiled the following days. I moved in a dull grey cocoon through the heat and the sunlight.

The police interviewed me again, but they didn't query my story: that she'd been a friend of my parents, to whom I'd been paying a dutiful visit. And why should they have doubted me – it was the truth, after all, if not the whole truth. They'd decided, in any case, that Violet had surprised an intruder, that her murder had been unpremeditated – just one of those commonplace crimes that didn't even make the national dailies.

It was headlines in the *Camden Bay Chronicle*, of course. I refused them an interview. I didn't want to put my head above the parapet, and I was irrationally relieved that they didn't mention me by name. This was irrational because of course whoever had done it knew all about me.

I thought about him a lot. There he was, somewhere in the city, somewhere in a room in a house or a block of flats, or driving around in a car, or sitting in a restaurant, or walking along the beach – doing all those things, and knowing. And waiting, for me. It gave me the creeps to think of him reading those headlines. What would he be thinking? He'd be laughing, that was for sure, sitting pretty with no finger of suspicion pointing at him.

I hid in the Ocean View Hotel for several days, but their prices were making a hole even in my bank account, and anyway I knew that sooner or later I had to face the Lost Time Café. It wasn't the Café, it was Adam, and when I gritted my teeth and pushed open the door he was as bad as I'd imagined, fussing over me in a way that made me feel not stronger but weaker.

'Now don't do anything crazy, Justine, just leave it to the police, they know what they're doing.'

You bet they did. They were covering up, that's what they were doing – but when I suggested as much to Adam that pained, worried, shifty look flickered across his face; he was humouring me again.

I found I was telling him less and less of what I was doing.

The newspaper division of the National Library was housed along with the main book collections in the former Royal Northern Hotel, a red-brick Victorian castle. The frontage was a replica of the Doge's palace, and had gained, since the Venice floods had destroyed the original, a kind of architectural cachet. The new wing was built on the site of the disused goods yard at the back, and this housed the newspapers.

The tiled hall was cool on a hot day, but a design error – too much glass, and the automatic window shades had a chronic malfunction – made the newspaper section an uncomfortable and tiring place to work. Upstairs, the sun poured in on to long tables at which readers sweated as they scanned giant volumes of bound newsprint.

I ordered my volumes of *Workers' World*. Then, since I'd forgotten to bring anything to read while I waited the half hour or so it took them to fetch the volumes up from the stacks, I descended to the basement coffee shop. It felt chilly after the heat upstairs. The only other customer was a young man seated in one corner.

The cold made me shiver. My stomach constricted

117

suddenly, and I felt ill, anxious, jittery. It was part of my state of shock, I supposed, to be feeling all the time as I'd felt in those first minutes, staring at Violet Frankenberg as she lay on the floor.

Now, though, I was staring at the young man. It was Lennox. He looked up from the book he'd been reading. He showed no surprise. He smiled his slow smile, and just waited for me to walk over to him. And of course I did. I wondered if he could tell that my legs had turned to water.

Coincidence has a way of seeming momentous, like – 'it was meant to be'. So seldom is. You chat for a moment, you might even have a drink, but then you and whoever it was you met by accident go on your separate ways, and that's the end of it.

Afterwards, I used to wonder if this meeting had been a coincidence at all, or whether he'd come to the Library on purpose, to lie in wait for me. He could have found out I'd be there. Myra knew.

Afterwards, much later, all I knew for sure was that that was the moment at which the die was cast. Everything that happened later grew from this. Yet I made the choice without allowing myself even to know what I was doing.

At the time pleasure triumphed over nerves. I felt as if I'd been lit up from inside. The simple act of buying him some cake seemed like a gift from heaven.

'Why aren't you charging round on your bike?'

'Oh . . . I had some research to do,' he said vaguely, 'I only do the messenger stuff when I'm really desperate for cash.'

I sat there, drinking him in.

'I'm glad I met you,' he said, 'it's so difficult to talk at the Café. And anyway you haven't been there.'

So he'd noticed. My eyes met his. His look was unreadable: intent, serious, shy; it could even have been what I hoped it might be.

Almost at once he looked away, his eyelids weighted with their dark lashes. It was as if he'd pulled down a shutter, withdrawn into himself.

'I've been wanting to talk to you,' he said, 'let's go outside, it's cold in here. I hate the cold. It was always cold in prison. Funny really – it was because they'd installed air conditioning. The screws insisted. It was so hot before. But afterwards it was like living in a fridge.'

We went out into the white glare of the courtyard and sat on some shallow steps. I was tempted to lie right down on the paving stones and have the heat roll over me, flatten me into the ground.

They were taking up the road beyond the railings. The intermittent stuttering of the pneumatic drill came from the far end of the street, but just beyond the railings the steamroller pounded the fresh tarmac. It glittered black like treacle. The air shimmered with heat above the surface, and you could smell the tar.

'Less likely to be overheard out in the open,' said Lennox, 'though I don't suppose it matters, it's naff the way some people go on about that sort of thing. Being paranoid can be so self-important.'

My skin felt warm like a baked biscuit. It wasn't, of course, it was covered in sunblock make-up.

'I heard about the woman you found – the one who was murdered. Sounded pretty rough.'

'It was horrible.' Again I saw her lying there – the blood – the blue eyes in that red mask of a face – her croaking last attempt at speech. 'I don't want to talk about it.'

He said, 'I just thought it must have really upset you. Myra told me about your old man, too – like someone could have offed him as well –'

How could I not talk about it? It was there all the time. 'It must be connected,' I said. 'Until this happened I wasn't sure, it could all have been – well, I think Adam still thinks it's all my imagination. But now – there was nothing imaginary about the way Violet died.' Tears swam into my eyes, but I managed to keep them from falling.

'It sounds feeble, but I am sorry. Maybe I shouldn't have mentioned it, I just thought –'

'It's okay.'

I sat there and thought about Violet. I forgot why we were sitting there. I even forgot about Lennox.

When he spoke again it startled me.

'The way I look at it, those old Communists, they fucked up in the end. Sold the pass. Bottled out. Couldn't go the whole distance. But we won't make the same mistakes – though it's so much harder now. We're starting so far back from where they were. From where we are you could say they had it all going for them. And still they managed to fuck everything up in the end.'

His words annoyed me. 'You underestimate the difficulties, I think,' I said drily. 'Actually, being in a Communist family, it turned me off the whole thing. And yet when you attack them like that I want to defend them. They were serious about they were doing, you know. That's why they were careful. And it was never easy, it was never like you say.'

'It didn't work, though, did it?' he said. 'And now we have to start all over again.'

'Who's we?'

'Oh, there are lots of groups – I mean, there has to be some opposition, doesn't there? Left-wing opposition. The stakes are getting higher all the time. Like – with the coalition – there's no official opposition at all, no legitimate alternative, the rump of the left, that's all, in collapse. And now the PP and New Albion are coming on really strong . . .

'But we're quite big – we're growing all the time. Different groups do different things. We're planning a pirate radio station. And one or two other ideas. Things have hotted up while I was inside. There was quite a lot

going on *in* prison, anyway. I met some good contacts.'
His lips twitched in a little reminiscent smile. 'There was a
New Albion type – he wasn't in for that, they didn't know.
I talked to him a lot. Interesting. Albion's politics are shit,
of course, but they do have some good ideas when it comes
to methods, propaganda, agit prop, that sort of thing.'

Now he was being stupid. 'You think so? Terrorism?
Oh, come *on*, Lennox, you're not into that kind of crap.
How old are you – nineteen? You don't want to spend
your life in and out of prison.'

'I'm twenty-one,' he said, offended. 'And it's all right
for you, for people like you, but look all around you, how
do most people live – shitty, fucking awful lives.'

'I do know.'

'Anyway,' he backtracked, 'I'm not saying terrorism,
terrorism's just a word, anyway. But surely we do have
to expose the authoritarian state. We need mental bombs,
to blow their credibility apart, to destroy their power to
define the situations.'

He was beginning to quote some party line, I could
tell. Those weren't his own words, he was repeating
something he'd heard. He went on like that for a bit.
Then he fell silent. I didn't know what to say. My CP
upbringing was more enduring than I'd thought. I'd long
ago learnt a name for what he was saying: adventurism.
Yet with all my heart I wanted to believe that there was
something serious about him.

But the heat made thought and conversation too much
of an effort. And I liked just lying there, so close to him;
except, of course for the sword that lay between us. He
was so close, but he was remote, untouchable.

The pneumatic drill burst out again. My volumes of
Workers' World would have arrived by now. I ought to go
back into the prison house of knowledge.

'The trouble is,' he said, 'the question of violence. That
is the cutting edge in the end. Gradualism and parliament
just haven't worked. So maybe the Situationists were

right, maybe staged violence – the spectacle of violence – how else are you to shake people out of their apathy? They've lost heart in the voting process. People want something different, something more radical.'

'They want a bit of hope I suppose. What's the good of a spectacle?'

'So why do you sit in the fucking Lost Time Café? That's a spectacle, isn't it? You get off on that.'

'Oh, well – me. I'm not political at all – like I say, I turned against it.'

'Your father can't have liked that.'

'He didn't.'

'How *did* they think the world was going to change? What *was* their theory of change?'

It dawned on me he really wanted to know. 'Some of them are still around – you should talk to Jack Morris.'

'Oh yeah, the Port guy. Trouble is, it's a bit late for that sort of thing. You can win a little here and there, of course, but . . .'

'It's a pity you couldn't have talked to my dad.'

'Someone must have done him in – but how could you find out for sure?'

'Lennox! That's what I'm trying to do!'

'My first time inside I was sent to an open prison – lots of grasses, bent cops, white-collar-fraud types, that sort of thing. Rather different from Bentham Prison. There were even a couple of politicians there, been caught with their pants down.'

'Adultery? You're joking – they were in prison because of *that*?'

'Of course not. Political scams, corruption, things that had just got so embarrassing they couldn't be overlooked. There's lots more of course, things that never come out, that's what I'm researching now – some of the big boys.

'Anyway, I met someone there, he'd been in the secret service, passed information to someone he shouldn't. Nothing big, but he got found out. Doing three years.

He was weird. Out of his head – but he told me some useful little bits and pieces.'

And as Lennox talked, a whole shadowy web of secret connections, of things I'd never dreamt about, floated into vision. 'It was like lifting one tiny corner at the very outside edge of something huge,' he said, 'I used to feel, when he told me things, it was like a curtain, and behind the curtain there was a byzantine underworld of intrigue and manipulation. The way he talked, I used to wonder if *any* of them understood it all, it was a world that no one in the end controlled, it just ran of its own volition, reproduced itself, pulsating in the dark like some rogue bacterial culture in history's boiler room, like something in a horror movie.

'And you know, maybe someone *was* interested in your old man. They did keep tabs on them, you know – he told me, he thought it was a big joke, he really fancied himself – I might look him up, he might know something – bit of a long shot, because of course he was sacked, still –'

'Would you? Be good if you could.'

'I met someone else, too – not in prison – just a journalist I know – met him down on the beach one night.'

This was what I wanted to hear. I was sceptical about his contacts: it was the gesture that thrilled me, the fact that he was prepared to help me.

He stopped talking again. In the silence the tension built up; my tension, but maybe his too. I could have sat there for ever, stoned mindless by the heat and by him, but it was smarter to move first. If I broke the spell, he'd show his hand.

'Better get back.'

'Don't go . . .' His hand shot out and landed on my knee. 'There's something I wanted to ask you.'

'Yes?' Deliberately I took his hand in mine. It was a fine hand, strong, with long fingers. I turned it over. 'A double heart-line,' I said, and drew my finger slowly down it.

'Another fortune teller.'

I let go of his hand. 'What was it you wanted to ask me then?'

'This group I'm involved with, I – like I said, things have been developing while I've been inside. The pirate radio's really ready to go, we just don't have the cash.'

'And so you thought of me.'

'Yes,' he said, simply.

At least he didn't beat about the bush like Adam.

'It *is* a good idea. But you'll have to tell me more.'

The way he told it, it really did seem good. Someone – mainly Baz, by the sound of it – had done a lot of work on this.

'How much do you need?'

I hadn't got used to écus yet, but surely the sum he quoted was huge for even the best equipment.

'I'll think about it,' I said. 'It would take me a little while – I'd have to sell some shares.'

'Oh, say you'll do it, that'd be sublime . . .'

'I'll think about it.'

He took it coolly, but I could see he was terribly pleased by the way he smiled. I could see he knew I'd succumb. He felt confident he'd get it in the end.

And I – what did I feel? I watched him smile and wished I could have kissed that beautiful mouth. I watched him, and he caught me at it.

'How can I thank you?' he said. But the smile faded. 'It's wonderful – if you'll do it.' Now he sounded quite sombre. 'I owe you.' He stared at the paving stones.

'When I was in prison I read this novel,' he said. 'A man comes to a mining town. The workers have nothing, they spend twelve hours a day – maybe more – down the pit, but they're starving. They dress in rags and live in hovels. Life is grim beyond imagining. The man lives and works among them. He is a revolutionary. They don't know it, but he has come to liberate them. He's dedicated to the cause, one hundred per cent, and so he permits himself no feelings, no emotional ties, no lovers, no friends. The one exception to this is that he has a pet rabbit.

'One evening, there's even less food than usual, in desperation, his landlady kills the animal and serves it up to her lodgers. For once they have a square meal. Afterwards, someone asks: but how was it we had meat today? There hasn't been meat in weeks. She tells them – whereupon the revolutionary goes outside and is violently sick.

'At the end of the novel he goes down the mine and blows it up, but of course he kills himself in the process.'

'An even less encouraging example than my father, I should have thought.'

He smiled. 'The moral is – don't have a pet rabbit. No chinks in one's armour.'

'You have lovers, though.'

He shook his head. 'Not really.'

'Let's go inside,' I said.

My volumes of *Workers' World* had arrived. Soon they wrapped me in another time. Lennox was forgotten in the bleakness of that world of 1947. It was so strange and other, that world, yet so strangely the same as our world of the millenium. Between the two, the world I'd grown up in, the world of the seventies, had disappeared, and we were back in something much closer to that smudged, black and white universe of old newspaper, that world of chaos and war.

In 1947 Central Europe was one vast camp for displaced persons. Cities were heaps of rubble. Nazis were on trial. The British had destroyed the Greek Resistance – on one front page there was a photograph of two partisans. The handsome man with a pointed moustache stood there casually on a hillside dressed in pyjamas and an overcoat. He was holding the hand of a young woman in a headscarf. They gazed with mild stoicism at their executioners, waiting to be shot.

The West was getting sucked into the Cold War, and was in the grip of an icy winter as well. I leafed on. There were strikes and the troops were drafted in. It was as if the triumph of Hitler's defeat had been forgotten. All that was left was the desolation of victory.

I was looking for a journalist whose name was Colin, but most of the reports were signed simply 'Workers' World reporter' or 'special correspondent'. It was discouraging, boring, my fingers began to feel soiled, but I went doggedly on, and eventually I did find the dispatch I was – maybe – looking for: an article by someone called Colin Fox. There was no proof that this was the Colin of the photograph, of course. It was merely a possibility worth pursuing. I read carefully on through the heavy volumes. No other Colin appeared. I worked at it for over two hours.

Then I just sat there, thinking. Perhaps the thing to do was to interview the ex-editor of the *World* – not the man who'd been editing it in the forties, he was dead years ago, but Maurice Kavanagh, the editor from the 1960s to its demise, a long stretch, and he might well remember something useful, or know what had happened to Colin Fox.

Jack Morris could probably put me in touch with Kavanagh. I'd find him at one of his meetings. I stood up, preparing to leave, and looked around for Lennox.

But he wasn't there. He'd gone.

Chapter
Twelve

The Port campaign group meeting was in a room above a disused pub which had been converted into a community centre. Less than a mile further along the shoreline from the Café and its habitués, it belonged to a different world, to a declining area of boarding houses and cheap hotels, blocks of ex-municipal housing, faltering caffs and low-income supermarts.

A dozen men and women sat round a table, with a second half-circle of mostly younger people ranged behind them, including a woman in shorts with a toddler on her lap and a baby in a buggy. Jack Morris was chairing the meeting. Adam was seated to his left, and to Adam's left a woman with a grey pudding-basin haircut and a grey, unravelling cardigan was speaking as I entered.

People looked up as I squeezed past, miming my intention not to disturb by hunching my shoulders and tip-toeing stiffly, but the grey-haired woman just carried on talking. I could tell, once I'd settled myself, that she'd been droning on interminably, by the way in which members of her audience were frowning out of the window, or examining minutely a thread in a sleeve or a scar on a limb or fiddling with their hair. Jack tried to nudge her along.

A bent tortoise-like character with a shock of white hair and old tweed jacket was seated on Jack's right. I hadn't seen him for years but I recognised him at once as Maurice Kavanagh, in better days the editor of the *Workers' World*.

One of the tearaways at the back was pressing for more militant forms of direct action. 'They don't give a fuck about legal protest, that's just a ruling-class safety valve, we gotta *do* something.'

There was a flurry of agreement and disagreement. Adam said nothing. Maurice Kavanagh's neck moved in and out of his tweed collar as he tried to get a word in. This made him look even more like a tortoise. Finally he said, 'As revolutionary socialists our guiding principle must always be – CAUTION.'

Titters from the back.

'No – no, I'm serious, we're not playing games here, these are serious issues.'

It was Jack's job to coax the meeting back to practicalities. To organise these local residents couldn't be an easy job, since many of them were already organised to different ends. Beggar gangs operated from this part of town, fanning out towards the waterfront and the city centre; women got involved in prostitution; youths were recruited to New Albion. Those who lacked the energy to engage in a life of crime were also too impoverished and undernourished to protest about any aspect of their miserable lives; grousy old women with nothing to look forward to, desperate mothers quietly going mad, unemployed men who'd given up and sat around drinking.

Yet Jack managed to convert at least some of the fear, graft and apathy into anger. The pensioners, for example, were attached to the area in which many of them had lived for almost all their lives, as the woman with grey hair had been saying when I came in. The young mothers had realised that the state no longer guaranteed them a home once their gruesome lodgings had been demolished. The jobless young men, who weren't all petty criminals or Nazis, longed for action. In fact, as Kavanagh had implied, the problem was more in holding them back.

Jack struck a personal, friendly, calm note. He didn't

talk down to anyone, and as I sat there I could see how he held the group together. Plans were soon made to draft a leaflet; a woman volunteered to represent the tenants and to approach the local paper; others were pledged to organise small tenants' meetings in their street, block, or even rooming-house. The beginnings of a plan for a demonstration took shape.

The meeting moved on to discuss the financial backers of the development scheme. Now Adam spoke, flourishing his contacts with the Ministry of the Interior (due to his employment of Russian migrants), and the Ministry of Trade, Industry and Development (thanks to his plans for expansion).

'Bastards,' said another of the young men, 'they make like you should expand, lay out good money, bring all these Boris types over here – and all the time they're planning to knock it all down.'

Adam smiled. 'I suppose their answer would be that I'll get compensation. In fact, of course, it won't anything like cover my losses.' He shrugged – cynical, deprecating, self-effacing all at once.

Once more, Jack brought the meeting back to its main business. When he rounded it off everyone had a task and knew what they had to do.

I hung back to speak to him as the others loitered away. 'You had them eating out of your hand, Jack.' But it was a mistake to have said it. I could see he didn't like it.

'Just a matter of bringing people together. It's them doing it, not me.' Gathering up his papers, he added, 'We're finding out a few things, you know, a familiar story in a way – quite interesting, though.'

The whole saga of the port was a familiar story. Nation-alisation of the docks after the Second World War; a new era for the dockers; union recognition, pay structures, de-casualisation. Then twenty-five or thirty years later, new processes revolutionised the work and the docks were run down. Deregulation followed, demobilisation of the unions, decimation of the labour force, finally, closure of the docks. Meanwhile the overhead expressway was built alongside, creating a no-go zone beneath its entrails.

'The freeing of both lots of land together is an absolute bonanza,' said Jack, 'once in a lifetime thing.'

From the beginning, there was strong grassroots organisation to obtain the land for community development: housing, new factories, jobs, recreation. He told me they'd even got a benefactor, local boy made good, so there was money on the table. The planning permission couldn't be blocked, because under new legislation (drafted specifically with the Port in mind), if there was private financial backing for local plans then it was to get the go-ahead. It was sweet – the local group would take advantage of the deregulation of planning to make the best bid, supported by the benefactor's money.

At the last moment, something went wrong. A tabloid blew the benefactor's cover, outing him as a gambling promoter with a shady past in the pornography business – or worse. That was bad enough, but it became a much bigger scandal when someone put a bullet through him. Ironically, the bullet went straight through his body and out the other side without touching a single vital organ, but the government whipped the whole thing up to a level at which they could use their special powers to veto the community consortium offer.

'Interesting thing is,' said Jack, 'the frontrunner is this outfit Forest Brothers Investments. We've dug up some dirt on them – it's been funded massively by banks, but not only by banks; by government sources as well – money to develop housing associations, hostels and so on as an offshoot of its more general, much more important property development enterprises. A few years back the government was simply shovelling money into it. That was when Alex Kingdom was Minister of Housing. I thought that was pretty interesting. He's got a lot of directorships. Some of them we've traced back to

Forest. He's in it, he's right in there. *Must* mean there's a corruption issue. Some of this is sure to be illegal. Mind you, it's pretty hard to make anything stick these days . . .'

He stood lost in thought for a moment, then he added, 'Of course, we can always do with funds. I don't know if you'd thought – I mean, Charles gave us a bit from time to time.'

So here was another one who thought I was a a soft touch. I smiled, remembering Lennox. I didn't resent Lennox asking, the way I did the others, in fact I wanted to boast about it. 'You're too late, Jack,' I wanted to say, but of course I didn't. I ought to make him a donation. I could easily afford it. In fact, I wrote out a cheque there and then.

We were standing at the bottom of the stairs. Maurice Kavanagh seemed to be on his way out.

'Oh Jack, I wanted you to introduce me . . .'

But Adam came up to me and took my elbow.

'Didn't expect to see you here,' he murmured.

Maurice Kavanagh was going out the door. I tried to make a move, but Adam's hand was still on my arm.

'Where have you been? I haven't seen you –'

'Oh, for Christ's sake, Adam, I told you, I just needed some time on my own!'

'Yes, but –'

'Look, I have to talk to someone. I'll be right back.'

'Oh? Who's that?'

'Oh, never mind.' It was too late now. Kavanagh had gone. I went over to Jack anyway.

'I was hoping to talk to Maurice Kavanagh,' I said.

'He had to rush home. His wife's been ill. What's it about? Your dad? Doubt if he could tell you much. They never got on.'

'You could give me his phone number, all the same.'

'Yes, I think I can help you there,' and he took out his little leather notebook, which he leafed through until he found the relevant page. I wrote the number on the back of my chequebook.

'Something came up,' I said, 'about a man named Colin Fox. I don't know if you knew him –'

Jack frowned. 'Name rings a bell, but . . . No, don't think so. But Maurice might know. He was always on the inside, knew everyone, bit of a schemer, to be honest, behind the scenes man, you know.'

'I thought you might like a drink.'

Adam handed me a glass of wine I didn't want. I hadn't noticed him slide up behind me, and I wondered how much he'd overheard. I didn't want Adam to know everything about what I was doing.

'What were you talking to Jack about?'

'Oh – nothing –'

'Shall we go? When you've drunk that, of course. I need to get back to the Café – could you give me a lift? I walked over here. It's not far – but if you're going in that direction . . .'

'Sure, I'll drop you off – but it's the clapped-out Lada, you know. Thought you thought it wasn't safe to drive.'

He had to smile. In the car he said, 'They're coming to do a feature on me for the arts programme, the new one, *Vanguard*. A laugh, isn't it? Programme's about "the new Bohemia". You could be in it if you want – you've got the personality – you should come and hostess sometimes, it'd be so great, you'd be a bi-ig big asset to the bar – you've got the right sort of looks, off-centre. If you grew your hair again you'd be great. Really.'

Maybe he meant it. Or maybe, like all the others, he was first and foremost interested in my money.

I dropped him off and then I drove up towards the University. I let myself into my father's house, and stood there for a moment, unnerved as usual by the waiting silence. With a sense of dread I picked up the oddments of mail that kept on coming, but there was nothing for me this time.

The first thing to do was telephone Maurice Kavanagh. He'd have reached home by now. He answered the phone almost at once, his flat-vowelled, creaking voice tinged with self-importance.

'Of course I remember you,' he said when I'd explained who I was – although he'd shown no sign of recognition in the meeting. He was cordial until I told him what I wanted, and then he just said, 'Sorry, I'm afraid I can't help you there. Long before my time. And Hilary Cohen, who was the editor in the forties and fifties, died years ago.'

He hung up. Why so curt? It was odd. I sat down on the narrow divan in my father's study. Colin Fox might be a gigantic red herring, a complete diversion, but I began a more systematic search through the boxes for any mention of him.

I was sorting through a box which contained material from 1956 – the year of the famous Twentieth Congress of the Communist Party of the Soviet Union, the one at which Krushchev had denounced Stalin and admitted to the existence of the labour camps, the show trials of the thirties, the political prisoners. It had also been the year the Soviet Union had invaded Hungary.

As I read through the documents it was borne in on me that my father had actually attended that historic Congress. I wondered why. Was it because he spoke Russian? Or perhaps he'd played some role in the Party that I'd never known about. I came upon some detailed long-hand pencilled notes, and I looked over them, without reading them properly, but carefully enough to form the impression that they were simply factual. It was frustrating: he'd actually been a witness at one of the more important events of the twentieth century, one of the few witnesses from the West. Yet there was nothing, no comment, only in one place had he written in capital letters: FUDGE AND COMPROMISE!

He'd stayed in the Party after that traumatic year. In

the end he'd been known as a 'hardliner'. The more I delved into this past the less I understood it. The great wall of history rose between me and them – my father, my mother – and obscured what they'd hoped for and worked for.

The telephone rang, shrill and unexpected. I hate the sound of a telephone in an empty house. And essentially this house was empty. I was simply one of its ghosts.

I answered – half expecting it to be Adam.

'This is Maurice Kavanagh again. I'm sorry if I appeared rather abrupt. Your question came as a surprise. For some reason I had expected you to be interested in the more recent events at *Workers' World*, matters I could have helped you with.'

Ah, so his curtness had been due to self-importance. He'd been miffed because I hadn't asked about him. It wasn't just self-importance, though: he had a story too. He'd visited Brezhnev, had interviewed Castro; all that history that was being swept away even from the great collective memory. Yet I cared for nothing but to dig up some insignificant character from the past.

'As I say, there's little information I can give. I thought you might like to know, though, that the police have released Violet Frankenberg's body, and her funeral will take place the day after tomorrow. At the crematorium. I believe it was you who found her. That must have been most upsetting. It's possible you might find someone there who'd have known the person you mentioned. It will be a public occasion. Might be nice if you went anyway. In the circumstances. She was a friend of your parents, wasn't she?'

A funeral – it seemed appropriate enough. I felt a bit shaky about it, but it was obvious that – Colin Fox quite apart – I had to go. I wondered why Jack hadn't mentioned it.

My muddled search for some clue in the boxes of papers became wearisome, and my hands were sticky with the greasy dust that accumulates on stored papers. I went upstairs to wash, and afterwards, on an impulse I turned down the dark corridor that led to Anna's room. I hadn't been near it since that first early morning with Adam, but I had to be able to go in there alone.

I looked carefully round. Adam had searched in the chest of drawers and the wardrobe, but we hadn't investigated the bookshelves or the desk.

The top shelf was stuffed with papers and folders. I pulled at a folder, and the whole lot ejected to the floor. I knelt down to look through the scattered essays and notes, and picked up a hardbacked exercise book, A4 size, at random. Only the first few pages had been written on in her large, round script:

Bonfire night in the Park. People streaming up the hill. Traffic jams. Smoke charred the air. Fire like witchcraft – wild, tattered flames.

A crowd stood in darkness on the hill and looked across a black ravine to a line of lit-up buildings on the horizon, shimmering, insubstantial towers and skyscrapers. Beyond them again the occasional burst of golden stars from another, distant firework display.

With a high-pitched whine the first firework catapulted into the air with demented force and exploded into a powder-puff of stars. A great low murmur of appreciation prowled through the massed and indistinct ranks of spectators. Another and another – soon a fountain of fireworks was rising from the far-off depths of the ravine. Each ball of fire burst into stars, which sprang silently towards the upturned faces and then melted away just out of reach – bouquets of stars, green, white, magenta.

I'd come with some other kids from school.

'Oh, golly gosh.'

'That one looks like hair, like dreadlocks.'

'Dreadlocks in the sky with diamonds.'

'Like a palm tree –'

'Aaah – look at that one. Wicked.'

'My dog won't like the bangs, he'll be cowering in a corner.'

'My cat too.'

We swayed with the crowd, all children for a while.

In the road that led back down from the park – people streaming down again after the magic of being innocent for a while, recapturing childhood, the front room of one of the houses was brightly lit, no curtains or shutters, you could see right in. It was empty but for an almost life-size rocking horse. A man was seated on the horse and rode backwards and forwards, rode it frantically, naked from the waist up. With his long hair and gipsy trousers, waving his whip as the horse neighed forward, he looked somehow mad, and it was also the most sexual thing I'd ever seen. Others must have thought so too, for lewd shouts came from the road, and someone was filming him with a video camera.

I lingered behind, it was easy to get lost in the crowd. I walked up to the huge black front door. It was ajar. I slipped in. It shut behind me with a hollow bang. I was alone in the dark, but a shard of light came from the door of the front room. I pushed it open.

That was all she'd written. It was just another fragment, just another non-clue.

Chapter
Thirteen

I left the house and walked towards the campus. How could this city be so many places? Up here it was as quiet and peaceful as in the grounds of some great country house: decorous footsteps on the flagstones, laughter and voices as cool and soft as the water spouting from the fountains. Yet a year ago there'd been occupations and outrage, ending in riots when a student had been shot. My father had sent me the newspaper cuttings, and I remembered a photograph of the front quad as it had been then: draped in black, with a gigantic 'coffin' in the centre.

I walked into the front reception area. As I'd hoped, Star was lounging behind the desk. 'Can I talk to you?'

She glanced at her fellow student behind the desk, another huge, rangy guy. 'Back in five minutes, okay?'

'Don't worry, it's dead here. I can take all comers.'

We walked off down a corridor in the direction of the library.

'It's nice to see you.' She squeezed my shoulders. 'What's the problem? Or is this a social call?'

I smiled uneasily, and ignored the arm, but she must have noticed me stiffen. Then I thought – what the hell. I wasn't using her, not really. It was simply that I had to know about Anna. I had to do everything I could to find out, and Star could help me. I hoped she could, anyway. So I relaxed and willed myself to be just a little more approachable.

'Remember that student who was staying in my house – she never turned up, you know.'

'And you've had all this other stuff – I heard –'

'I'm sure there's some connection. And I wondered – I mean, could you somehow find out about her? Anyone who knew her, any gossip – anything.'

'I could try. Tell you what. I know someone in Admin. The Registry. You could look at the file, for a start.' She put her arm round my waist now. 'Are you okay? You haven't been around. I was going to call you.'

She opened a door and we were in a large, light, cluttered office. Seated at a desk was Jade.

There seemed to be a jagged tension between them. She gave me a big smile, though. 'We've met, remember,' she said, as Star tried to introduce us.

Star looked annoyed. 'Of course, how stupid of me. I forgot.' She leant against Jade's desk and smiled down at Jade. Not a very nice smile. 'How's Wilma?' she enquired in silky tones.

'She's having a party this evening. Want to come?'

Star looked at me. 'Fancy it?'

I wasn't sure, but I wanted to keep her sweet. 'Could be fun,' I said.

'Justine needs to look at a file. Thought you might help,' Star said to Jade, staring just as insistently at her as she had at me when I walked through the portico of the grand entrance hall. There was a message for Jade in that stare. Were they rivals for Wilma, or lovers – or both?

'Well, you know I'm not supposed to . . .' Jade turned uneasily to me. 'I'm not trying to be unhelpful –'

'Please,' said Star, 'it won't take a minute.'

'Okay, if it's really important. What's the name?'

She keyed it into the computer and wrote down a number. Then she went away.

'You coming to Wilma's party then?'

'Should I?'

'I think you should.' She smoothed a finger along my arm and smiled.

I shivered. 'Air conditioning's freezing in here.'

Jade came back with a thin beige file. 'You can sit over by the window – at that desk.'

I looked through Anna's file. So little there. Nothing about a husband. Yet the diary entry had read 'How I met my husband'. Maybe application forms didn't ask for that sort of information any more. In any case she must have been separated from him, or she wouldn't have been living in my father's house. Marriage would account for the two names, though, Fotiriou and Musgrove – a disappointingly mundane explanation. And it didn't tell me anything useful. I stared at her photograph. She stared back, as people do in passport photos, a blank, yet slightly anxious expression on her face with its thick eyebrows and black eyes, curtained by the long black hair.

There was absolutely nothing there. There was no note that I'd reported her absence, nothing from the 'placement'. I felt slightly baffled. Maybe that was bureaucracy – perhaps the University was like the dinosaur, which became so huge that it had to have another brain in its bottom because the brain in its head was too far away to communicate with its tail.

I returned the folder to Jade. 'Thanks. Have the police been around?'

Jade stared at me. 'Not when I've been here.'

'Well, thanks anyway. Look, could I make a phone call?'

'Sure. Help yourself.'

I'd lost the number of the residential placement, but it was in the file. The same man answered. He was as aggressive as before, although this time I pretended I was from the University.

'I don't know why you've rung again. I already informed you she's withdrawn. Her tutor rang to confirm it just a few days ago.'

'A few days ago? Could you tell me exactly when?'

No. He couldn't.

Star put an arm round my shoulder again when we were once more in the corridor. 'Anything useful?'

I shook my head. 'I'm completely baffled,' I said.

'D'you want to go back to the department?'

I shook my head. 'I want to look up something in the library – something different, not to do with this at all. You go back to the desk.'

'Okay, if that's what you want. But I will ask around about – what was her name? I'll see what I can find out.'

'That'd be great.' I gave her a big smile now.

'I'll see you later at the Café, and we'll go to Wilma's. Promise you'll come?'

'Yes, I'll come.' Why not – Lennox might even be there.

I went down the long corridor in the general direction of the library, and all the while I was wondering what to do. The telephone call to the placement could not have been from the University, for there was nothing in her file. Someone else must have made that call. But who? Who could have done it? It must have been – yes, it must have been her murderer. The University thought she was at the placement, and the placement thought the University had told them she'd withdrawn. Sooner or later they'd all discover their mistake, but by then the trail would be cold. I alone knew. No – not I alone; I and the murderer.

To go to the police was the obvious thing to do, but I didn't want to. You never got what you wanted from them. They bullied or patronised. They didn't tell the truth. They always had their own agenda. Willingly to present yourself to them, to draw yourself to their attention, was to be asking for trouble. In any case, I'd already found one dead body. If I went to them about a second, they'd have the Adam reaction. They'd say I was crazy.

I turned a corner, and came to the library, signed myself in, and went down to the lower floor. A velvety hush wrapped the place in an atmosphere of luxury. The carpets were so thick that you could turn a corner of the stacks and bump into another silent browser of whose existence you'd been completely unaware. On this brilliant afternoon the vast spaces were empty, and the silence unnerved me. I'd decided to continue my search for Colin Fox here, rather than in the National Library, where you had to order books in advance. Here I could roam through the stacks and pick out whatever looked interesting.

I made for the on-line catalogue near the entrance, and looked up 'Communism'. Thousands of entries. I ran through the first few, and, seeing that they were mostly catalogued under the one numerical series, I looked up the location on the map, and set off. Of course, I could probably have done the same in my father's house, in fact it would have been more sensible to go through his books first, but the house still upset me. I had to keep going back to it, but I could never bear to stay for long.

The front part of the library, with its carpets and study nooks and carels and comfortable tables and chairs in the window embrasures housed only a small part of the total collection. I came to the door into the stacks. It shut behind me with a hiss and I was now in an underworld of metal bookshelves and rattling wrought-iron stairways, or ladders, floors and floors of them, interspersed with narrow metal runways through this endless, appalling warren of unread books.

As I went further in, the silence began to get to me. Was anyone else here at all? I'd come here to get away from the silences of my father's house; it had never occurred to me that it might be just as creepy here – in a library – but I began to feel a chilling unease. I pressed on, advancing further into the warren, looking for the numbers I wanted, but also looking over my shoulder from time to time. Far away the door hissed again. I wasn't alone, then. Someone else was lurking in the stacks. Someone had followed me, perhaps. Was following me. I stopped. Should I turn back or go on? I began to panic. I heard up above me a rattling of someone walking along the wrought-iron gangways. I retraced my steps, trying not to run, sweating with fear, and rounded a corner.

I jumped; my heart pounded. There *was* someone there. A woman had her back to me. She heard me coming, and turned.

Anna. She stared. I couldn't believe it, and yet – she was wearing dark glasses and a scarf, but there was the long black hair and something about the way she held herself, slight, a little shrinkingly.

She gasped, pushed back the book she'd been looking at and ran away. She was several yards in front of me but when I quickened my step, so did she, dived round a corner and I heard her footsteps on the ladder.

'Anna!' I called softly, and I turned the corner myself and came helter-skelter down the ladder after her.

When I got to the bottom she was nowhere. I could still hear her footsteps, but there were two narrow corridors between the stacks, running in different directions, and I must have taken the wrong one. I didn't catch up with her, anyway. I was beginning to lose my bearings. The stacks were like a maze. Far away I heard the door into the front library hiss to. I turned and hurried back, to try to find the place where I'd first caught sight of her, to discover what she'd been looking at, but I couldn't find it, I was lost.

The stacks were silent and empty again. I stood still, mesmerised for a moment by the swelling silence. Then I ran, ran round corners and down ladders, along rat runs and into dead ends, until at last, on the verge of panic, or well beyond it, I came to the hissing doors and entered reality again.

Here was normality. Everything was okay. Star was

back at the desk in the front hall. I was so pleased to see her, I thought she'd think I was doing a big come-on. But all she said was, 'You look like you've seen a ghost.'

Wilma Hecht's glass penthouse would have held a large party, but only a dozen of us hung about in corners in the big double reception room. I was bored, although several margaritas had taken the edge off it. Now I just wondered why I was here.

Wilma had slotted some very throbby music into her player. Underneath it sounded like breaking waves, over it the heartbeat of a monotonous sobbing lament. Wilma seized Star and was swaying to and fro in the centre of the room. They were glued together. That was a relief – and yet I resented it. I hoped I wasn't a pawn in some game that Star was playing. That wouldn't suit me at all. Okay if others were pawns in my game, of course.

The trouble about my game was, I was making up the rules as I went along. Yet still I didn't seem to be winning.

Jade did seem to have some prior claim to Wilma. She was scowling as she chatted in front of the chimneypiece with two women who had obviously cast themselves as the perfect butch/femme couple. One had brilliantined hair and a white tuxedo, the other wore a red satin slip dress with lots of narrow straps that crossed her back like whiplash marks.

To say that Lennox looked out of place when he strolled in with a teenage People's Army type in tow, would have been an understatement.

Wilma pounced on him. I suppose she counted him as part of the aesthetic spectacle. Eccentrics, colour, life, suffering – other people's suffering; she loved all that. It was all grist to her mill. That and his beauty, of course. It was only an hour since I'd met her, but I reckoned I had her number. Queen bee, queen voyeur.

She let go of Star, almost flung her aside in fact, and

stretched out her hands to the two youths, leading them to the table with its many opened bottles.

One of her friends was offering us coke. I declined. So did Lennox. But his friend was soon squatting in a corner, sniffing the stuff with a little leather dyke.

Lennox sat on the sofa beside me. 'How'd you get on at the library? Find out anything interesting?'

I shook my head. 'Dead ends, blank walls.'

'I'm seeing that guy again, the one I told you about. I'll see what more I can find out from him.'

'Oh, would you?'

'For you, anything.' Ah – so he was back in the campy flirting vein. Unfortunately, there was a crash as his friend slumped sideways and broke some glasses that had been set on the floor. A red stain seeped over the spotless pale carpet. Blood or wine.

'Christ, better see to this . . .'

He and his lover staggered off in disorder. Wilma took it well. 'Don't worry, darling – it's a rented place, who cares about their fucking carpet,' she was saying to Star. Not that Star seemed to be apologising. Wilma wrapped an arm around the girl who was one half of the most perfect butch/femme couple in the world. This woman looked like Jean Harlow. Her bobbed hair was white with peroxide. Her eyebrows had been plucked to two black antennae.

'I think I want to go,' said Star to me. 'Give me a lift?'

I'd have stayed, in spite of my boredom. I certainly didn't fancy being back at the Café in Adam's monastic spare room, and the thought of my father's house filled me with dread. And as for Star's flat, well, Lennox might be there, and that could be embarrassing or dreadful. Yet the one place I wanted to be was wherever Lennox was.

'Shall I drop you off at Avenue West?' I said carefully.

'I don't want to go to the flat . . . Lennox's rent boy'll be throwing up all over the show.'

'Rent boy?' I didn't like that.

'Oh, sorr-ee. Lover then.'

'Where shall I take you then?' I sounded cold, because I was upset. We stood uncertainly, not looking or touching. I was conscious of her narrow yet heavy body – muscular, not fat, and so like Lennox, but it was all wrong, it was hopeless, and at the same time, so strange.

'Can't I go where you're going? You've got a house, haven't you? What's wrong with that?'

'I don't desperately want to go there.'

'Oh . . . we could go down to the beach, I suppose – a bit dangerous.' She put her fingers on my shoulder, and drew them down over my nipple.

I didn't want to go to the beach either. 'Look,' I began. Then I laughed. You had to laugh, really. 'Okay,' I said, 'I'll take you back to my place.' After all, it wouldn't frighten me so much if someone else was there. 'If you think you deserve it,' I said.

'Are you going to give me what I deserve?'

I placed my hand on the back of her neck. 'What do you think you deserve?' The suggestive words were worn smooth like old money.

What the hell was I doing? I guess it was the margaritas. And she did look like Lennox, after all.

It was hotter out of doors than it had been in the air-conditioned apartment, like going into the baths. Her arm crushed my shoulders. I was feeling curiously light-headed and detached.

'Listen, I asked around about that woman – Anna – chatted up some of the soc. adj. students.'

'Anything interesting?'

'Not much. They said she was unfriendly, very quiet, kept herself to herself. One woman knew her a bit, she seemed to have got the impression Anna was close to your father, said she'd told her she lived there rent free.'

'Rent free?' My father wasn't a mean man, but I should have thought he'd have charged something.

'That's what she said. There was another thing. Anna never had boyfriends, never went out with men. But recently – just two or three weeks ago, just before she disappeared, one woman saw her in the town with a man, not from the University. And she said when Anna saw her she buggered off quick.'

'What did he look like? Did she say?'

'Yes, I asked her.' Star looked pleased with herself. 'Good looking, she said, medium-coloured hair in a little bun, smart looking, dark-green shirt – well, it's not much, is it? Could be anyone really.'

'Sounds like Adam,' I said.

As I locked the door of the Lada a man got out of a car parked opposite the house. A big dark car. It glimmered in the monochrome of the city at night. He called my name.

'We've been waiting for you,' he reproached me, and showed me his police badge. 'Detective Inspector Markfield,' he said. 'And this is Detective Constable Trask. A bit late to be coming home, isn't it?' There was a third man with them, who wasn't introduced.

'There's no curfew up here is there?' I posed the rhetorical question as politely as I could.

'You can't be too careful, Mrs Unwin.'

He was tall, heavy, dark. His partner loomed behind him. The third man loitered in the rear.

'We wanted to ask you a few questions.'

'At this time of night?'

'I'm afraid the body of your lodger's been found. Your father's lodger. Dumped in the ditch near the bottom of your garden – well, half a mile or so towards the campus. Seems a bit strange you never reported her missing.'

'Oh, but I –' My hand was shaking as I unlocked the front door. I suppose they like to spring it on you, to see how you react.

Star nudged me, and hesitated. I took no notice, and she followed us in.

We stood in the hall. I didn't show them into the drawing room or ask them to sit down. I didn't introduce them to Star either. So they did it all for themselves:

'And you are?'

Star muttered her name.

'Romano? That sounds familiar,' said Markfield pleasantly, and glanced at the man he hadn't introduced.

'Mind if we make ourselves a little more comfortable?'

Some of them are quite smart at taking the initiative. I couldn't refuse, so they were one up on me. The four of us sat in the abandoned drawing room. The nameless one took up a position leaning against the wall near the door.

'Mrs Musgrove was found in the ditch between here and the campus,' said the one who called himself Markfield. 'We need to make some further checks, but it seems fairly conclusive.'

'So why do you need to see me?'

'This is a murder investigation, Mrs Unwin. Cause of death isn't clear, but she'd probably been suffocated. And, as I said before, we wondered why you didn't tell anyone she was missing.'

'But I did – I went to the University but they told me she'd gone on some sort of residential part of her training, or something.' To myself I sounded bright, too bright, tinny, ingratiating. 'I hardly knew her. It was my father who rented her the room. I've only just come back – he died – I didn't even know if she was actually staying in this house any more or not,' I said, 'though she did leave some of her things.'

'Ah – we'd like to see those, if you don't mind.'

'Now?'

Markfield ignored this. Instead he asked suavely: 'Did you know that Mrs Musgrove was a drug addict?'

This was so utterly unexpected that I felt like he'd

kicked me in the stomach. 'No,' I said, when I was breathing normally again.

'So you do see why we need to search her room. Of course, if illegal substances should be found there, that could have serious consequences for yourself.'

It sounded like a threat, but maybe it was just the bleak truth.

'I hope you're not implying –'

'I'm not implying anything – I'm simply here to conduct an investigation. So – if you don't mind showing us her room, we'll start there.'

'Do you have a warrant?'

He laughed. 'Mrs Unwin, I told you, we're treating this as murder! No-one goes and lies down in a ditch and dies while they're barefoot and wearing their dressing gown.'

'But what made you think it was her?' I was trying to work it out, but my mind was frozen, slow.

'The University authorities established that no one had seen her for some time. And then –'

'But what made you go to them in the first place? What made you think she was a student? I don't understand –'

Markfield gave me another chilly look, but Trask was more forthcoming. Perhaps this was their idea of the nice cop/nasty cop routine.

'Student I.D. card was found on the body.'

'But she was –' I looked at him. An I.D. card? 'But no-one carries an I.D. around in their dressing gown!'

He looked at me. Long and hard. As if that was my problem. Then he smiled in a nasty kind of way. He was trying to rile me, that was for sure.

'In answer to your earlier question, Mrs Unwin, yes, we do have a warrant.' He flashed it at me, but it had disappeared again before I had time to read it.

Star neither moved nor said a word. I left her there while I took them up to Anna's room. The anonymous one had roamed off into the study. I didn't like that, but there wasn't much I could do. Later he followed us up.

I leant against the wall and watched them. 'What makes you think she was an addict?'

'Full of holes as a sieve,' said Trask. 'Needle marks everywhere.'

Yet it would have been somehow unlike my father to have offered house-room to a junkie. He was old-fashioned, and not very sympathetic to addiction, or to self-indulgence in any form. No liberal, he, when it came to what he'd have considered to be irresponsible, stupid behaviour. Then why had he let her have the room rent free? That suggested some charitable purpose, but unless there was a political connection I couldn't account for it at all.

'I don't believe it,' I said, 'my father was – he hated that sort of thing.'

Markfield laughed again. 'Don't suppose he knew. They're very cunning . . .'

I didn't argue. He could be right; except that an addict wouldn't even have to be cunning with my father – he was an innocent about that sort of thing.

I also didn't argue because I just wanted them to go, and I thought that would be the quickest way – but they spent what seemed like forever poking in drawers and shaking out books and rummaging through her clothes.

I watched them, and all the while I was thinking about the thread of blue I'd found on the twig. I was also thinking about the University library. I'd seen Anna in the library. Thought I'd seen her. So I was going mad, after all. Except that I'd also seen the body, the body lying on that bed.

'Are you absolutely sure that it –?' I began.

'That it what, Mrs Unwin?' Markfield's stony eyes gave no quarter.

I shrugged.

'I think you were going to say something more, weren't you.'

'It's just – I mean why should anyone do that? It's so terrible,' I improvised wildly, 'she never harmed anyone, she was so harmless, so quiet –'

'I thought you said you hardly knew her.'

They seemed to linger over her possessions forever, but at last they were through. Markfield looked around the room. 'Well, nothing much here. We'll take her passport, if you don't mind – I see it's in a different name.'

He made even that seem suspicious. I felt angry, but I was vulnerable. They could easily plant some stuff – any time they wanted.

'Big house your father had,' remarked Inspector Markfield as we descended the stairs. 'He normally had lodgers, did he? A widower, I understand.'

'So far as I know Anna was the only one.'

'We may need to search the whole house –'

'Oh, you're surely not going to do that now! It's nearly two o'clock in the morning!'

'I appreciate the inconvenience. Perhaps if Detective Constable Trask were to have a look around while I check up on one or two points. There are just a few more questions.'

We were standing in the hall. He said, 'Shall we?' And gestured towards the sitting room.

It was empty. Star had gone.

'I wonder what happened to your friend.'

'I expect she's gone to bed.' I didn't want it to seem as if she was scared.

'So you do have another lodger now?'

'No. But I don't like being here alone. It's lonely.'

'I'm sure you don't need to be lonely, an attractive woman like you, and I don't imagine you need the money either, Mrs Unwin.' I hoped my look froze him – but I could have kicked myself for having given him the opening in the first place.

'She's not a lodger – just a friend.'

'But then I don't suppose your father needed the money either.'

'You seem to know a lot about us.'

But not that much: the money I had was left me by some relative of my mother – nothing to do with my father. He wasn't rich at all.

'Perhaps your father was . . . *lonely*, too.'

Markfield went through all that had happened since my return. His questions were fairly perfunctory, he was just picking around. Yet there was always that chill hint of menace. It wasn't anything he said. It was just his manner. But perhaps they're always like that – assuming the worst. And I suppose I could be a suspect. And I lied about the date of my return – or rather, I said nothing about the accident, the time in hospital. I lied without even knowing why. At least they didn't mention Violet Frankenberg. That must be because they hadn't made the connection.

Why hadn't I reported Anna missing? He came back to that again. What was my relationship with her? We didn't have a relationship. What was my father's relationship to her? Simple, direct, unfriendly questions. No finesse. He hadn't a way of gaining my confidence, of getting me to open up. So it was mainly a test of endurance, of getting through it.

And Trask was gone a long time – he and the cop without a name. I could hear them moving about in the other rooms.

Then they came back, and it was all over. Markfield stood up. He walked towards the front door. I followed him, like a good hostess.

'There is just one thing, Mrs Unwin. You were recently at the scene of another murder. A woman down in Camden Bay, I believe.'

It was like we stood there, frozen, four figures frozen to the floor.

'Nothing to say about that? Funny coincidence, isn't it? I'd say it was a bit of a bad move, going around stumbling over dead bodies. What d'you say, Jimmy? Not the sort of thing a healthy young woman would make a habit of doing.'

Trask smirked.

And they went away. I was alone in the house. I called Star's name, but I knew she wasn't there. She'd been that scared that she'd fled into the empty, lonely, city streets in the middle of the night. I wondered what she had to be so frightened of.

I had things to be frightened of. I was alone. I didn't dare walk up the shadowy stairs to the bedrooms. I lay down on the divan bed in my father's study. I lay there, listening, listening to the silence that was so slow and so palpable. It was a silence like the silence that first day, the day I returned from California.

Chapter
Fourteen

Gouged open like a water-melon clustered with flies, Kakania rotted. As it sank slowly into the sea a stench of superstition and violence rose. It should have hung above the city in a pall of yellow pus; but the blue sky was cloudless.

On my way to Myra's, I picked my way through the crowd that swirled around the stalls on the plaza. The Child Goddess stall was draped in red and pink satin with swags of grass-green fringe. Across the top stretched a banner with glittering letters: 'Behold the Child'. Photographs and mementoes of the Child were set out on the stall. Books told the story of her miracles. I picked up a tinsel-edged tin heart.

People's Army types were milling around with their blond dreadlocks or cropped hair, and their combat boots and fatigues, and their mean-looking mongrels led on bits of string. I looked into their faces, wanting and not wanting to bump into Lennox's friend. One was arguing with the Child Goddess stallkeeper.

'A three-year-old kid!' yelled the young man. 'It's against the bloody law! You should be had up for cruelty!'

I'd seen a newspaper photograph of Behold the Child on one of her holy train tours. The train had stopped before a large crowd. From a richly-curtained window a small face peeped out, a doll in a mitre and heavy robes.

*

Myra and I left the train at Snake Beach. We sat beneath
the pink umbrellas of one of the waterside salons. Myra
spooned up the cream off her Café Liégeois, I sipped a
margarita, and we talked about 'it' – the mysteries of my
father's house, Anna, Violet Frankenberg, Colin Fox.

Myra said, 'It's just a series of random events . . . well,
so far as Anna and your father are concerned. There
doesn't seem to be any link between them except that
they were both living in the same house.'

Myra never admitted defeat. The more baffling the
situation became the more she seemed determined to
unravel it.

I hadn't told her of my encounter in the library stacks
– how I thought I'd seen Anna. That might be too much
even for her.

'I'm dreading this visit,' I said.

'Are you? I'm looking forward to it. Friends' families
are always fascinating. I know the same can't be said of
one's own.'

'Oh, I thought . . .' I'd thought Myra would wait for
me in the town, I'd brought her along for moral support
before and afterwards. She was the sort of person of whom
my aunt was bound to disapprove.

Aunt Susan had disapproved of my father, of Communism, of my upbringing, and incidentally, of Occam, under
the mistaken impression that he was a communist too. Yet
she and my mother had been close, in spite of everything;
she'd been kind when my mother died, I remembered her
then. My father had pushed her away, though, hadn't
wanted her sympathy.

We wandered up into a hinterland of white-painted
dolls'-house terraces, a different world from the great
city sprawling eastwards. It took me a while to find
the right road, and Myra was breathing heavily by the
time I spotted the house, with its newly painted but still
deep-blue door and wisteria floating from the trellis.

Aunt Susan looked astonished when she opened the door, but she held out her hands in welcome, and seemed genuinely pleased.

She ushered us into the sparkling little drawing room with its polished furniture, glittering objets d'art and yellow taffeta curtains. Like the front door, it all looked new, yet was the same as when I'd last visited, which must be all of – how many years? Seven? Eight?

'You haven't changed at all, Aunt Susan. You don't look a day older.'

'Well, you have – your hair! So short!' But her laugh was friendly. 'You'd like some tea?'

I'd planned my story in advance, and told it over the tea cups. While clearing out the house, I said, I'd found mementoes of my mother, things that had belonged to her, and which Aunt Susan might like to have. I'd also found some letters and a valuable-looking watch. I wanted to return them to their owner; I believed they'd belonged to someone called Colin Fox. It was a gamble. Even if Aunt Susan had never heard of him, I hoped to get her chatting about the past, and surely we would glean useful information of some kind.

Aunt Susan didn't say she'd never heard of Colin Fox. She frowned. 'Isn't it best to leave those things be? And anyway, who knows what happened – he may have died years ago.'

'But he might have had children; his watch, after all – it's obviously valuable. I could say Dad forgot about it.'

'People often don't like it if you rake up the past.'

'It's important to me, though,' I said, 'they were my parents, after all. I suppose it's all this going through things – finding letters – all the old photographs –'

'Oh, you poor thing, that is distressing – I know when your grandmother died . . .'

She started to talk about my grandmother, and slowly the reminiscing mood began to work. People do like to discuss the past, and gradually she began to talk about my mother.

'Joyce was always streets ahead of me,' she said, 'very much the successful older sister.'

In 1948 the two sisters, Joyce and Susan, were just ready to take wing in the gloomy climate of post-war austerity and socialism. Although the great University up on the hill, to which Joyce soon went, was stricken, like everywhere else, with the cold, dank atmosphere of shortages, power cuts and rationing, it was also enlivened by the presence of ex-servicemen with sexual clout and glamour. Beyond the unheated corridors, and struggles with scholarship in a Literature faculty soaked in Christianity and medievalism, left-wing ideas beckoned brightly. It wasn't long before she fell in with my father and his friends.

Susan, still at school, was soon the fascinated witness of unaccustomed family rows as a cocktail of sex and socialism exploded in the face of traditional family life. Rebellion only made Joyce more glamorous in Susan's eyes. She was taken to meet the new friends one afternoon after school, on the sly.

'He's the most wonderful man,' Joyce told her, 'he's the love of my life.'

That wasn't like Joyce, such excessive, extravagant language. But Joyce's language at this time had undergone a profound change, and included words that brought a whiff of gunsmoke from the wider world to the chintz and furniture polish of home.

'You know, it sounds odd, but I was never quite sure which one it was, the one she was fond of. I hardly met them, of course. But it wasn't your father – not at first.'

'Colin Fox?'

'I didn't take to him,' said Aunt Susan, 'there was something coarse about him. He made an impression, though. I just met them at the tea rooms where they used to congregate, two or three times after school, that's all.

I remember him, though, because he *was* amusing – told wonderfully funny stories, outrageous escapades, things he'd done, he could tell a joke against himself – that's always engaging. But there was something fundamentally rather destructive about him. Gallows humour. Nihilistic. And there was a – bitterness about him, even then. There were two or three others – but I don't really remember them. I think they must have faded out quite soon.'

So why had she married my father? On the rebound? A lover's tiff? And what had happened to Colin Fox?

Susan went to secretarial college. She was the dull one, the ordinary one. While Joyce did literary research, campaigned politically, and 'became rather intense', the younger sister went to inhibited cocktail parties and was sometimes invited to the races, to weekends in the country.

Once Joyce and Charles were married her parents made the best of it. Charles might be a Red, but he seemed to be embarking on a reasonably respectable academic career. 'They seemed happy enough, you know, and they were always so busy, and then much later you were born – they tried for ages – and they seemed very close then, she and Charles.'

'And then one weekend,' said Aunt Susan, 'this is years later, Joyce rang up in a state of agitation. I'd never known her like that before, not as tense as that.'

Her sister's distress frightened her. 'You see I always felt Joyce was the brave one, the clever one. I wasn't strong enough to kick over the traces. And I suppose I didn't want to. Not really, not the way she did. And I have to admit I sometimes felt resentful. She was so brainy, it used to make me feel stupid. All the same, it seemed all wrong that *she* should be upset and – yes, frightened. I could tell that it was something serious. Really serious.

'She told me Colin Fox had got involved in blackmail. He was blackmailing someone. Blackmail! Can you imagine. Something beyond my – I just couldn't *believe* –

Joyce was beside herself. "He's running the most terrible risks. And think what it will do to the Party if it comes out." I think the comrades had kicked him out by this time, but it would still have been a jolly good story, wouldn't it? That's what Joyce thought, anyway.'

'"He's a drunk, a total wreck," said Joyce. "Someone else will have to go. *I'll* have to go," Joyce said, "I'll have to go and sort it out, but – oh Sue, I'm scared, I want someone with me. I want you to come with me. It can't be Charles. He doesn't even know about this, he'd kill me. And you mustn't tell him. But you will come with me, won't you?"'

Aunt Susan looked at me. 'You know – I refused. I've often wondered since if I did the right thing. And as time went on – well, after Joyce died, I was quite sure I hadn't. Hadn't done the right thing, I mean. Yet at the time – well, I simply couldn't believe my ears. I thought she had taken leave of her senses. Me! With two small children, a husband on the stock exchange. How could I possibly get mixed up in something completely illegal! Such a revolting crime too. It just seemed out of the question. We quarrelled. I thought she was mad. But when she began to be ill – so soon after – as I say, it troubled me. The only time she ever asked for my help. And I refused.

'"Then I'll have to do it by myself," she said, "but I'd feel safer. He'd know *you* were just a go-between, whereas me, on my own – who knows what might happen . . ."'

I stared at Aunt Susan, but I hardly saw her, for in the old moviedrome in my head – where they only show archive material – a memory began to unreel.

It was that old quarter of the city, where the pavements are high above the street, protected with solid, eighteenth-century railings at the top of little flights of steps, and where there are square, old eighteenth-century, seventeenth-century houses turned into offices. My mother wore her best suit, it was gentian blue. We climbed the steps of one of the houses. We waited in a room. Red velvet chairs were set round a mahogany table. On the table were back numbers of magazines. We waited a long time. A man in a black suit entered the room. He murmured her name and she went away. When she returned she looked even more white-faced and tense. Now she was with a different man. He seemed so tall. He bent towards me. 'And so this is the little one,' he said.

My mother was flustered. 'Come along,' she said. We went home. She never talked to me the whole way. But when we got out of the bus I saw she'd been crying.

Aunt Susan continued, 'And that was all I ever heard of it. It was never mentioned again. I think she was telling the truth – I'm sure Charles never knew about it. He wouldn't have allowed her to – he was a man of principle after all. In his own peculiar way.'

There was a silence in the room. Was my mother not a woman of principle then?

'It's a strange thing,' said Aunt Susan, 'She had all that promise, she was brilliant, and yet in the end . . .'

I thought of my mother, faded and quiet – but then she was ill so soon and died at fifty, of cancer. Before that though, strangely for a woman who'd been so gifted, independent, a rebel, she hadn't continued her research; after my birth she stayed at home, and then, later, taught English at a girls' school.

She'd been dutiful in the Party, dutiful at home. Perhaps she'd had to be especially good, especially right, in order to make up for that great wrongness, that great badness, of her fatal – futile – love for Colin Fox.

But what happened afterwards? Aunt Susan's reminiscences grew vaguer. Did Colin figure in my parents' lives? Or did the links of past obsession, comradeship, and the links, just as powerful, that betrayal, exasperation and pity could forge, did those ties of feeling crumble and erode?

'I think he was left to drink himself to death along the

coast. He fell off a cliff in the end.' Aunt Susan smiled. 'Your mother said she wouldn't be surprised if he'd been murdered.'

Myra shifted in her seat. I'd forgotten about her; she'd managed to efface herself, emotionally if not physically, allowing my aunt to forget she was there. Now we exchanged looks, but Aunt Susan seemed unaware of its being more than a throwaway remark.

'Aunt Susan, I don't know what to say.'

'My dear, I hope I haven't upset you.'

'Thank you for telling me.' But I did see what she meant about letting sleeping dogs lie.

There was the deep silence of a story ended, and the two of us sunk in our different thoughts – disrupted as the front door banged. 'Hullo darling!'

Uncle Henry was red in the face and mopped his brow. 'Good heavens – it's little Justine!'

He plied us with gin and tonic, and breezed on in his genial, brisk and well-scrubbed way. He'd been out sailing; a wealthy man, enjoying good health in his retirement.

Myra sat opposite me in the train and fanned herself. Like Uncle Henry, she was red from the heat, and the tissue with which she repeatedly dabbed her forehead came away smeared with make-up. 'All this *past*,' she said, 'it's upset you, hasn't it? It's bad for you, all this dwelling in the past, raking it up. You have to move on.'

'But Myra, how can I? How can I move on?'

Chapter
Fifteen

In the Café Wilma held court at the big round table. She wanted to film in the Tunnels. The group was arguing about it, although so far as I knew only Lennox had ever been down there.

'It's only a matter of time before they bust the whole thing up,' he said. That's all they need – a fucking film crew. They'd never co-operate.'

'All the more reason to get in there soon.'

'You should film Behold The Child', I said.

'Behold the Child? What is this?'

When I told her, Wilma exclaimed: 'But this is really *sublime* – a marvellous idea! White of you, darling. We must talk about this.' She snapped her fingers at Gennady and ordered food.

It came gradually, in a series of little dishes: raw fish, cherry salad, rice cakes with sour cream, tiny spinach croquettes.

'Where's Star?' I asked Lennox – a bad move, but I made it anyway. 'She came back to my place – the cops were there. She got scared and buggered off.'

'Are you on with my sister, then?'

I hesitated. 'No . . .'

He raised his eyebrows sceptically. 'She likes you,' he said, and placed his arm along the back of my chair. 'She'll be along later.' And his smile was melting as honey, and tantalising, as he held himself just out of reach. Was it deliberate, or was it just the way he was?

'There were these two cops came to the house,' I said. 'But there was a third guy with them, never got introduced. He just hung about. He was creepy.'

'Intelligence – they're all over the fucking show these days.'

Neither of us spoke for a while.

'Have you found out anything?' I asked him, remembering the story of his contact. He shook his head. 'Nothing about that – but I did meet someone in the Tunnels. Someone who wants to meet you.'

'In the Tunnels? Tell me,' I said, even more quietly. It was like making love to him, having this secret conversation, cocooned away from the others by the noise.

But Wilma broke in. She was wanting to take us all to some nightclub. 'Come with us,' she murmured, with her arm round me. 'It's so *transgressive*. You know?' She laughed. 'I just love that aesthetic of defiance. Such a *frisson, mein liebling*. Know what I mean?'

'Not really.'

But she twined herself closer to me. 'We must talk about my film,' she said with a brilliant smile, her lips, so thin and red, a pinched crack across her face. 'Maybe you will help me. *Das wär so schön, nicht*? You could be my producer.'

Money again.

We drove away from the port, and turned off the ring road on to a forecourt in front of a high wall. Jade told me it was the wholesale market. It looked more like a prison to me.

The concrete space stretched away in all directions, bleached in the glare of the lights high overhead, craning their antennae across the highway. There was nothing here, no houses, no people, no life, only the wall, and the vehicles that passed, with a hiss like tearing paper.

We climbed concrete steps, and through a door in the wall at the top we entered a black room. At first I thought it was empty. It was divided by long, cloudy streamers of crepe paper and strips of white muslin suspended from a line of string.

We passed between the gaps in this insubstantial curtain. You expected something new or surprising beyond it, but there was only the other half of the almost empty room, just a few figures leaning against the bar.

'So empty!' Wilma made a face. 'Perhaps we are coming too early – but at least this way we get a table.'

The room began to fill up. 'The scar people come here, you know, it is their venue,' Wilma murmured in my ear. She would be filming them, too. And certainly there were a lot, not only of tattoos, but also of deliberate scars – slashed cheeks, and puckered, raised scarifications on arms. One man had twisted knots of scar tissue across his forehead.

The show began with flickering images projected at high speed across the wall. They came and went too quickly to recognise – lips, eyes, hands, heaped concentration camp bodies, a silent movie Babylon, Siegfried, ancient Egypt all quivered black and white across the sheet, signalling in desperate, half-understood semaphore.

Next, a woman stepped on to a little stage. She wore a peaked cap, an SS jacket, a short skirt, fishnet stockings and high boots. Her lips were darkened almost to black. She sang, 'I love a man in uniform.' The rest of her words were lost in the hoarse, mournful music. The room was crowded now, and dimly red-lit. The refrain rose insistently again, repetitively: 'I love a man in uniform.'

'I love a man in uniform.' A girl of about seventeen was propping up the bar in the full Nazi rig-out: peaked cap, jodphurs, shiny black boots. It was all slightly too large for her.

Someone squeezed my hand. I looked up to find a stranger smiling down at me, a young woman in black leggings and T-shirt with bleached hair and a white face which appeared almost to float detached from her body. 'Dance?'

There was hardly room between the half-circle of tables and the rostrum on which the singer was now lifting her skirt. The blonde clung to me. I looked around the room. Lennox was propping up the bar, and chatting up some chunky blond leather queen.

I moved away from my partner who stretched out her thin arms too late. I slipped through the gap in the curtain and out of the door. I eased my way downwards against the tide of a party of those coming up, but at the bottom of the steps I was alone on the concrete runway between the high wall and the road. Lightheaded in this white-lit space, I leaned against a concrete wall.

When I went back inside, Star was sitting at our table now – in my seat. Lennox was still at the bar.

We watched the show. Now it was a boy dressed as a priest, and he was caning, or pretending to cane, a nun, whose habit had been parted to display her buttocks, which were divided by a leather thong. The scars were quite gruesome – patterned, the way people used to shave patterns into their hair. She meanwhile was sucking the dildo of a dyke in glam rock silver, whose painted face – a woman made up as a man made up as a woman – was all white and red, like a clown, with a shock of red and purple hair.

Later, I danced with Star. 'You like this place? Turns you on?'

'You turn me on,' she said.

'What's Lennox doing here – recruiting for the revolution?'

'Slumming, like you.'

'Why don't we go back to my place? Lennox could come too – and his friend.'

'What, that creepy house? No thanks.'

'You owe it to me, after the last time.'

'I meant to say I'm sorry but those bastards really chilled me.'

'You left me to it.'

'Look – I'm real sorry, I am.'

'That's white of you. As they say. But you wouldn't be frightened with more of us there.'

'Why Lennox? You want to have a party, ask all of them. Ask Wilma. I want to keep in with her.'

'What's with you and Wilma, anyway?'

'I just want to work on her film.'

'I think she wants me to put up some money.'

'Oh, how sublime! Why don't you?'

'I don't know.'

But I did know, of course. It was because the money was going to her brother.

She went and sat down by Wilma. I wandered over to the bar. Lennox said: 'Why do we come here? Jesus! Café society in the year nearly 2000. There has to be something better than this.'

'I quite like it,' I said.

'You *would*, though, Justine. The ideal occasion for your new leather trousers.'

'Don't bite the hand that's feeding you,' I said.

'Would I!'

We moved on to tequila slammers.

'I like them – the trousers I mean.'

'You've made my evening, Lennox.'

We had breakfast at the Poly Glut. 'Around the world in Eighty Tastebuds' ran the legend in fat kiddies lettering. This was an exaggeration, since only about fifteen dishes were on offer, Poly Glut aiming to capture the truth of each country in one predictable meal. Britain was 'roast beef and all the trimmings', a dish no one ate any more.

'What happened to you last night?' cooed Wilma when she saw me. 'I adored the – the show, the women, the boys. And we were having such sublime time all together. Only then you have disappeared. So bad of you.' She pouted, but she wasn't bothered. Nothing dented Wilma's confidence.

What had happened last night was no longer too clear, but I seemed to remember that Lennox and I had gone down to the beach. We'd smoked some dope and I remembered the clumsy, lurching feel of our discussion, like stumbling over the shingle.

'You have to remember, Justine, that all revolution-aries seemed absurd until they succeeded. Look at Lenin sitting in his café in Zurich, it wasn't even the right café, the one with the Dadaists, he never got to meet them. Or Guevara, hunted down in the jungle.'

Most of the words had gone, but the feel of the hard, round, hurtful pebbles in my back was still vividly with me, and the way the stars in the sky spun round as I lay, my hands at my side, with less than an inch, and a chasm of chastity between us.

'Didn't you think Star looked *wunderbar*, darling? She should have been in the show. You will be the *centrepiece* of the film, darling,' said Wilma, and put her arm around Star's waist.

But Star wanted to make a film, not be in one, didn't she? Or did she? Perhaps she didn't care which it was. Or thought it would be both.

'And now, with your friend's help . . .' added Wilma, smooth as silk. She put her hand on mine. 'We have transgression through music,' she said, 'here it is, S/M women; from Germany corpses – the new necrophilia cinema, I film them making the videos; for China my film of TaoMatan, the women anarchist group. It has been very dangerous filming this group. But it is a scoop, because they are hanged now.'

This seemed a source of great satisfaction.

'Around the world in eighty soundbites,' drawled Jade,

who was sitting there eating a so-called Californian fruit plate and wearing cut-off jeans and army boots.

'Lennox had to go,' she said to me, 'but he said to remind you you're meeting him.'

'Christ – don't remember anything about *that*.'

'That's what he said.'

'My headache is destroying me.'

'Some party.' Jade laughed. 'Was I *wired*!'

A TV screen above our heads unreeled pop videos, but now a news summary interrupted the flow: another bombing, two men and a woman killed, a child with its legs blown off, innocent bystanders, the Minister of the Interior on the screen again.

'Horrible,' said the Jean Harlow half of the perfect butch/femme couple. I wished I could remember her name.

'I'm afraid I've forgotten your name,' I said.

Wilma's arm was still around Star. 'Will your brother appear in my film also? My *next* film, that is. Such a wonderful-looking boy. We could make it around the two of you. Twins. It's such a marvellous theme. Twins. Mirrors. He looks in the mirror and sees you. Which is which – girl or boy. Gender fuck. You exchange. It has everything: narcissism, *doppelgänger*, reflections – *und* so *weiter*.'

Star shrugged Wilma's arm away. 'He wouldn't be interested. And we're not twins. He's years younger than me.'

Additional security measures to be rushed through by Parliament, prevention of terrorism act to be beefed up again, arrest on suspicion, suspects to be held for ten days without charge – it all reeled past and the Minister's upper-class face was long and pinched with sorrowful disapproval at the lengths to which he had been forced to go. Then he disappeared and they were playing MTV again.

I picked up a paper and read an unlikely article about

the return of the Ice Age, and another which described the royal families of Europe, consigned to the scrapheap of history, returning one by one to their thrones – was life going to be like *The Scarlet Empress*, all Tsars and Hapsburgs and snow?

'I am calling my film *Music of the Millennium*,' announced Wilma.

'I'm going,' I said.

'Stay!' urged Star.

I shook my head. 'I have to go to a funeral. I'll talk to you soon.'

She pulled at my arm. 'Meet me at the Café. This evening.'

'Sure – sure.'

Only ten o'clock, and the heat was infernal.

I had some trouble finding the Crematorium. It was way out in the suburbs, a series of long, low buildings with Spanish roofs in landscaped surroundings that reminded me of California.

The hearse parked outside was empty, and there were no uneasy knots of mourners in tidy clothes hanging around. It must have begun.

The chapel door creaked as I pushed it. I stepped into the coolness of the sanctuary. The rows were packed, but I found an inconspicuous empty space at the side.

The mourners were mostly middle-aged or older. A well-known left-wing politican was speaking of Violet Frankenberg's role in the peace movement . . . the 1940s and 1950s again. I couldn't get away from that dark, forgotten time.

Next, an old Party member spoke of her role as an organiser, in what was such a clear restatement of the values of the left, the language of my childhood – socialism, peace, democracy – that you wondered how such words and such ideas could ever have been so battered, ill treated and then forgotten like some broken toy. As he spoke he pulled them from obscurity, and made them fresh and new again.

What would Violet herself have thought of them, though – what would she have thought of this whole event, a celebration of the Party she'd turned against or wanted to be different? And what would she have thought of her niece, who spoke afterwards of Violet's love of children and devotion to her brother's family? Was it because of my father that she'd never had children herself?

The congregation rose for the Internationale. Both verses were sung, and everyone round me knew all the words. My elderly neighbour glared sideways at my mistakes.

The coffin slid away and we all came out blinking into the sunlight. Freed from social responsibility, since I knew no one, and no one recognised me, I watched the mourners chatting as they inspected the flowers, which were stacked in front of a hand-quilted peace banner. It gleamed silver and yellow.

I saw Maurice Kavanagh and went up to him. He again didn't recognise me, but when I reminded him, he led me towards a tall woman in a green dress.

'Myrtle would like to meet you – she's so very upset about Violet.'

When he touched her elbow she turned and looked at me with large, pale eyes. Earrings like drops of sea-water wobbled from her ears beneath an untidy mass of piled-up red hair.

'It was good, wasn't it? Violet would have liked it. You knew her, did you?'

'It was Justine who – Charles Hillyard's daughter.'

'Oh.' Her eyes grew even larger with the tears that filled them. 'Yes, let's –'

'Shall we find somewhere to sit down?' I suggested uneasily. The woman's grief unnerved me, as well as bringing back my memories of Violet's death.

At the far end of a Spanish cloister we found a deserted paved garden with wooden seats and lavender bushes in tubs.

Myrtle's heavy cotton dress looked as if she'd made it herself, most likely from curtain material. She spread the skirt round her and crossed her ankles. The purple slippers had once been nice, but the suede was rough and soiled and they gaped at the sides to show her dry, veined feet.

She started to talk, nervously, but fast. 'We live in a strange world, don't we? Between democracy and fascism. Neither one thing nor the other. It all seems – temporary. A temporary world. A temporary life.

'My father – he edited *Workers' World* after the war – he visited the refugee camps at the end of the Second World War. Well, that's what they called the camps – a temporary life. That's what the inmates called them. And the inmates themselves were referred to as Displaced Persons. Did you know that? I don't expect so. No one does. It's all forgotten, all that chaos, and yet it's all coming back again. But then every life is temporary, isn't it? And I suppose we are all displaced persons. So many people – I know I feel displaced. Since the Party collapsed –'

The tears started to spill over. I felt embarrassed, hopeless, I didn't know what to say.

'You were close to Violet?'

'I wanted to know – did she, how much did she suffer?'

I did what I could, said what I had to say, put my hand over hers. I was crying too, and that made it better, for the tears dissolved my embarrassment.

Then, when the time seemed right, and it didn't feel too instrumental, I slipped into gear with my questions about Colin Fox. I used the same story I'd used with Aunt Susan, the story about the watch and the letters. I showed her the photograph as well.

'Oh, that's Colin,' she said at once, 'the one in the middle. But who are the other two?'

'That one's my father.'

'Really? Oh, yes, I see now.'

'I wondered what sort of man he was, this Colin Fox. He must have been – that is, I have a feeling he was important to my parents, yet I can't remember that they ever talked about him, and I just wondered . . .'

'He came to our house a few times. I adored him, he knew how to talk to a child. I was about ten, I suppose. Even at that age, I realised there'd been some sort of scandal. He wrote about the socialist countries.'

'D'you know where he is now?'

'He died years ago I should think. Drank himself to death – he didn't last long on *Workers' World*. Dad did what he could, I think, but – I daresay your parents tried to help, they were quite well off, weren't they? But – he just gradually disappeared from view. In the end he was living along the coast somewhere . . . married some very young girl, or something.'

'Is she still around?'

'I haven't the faintest idea. She wasn't Party or anything. He'd completely lost touch with all of us by then.'

It seemed like I'd hit another dead end. I sat there, depressed, but Myrtle's tears were spilling over again, and I had to say something.

'I am so sorry about Violet. People have been nice to me, said how awful it was for me, to find her like that, but I didn't really know her, much worse for her friends.'

Myrtle pressed her handkerchief against her eyes. 'I don't believe it was burglary,' she said. 'The police seem to think it was, but it wasn't, I'm sure. She'd rung me. She said she was worried. Some phone call she'd had, or something. She was upset.'

'*What?*' I was about to pounce again, when –

'Myrtle – oh, there you are.' A woman appeared at the

mouth of the cloister. 'I think we should be getting on, dear. The reception will be starting, and Maurice has offered us a lift.'

I grabbed Myrtle's arm. 'Can I phone you or something?'

She looked at me with mild, startled eyes, bloodshot now. 'You can always reach me at the Peace Union office – but there's nothing more to say. She said she was worried, that's all she said – she was upset . . . I don't know why.'

And now Myrtle was upset too, even more upset. She made a feeble effort to pull away from me, and her friend frowned at my gross insensitivity.

'Myrtle, I don't think we should hang about, Maurice will be waiting –'

And she led Myrtle away.

Chapter
Sixteen

I didn't see Lennox for days. I issued instructions to brokers and banks in order to get his money, but he himself was nowhere to be found. Not even Star knew how to reach him.

Also, I was living nowhere, neither at the Café, nor at my father's house, nor in an hotel. If things went on like this I'd be living in my Lada, the way homeless Hollywood divorcées live in their Cadillacs.

Also, my investigations were stalled, but I drove Myra up to the house one afternoon to help me look through the books.

'See this in the paper?' she said, 'about your lodger. They've tracked down her husband, or at least they've found out where he lives, but he's gone missing.'

'I thought they'd lost interest,' I said, 'they never came near me again.'

'D'you think it could be her husband?'

'Two unconnected murders in one house? Come on.'

I still said nothing about the woman I'd glimpsed in the library stacks, the woman I'd been sure was Anna. It seemed so mad: first I'd been the only person to see her corpse, then when the corpse was found I started to see her alive.

Myra sat on the divan and talked, while I did all the work of looking at the books. I was searching for names, for subjects, anything to give me a lead. The problem was that everything so far led only into the past, and I had no more sense of anything my father could have been mixed up with in the present than I'd had when I read Violet's letter. I'd hoped that Lennox and his shadowy 'contact' would help, but now he'd disappeared.

'What's happened to Lennox?' I said. 'Is he down in the tunnels?'

'I doubt it,' she said. She gave me a straight look. 'You wouldn't really get hung up on Lennox. You wouldn't be that stupid.'

'He said he might help me, that's all.'

'Of course he would. That boy has too many ideas. And he'd think it was worth trying to butter you up. Of course he would. Talk about the great impostor! He's such a little teaser in his own quiet way.'

'Who said I was hung up on him anyway?'

'Oh, no one *said* anything.'

'Who are they, anyway? Where do they come from? Him and Star?'

'Oh dear, oh dear!' Myra rolled her eyes heavenward.

'I just want to know, that's all!'

'Know what? Father was Italian, went back to Italy soon after Lennox was born. Mother struggled along, shacked up with some other creep, that didn't work out, he hated the kids, Star stuck it out, she was older, Lennox left home – is that what you wanted to know?'

'There's no need to be so cross.'

'Cross! I'm just being real. Look, don't get hung up on him. In the first place he likes men. Really. He may go with women occasionally, or he may not. But deep down he's for men. And deeper down still, he isn't for anyone. He has other fish to fry.'

'The radio station?'

'Radio station?' Myra looked puzzled for a moment. Then she said, 'Oh – the radio station. That's Baz, really. He's done all the work on that and I think he's really going to get it off the ground. But Lennox . . . well, I suppose he might be a bit involved in that. But – who *knows* what he's up to.'

'What d'you mean? Are you suggesting something dodgy?'

'Oh, of course it's dodgy, bound to be,' said Myra carelessly, 'that's not the point. It's – just imagine him in ten, fifteen years time. Men like that get seedy so quickly. He thinks he's a revolutionary, but he'll probably get involved in petty crime, or not so petty, or maybe he'll get ill.'

'That's a horrible thing to say.'

'Anyway, everyone fancies Lennox. Couldn't you pick someone less obvious? What's the matter with you? Suddenly all these problems with men, Adam, now Lennox, and you spend all your time with men, no women friends, you've no time for Star, what's wrong with her, she's nice, she even looks a bit like him.'

'Lesbians don't have women friends,' I said, 'they only have women lovers.'

'Well, you don't even seem to want that any more.'

'Oh, let's start on the books.'

There were rows of complete works of Marx and Engels, in white paper jackets; and Lenin, in faded orange cloth. There were translations of other Bolsheviks, Hungarian Marxists, works in German and French, Marxist historians from the sixties and seventies, other historical works, rows of stuff on Marxism and science, and on science itself.

I reached a shelf of works on the Second World War. One caught my eye for some reason: *With the Forest Brothers* by Edgar Baxter. With its hard, blue cover, thick paper and old-fashioned print it looked like any discarded volume you might have picked up in a secondhand shop. Published in 1950 by a press I hadn't heard of, it told of underground work with Baltic resistance movements at the end of the war.

The author described how youthful utopianism had

blinded him (like so many others) to the true nature of Communism. His experience in central Europe after the end of the war, assisting what he had at first perceived as a Marxist resistance movement in Lithuania, only to find that it was impelled principally by ferocious hatred of the Soviet Union, had been the key experience that changed his mind. I looked up the index. The name Colin Fox actually appeared. I turned to the relevant page. Baxter's reference to him was brief and enigmatic:

> Like many of the comrades Fox had his eyes opened in the tooth and claw world of post-war central Europe – or so he later hinted to me on one of our drinking evenings during a brief period when we both worked for *Workers' World*. His dispatches were always tinged with an irony that escaped our masters back home.

I wondered if this Baxter could possibly have been the tall man in the snapshot. I wondered if he was worth following up. I wondered if it was possible to follow him up.

I turned back to the flyleaf. On it was written: 'Joyce – from Francis.'

'Look at this,' and I showed the book to Myra. 'Someone gave it to my mother.'

'Who's Francis?'

'No idea. Another blind alley, I expect.'

I made some tea, and we sat and drank it. Myra was quieter than usual. After a while she said, 'I keep thinking there's something missing, like, didn't he have any disks? If he had that smart machine, and if he was writing something, wouldn't it have been on disk?'

'Yes, you're right.' He'd always been one for the latest gadget. No elderly grumbles for him about new technology.

'I looked already,' I told her. 'He may have hidden them somewhere, or possibly they were stolen, maybe that's what they took,' I said. 'And there's something else, you know,' I reminded her, 'whatever Violet was trying to tell me about when she died. I've been worrying ever since how to get back into her flat, or whether the police have got hold of it . . .'

'You should have acted at once. It's probably gone by now. Maybe he gave her the disks. Maybe she had them hidden. Though you'd have thought she'd have said in her letter.'

It was true that I'd spent too much time on Lennox and on digging up the past, when all the while that hidden something in Violet's flat could have led me straight into the present.

'Won't they have – don't they seal up places like that, where's there's been a crime, a murder, anyway? I don't suppose I could ever have got back in.'

'I don't know,' said Myra. 'Perhaps Adam could help. He seems to have contacts in all the right places.'

'I don't want to ask him any more favours.'

'Couldn't you bribe someone? Surely with all your money you could find at least one bent copper.'

We talked and talked, but we were getting nowhere. We went round and round in circles and always came back to the initial enigma: what had my father been up to when he died?

When depressed, I always went shopping. I bought some kelly green suede shoes with many buttons and straps, and then wandered into a book emporium in the city centre. The display tables with the new books were near the front of the shop, and I noticed at once a book by Urban Foster, *The Reinvented Man*. I opened it:

'I was born last night,' proclaimed Alex Kingdom, the day he left the army. Reinventing himself after an orphanage childhood, he went on to become a brilliant lawyer, financier and politician. He is the true self-made man of the twentieth century, self-made not in the vulgar sense of making his pile, but in the sense that his belief in individualism and in his own abilities enabled him to survive setbacks to which a lesser man might have succumbed.

In 1948, George Orwell published his classic novel, *1984*, actually intended as a parable of the times: 1948/1984 – the inversion of numbers was deliberate. To the just-demobbed Kingdom, post-war austerity in Kakania did indeed resemble Orwell's negative utopia. In a bedsitting room in the then slums of the East City . . .

It was a biography of Alex Kingdom. I was amazed, but it was as good a way as any, I supposed, for Urban Foster to augment his income. As I read on I had to admit that beneath the apparent adulation I detected at least a hint of irony, but all the same, I hadn't expected that even now someone with Foster's background would have been so totally in bed with the establishment.

It was also surprising to learn that Kingdom had been brought up in an orphanage – itself an oddly old-fashioned term. I'd assumed his background to be impeccably patrician. The story of his childhood was rather touching, in fact his life, as told by Foster, seemed to be a rags-to-riches fairytale. I bought the book, and several others, but after that I still didn't know where to go, or what to do with myself.

It seemed like a long time since I'd been in the Café – although it wasn't. I looked round and once again Lennox wasn't there. Adam was at his table, of course. He waved at me to join him.

'How's it going?'

'How's what going?'

'Sorting out your dad's affairs, of course.'

That seemed an odd way of putting it.

'Okay,' I said.

Jeannie brought me a ristretto. Adam said, 'Let's do

something, go to a movie, why don't we spend more time together?'

'Too busy,' I said uneasily.

'But isn't that just what's wrong with us? You turning up again – it's made me think about it – seemed like such an incredible piece of luck when you came in that evening . . .'

'Oh, Adam.'

'I'm worried about you, Justine – knocking around with that crowd. I'd even say it could be dangerous.'

I laughed. 'Dangerous? Depends what you mean by dangerous,' and I thought of Lennox.

'All this digging up the past – what's the point? You know – your father – well, he must have had a heart attack, an accident. Justine, he just *died*. That's all there is to it – so why don't you . . . You should let me take care of you. Help you at least. And you could help me so much, you know, there's so much we could do with the Café.'

I looked down at my feet in their wonderful new green shoes, and said nothing. What was the use? Polite disagreement he disbelieved, silence was interpreted as consent. It was hopeless.

One thing was clear: I had to get out of the Café. To him that must seem like some kind of commitment, some need, when all the while I was only stringing him along and making use of him because I was too cowardly to spend nights at my father's house.

Yet in itself the idea of the Café was so attractive. What if – But there was no point even thinking about it.

He put his hand over mine. 'On Mondays the Café's closed. We'll do something then, okay?' Then his voice changed. 'I almost forgot. Or – well, I didn't know whether to tell you or not, but Lennox rang earlier with a message for you.'

'Lennox?'

'Something about he wants you to meet him out at

Angel Point. Seven-thirty, I think he said. By the kiosk under the steps.'

'What d'you mean, you didn't know whether or not to tell me?'

'Like I said, you spend too much time with that crowd.'

'I think that's for me to decide. Don't know if I'll make it, though. Where can I ring him back?'

'He didn't say. He said it was important.'

I'd arranged to see some old friends as it happened – as Adam said, to get away from the Café crowd, to get away from the whole thing, the impossible enigma, the unexplained deaths. I sat quite still, and thought about seeing Lennox.

It might be because he'd seen his contact, and had something to tell me. It might be because he was expecting the money. Those reasons were important, but it wasn't very cool to trek out all that way the moment he snapped his fingers. I remembered what Myra had said: Lennox, the great impostor, sure to be up to something dodgy.

The best thing would be to give Angel Point a miss.

When I reached the Point I turned off the expressway. Empty land, a silent grassy landscape, waited once I'd left the steady roar of the traffic. The only building was the convalescent centre for the blind. Built against a hill, it jutted out, a monument to 1930s architecture, a huge white ocean liner, beached and forgotten, seemingly deserted. Its rows of windows looked out blankly towards the sea.

I parked beside a field, looked around and walked back to the tunnel under the motorway. I walked through it, looking back once to see if I was being followed. There was no one. I emerged from the tunnel near the cliff edge to find that I was all alone in the golden landscape, walking towards the cliff. Like Colin Fox.

I looked about me again. A faint wind rattled the long dry grass. To my right, concrete steps had been constructed – set into the cliff face to lead down to the beach far below. I looked down over the railings, and felt giddy. The tide was up. The waves hurled themselves at the sea wall, burst with an explosion of foam, retreating with a sighing, grinding noise and coiling up to launch themselves forward again.

The steps were protected by iron railings like scaffolding poles. Long ago they'd been painted turquoise. Now they were spotted with rust. The steps led down a covered staircase. My footsteps echoed in the well. Round and round I went, counting – thirty – fifty – eighty – a hundred – and at last with relief I stepped out on to the cemented walkway, a kind of promenade between the cliff and the sea wall, which stretched as far as the eye could see in both directions. It was deserted.

The sun was low and shone across the sea straight into my eyes. I could see almost to the city to the west, but in the other direction a sharp bend ended the vista about a hundred yards away. The evening light turned the cliffs yellow. Under the cliff the kiosk was boarded up, as was a row of what looked like garages, or old beach huts, the turquoise paint flaking off their doors. On one door someone had written 'Frank and Martin came (together!) here 2.2.95'.

I looked to the east, and then to the west. The promenade was still empty. The landscape was entirely man-made. Even the sea was landscaped. Close to civilisation – the expressway was moments distant at the top of the cliff – this place was abandoned to the weeds pushing up between cracks in the cement, and to the sea, hurling itself against the wall as if determined to destroy it. Here and there the wall was already crumbling. I wondered if the Port development was planned to stretch out this far.

In the pause between breakers as the sea sucked back

down the shingle, I heard a stone clatter down from above. I looked up. No one. I could see no living thing. And yet I hadn't imagined that stone. I stepped back, nearer the sea wall. This place had no way out. The stairwell was a death trap. Anyone could bar your way along the walk under the cliff. And you could be seen from every direction.

And then to my relief I saw someone coming. I squinted into the sun. Something moved far along the promenade. A faint drone – a motorbike driving towards me. Lennox. I stood by the wall, and then began to walk slowly towards him.

He was coming on fast. The noise increased. I waved. But instead of slowing down, the black machine with its black crouched jockey, a man with no face but only goggles and a helmet, accelerated – I heard the change of register – and he was coming nearer and nearer, tilted, terrifying, speeding towards me.

Almost too late I hurled myself over the low wall. As I sank beneath the water and swallowed a rasping mouthful of brine I hit my head against something with a sickening crack.

Perhaps I lost consciousness for a moment. The next thing I knew I was coughing and choking and the salt water was hurting my throat. I struck out with my legs, but was out of my depth, and nearly went under again. My clothes felt like weeds, dragging me down, but I somehow managed to start swimming alongside the wall, searching for a break in the stones, or a breakwater, so that I could climb out.

There was a noise I didn't recognise. I looked up. Gunfire. Someone was shooting at me. I dived down into the water again and stayed under as long as I could, trying to steer away from the wall now, and out towards the open sea, yet at the same time to move in the direction of the next breakwater in the hope that I'd be able to hide behind it where it emerged above the waterline.

I reached it, and, twisting carefully round so that I was partially hidden, I raised my head high enough to look towards the sea wall. There was no movement. I couldn't see Lennox.

I waited. I was beginning to feel very cold. My head hurt quite badly. There was also a sharp, stinging pain in one leg and it felt as if I'd sprained my left wrist. But all this hardly mattered. What mattered was that Lennox had tried to run me down.

The sun had sunk almost to the level of the sea. The shining path beckoned across an expanse of water rippled like a mantle of silk laid down for me to walk on all the way into its centre.

As a kid, I used to use the expression 'walking on the water' in my private thoughts, but it didn't mean a miracle, it meant I was out of my depth, attempting the impossible, hoping to survive when actually I was sinking.

Like now. When Lennox had nearly killed me. But that couldn't be true.

I looked towards the sea wall and the cliff. Soon the sun would have set. At dusk the place would be even more dangerous.

I felt my way along the wall towards the shore. The tide was turning. Soon the sea would be far down the beach. The breakwater would be naked and exposed. I'd have nowhere to hide.

Perhaps he was waiting crouched behind the wall, at a turn of the stairs, high up on the cliff.

The wind was getting up – I felt chilled to the bone. I crawled and crept alongside the breakwater, close to the sea wall now. If I stayed in the water I would soon go numb, pass out, drown. My head hurt, my throat felt raw. I had to get out of the sea alive.

I heaved myself out of the water, lay for a moment on the head of the breakwater, which broadened out into a platform where it met the sea wall, then crawled forward again. I was completely vulnerable. Anyone could see me, shoot me down.

'Lennox!'

Silence.

'Lennox! Lennox!'

I sat up. I looked up and down the promenade.

I saw the bike, crashed up against the cliff. And beside it his body lay in a pool of blood.

The sun had finally sunk beneath the line of the horizon and a great shadow was cast along the shore and the empty cliffs. I climbed stiffly down onto the path and stood upright, still dripping, shivering, hugging myself, to stop the strange noise that was coming from me.

I didn't dare start up the twisting steps to the top of the cliff. I just stood there. I couldn't even look a second time at where he lay.

I looked up the steps, which slanted off into shadow. I could not make myself step forward. I just shook, more and more violently.

And then high up on the cliff I heard voices like starlings at evening. I looked up and I could see what looked like a crocodile of figures snaking along the top of the cliff and beginning the descent to the beach. Each figure held on to the shoulders of the one in front, as if performing a dance.

I waited until I thought the leader would be about half-way down the long flights of steps, and then I started towards the foot of the stairs myself. They were talking and laughing rather loudly as they came down. I, too, purposely made as much noise as possible, excusing myself as I met the head of the line.

They were blind. The leader smiled and nodded, his eyes shifting sightlessly from side to side, and called to his troupe to make way for me to pass, so I squeezed as close to the wall as I could as I climbed past them, thirty at least, not wanting to touch them with my wet clothes.

I reached the top of the cliff, numb, finished. I didn't walk into the tunnel, instead I climbed up alongside the motorway, slithered down the banked-up sides to the hard shoulder, and made a dash for it across the wall of noise.

Lights were coming on in the great ocean liner on the hill. I saw the path, marked with a white handrail which glimmered in the dusk, leading up to the front entrance, down which the line of blind convalescents must have threaded their way.

I walked back to my car. I managed to open it, and slid my key into the ignition. I turned it. Nothing happened. I felt a sudden wave of nausea, leaned out, and was violently sick on to the road.

I sat there holding my bruised head in my hands, relaxing in the relief that comes after being sick, but shivering too, more violently than ever.

Then I heard footsteps coming along the road, alongside the car, and I saw a pair of feet in shiny black leather lace-up shoes, and legs in black trousers standing by my head.

Chapter
Seventeen

'You're looking at me like I'm Adolf Hitler, but I just save your life, you know.'

Taste of bile in my mouth. His shoes and mine, the green ones, stained and soggy.

'Move over – if anyone can start this car, it's me.'

I sat upright. 'Gennady – you don't understand – it was Lennox –' and I started painfully to climb out of the car. 'We can't leave him there. We have to get Lennox.'

'Are you mad – there's only me –'

'You killed him, you killed him.' I started to scream and to hit him. He grabbed and shook me.

'You're crazy woman. There's no Lennox, he never tell you to come here, that's why I come after you. I'm in the Café, I overhear Adam tell you, it's sounding all wrong – why should he want you to come out here –'

I tasted salt now. I must be crying. Or maybe it was sea water.

'You're in shock.' He pulled a flask of brandy from his pocket. 'Have some of this.' I took a swig, and coughed.

'And now to get the bloody Lada to start. Why your father of all cars on earth chose a Lada – and this one's for the scrap heap, darling. Won't last much longer, you know.'

'Don't say that. You're talking about the car I love.'

'That's better. Now you're joking. Move over. And here – take my jacket. You catch cold.'

After a while it coughed into life. 'I drive.' He turned

the car and stopped by the opposite verge, got out, fished a small folding bicycle out of the ditch, and put it in the boot. 'My secret weapon. I followed you on this.'

'Did Adam send you?'

Gennady laughed. 'No, for sure he didn't. Look, I take you to Myra's, you stay with Myra for little while.'

I shifted round in my seat to look at him. He had a straight, long nose, a slightly-receding chin, and his pale eyes, sea-coloured in his tanned face, protruded, giving him a droll look. Just another migrant worker, I'd never given him a thought till now.

'You're not just a waiter, are you?' I said.

He laughed. It was a risky, devil may care kind of laugh. 'I'm representative of Russian opposition movement. I come over here for one purpose – that's to get help for the anti-government forces. We are the left-wing, you understand, the socialist opposition. There are others, of course, many groups, but we are the Left. Our guerrilla movement is growing, every day we are stronger. But we need much more funds, more support.'

'Hardly likely to be forthcoming from the National Government.'

'Of course not, are you mad? I'm sent over to make connections here, anyone, any sympathisers at all, anyone at all who's still left-wing – and one obvious group, it's the old Communists. A dying breed, but still there are a few. And maybe they can still do some political work for us here, even lead to more influential connections, raise the issue in more powerful quarters. Your father is obvious person to approach. Respected scientist, etcetera. So – I'm coming over, and my first contact, it's your dad. And soon he tells me something that opens a completely different picture –

'Also, I get the job at the Café because it seems like I'm meeting many dissidents, oppositionalists in this way. Turns out it's not like that any more, Adam's gone for the smart trade, but I don't know that till I'm there. And

Adam – he turns out a bit different, too. Lucky I find out before I'm chatting him up.'

'Find out what?'

But he was silent as we negotiated some heavy traffic. I was cold and damp, and shivered, in spite of his coat.

'Your father was a nice man. I liked him.'

'What was this new perspective he gave you on it all?'

Gennady cursed a driver who cut in. 'Look at the bastard, he's wanting to kill us.'

'Why didn't you tell me all this before? You must have known I was trying to find out what happened to my father.'

'I don't trust you. To begin with seems like you're big friends with Adam, and that's bad news. Then when I'm going to tell you, you disappear. Myra says you were living in Ocean View Hotel, but I don't know that then.'

'I'm not living there now. Dunno where I'm living. In my Lada. But what did he *tell* you?'

'It's one long story, baby – I tell you later, we're nearly there already. But what he tells me, it means he's much more useful than I've ever dreamed.'

'You *must* tell me.'

'Look, Adam will have missed me – it's a big risk already that I left the Café at all. I'll walk you through the tunnel. Then I come back later, when I can.' He took my arm. We were in the tunnel now. It was dark and eerily empty.

'I have to go now,' he said as we emerged on to the plaza. 'Listen. Lie low for a while – I come back to Myra's place, maybe tonight, maybe tomorrow. Or maybe Lennox come.'

'Lennox!'

'Ah! Lennox.' He stopped and looked at me. His smile was mocking. 'Lennox, eh. The man with the lizard hips and the alligator eyes.'

'What's that supposed to mean?'

'Lennox is okay, baby – he never trick you, never come after you. The guy I shot –'

'So you did shoot him.'

'Of course.' He looked incredulous. 'I told you this all along. This is serious stuff, baby.'

'So what am I supposed to do? Just stay here with Myra?'

'Till you feel better. You're still in shock. Just be careful, that's all.'

I didn't tell him, but I had been careful. At first I had been going to take the money with me out to Angel Point. I'd decided against, for once I'd parted with that, I had no guarantee that I'd ever see Lennox again.

Well – not careful. Calculating.

I started walking. When I looked back, it was too dark to see Gennady any more.

I woke in the dark. The digits on a clock glowed green. Five to midnight. I groped around, found a robe that hung over a chair and slipped it on.

Myra and Emma were watching television news downstairs. More bombs. More coverage for Kingdom, the Minister of the Interior. The para-militaries had surrounded an estate where terrorists were hiding out.

With no make-up and dressed in old jeans, Emma looked about twelve years old, but less waiflike, more cheerful. This must be her night off.

'I'm hungry,' I said. I wouldn't eat Myra's lentils and brown rice; I made her make me an omelette stuffed with fried potatoes, and a big spinach salad.

'That's a good sign. You might have been concussed.'

She made me drink one of her horrible tisanes. 'And now,' she said, 'I think we need a reading.'

We settled down to the cards. 'So, tell me what happened. He just dragged me off my pitch and said I'd got to wait for you at home.'

In spite of the ache above my ear, it was a fading nightmare now, and, like a dream, although I could see it all so clearly in my head, it slithered away when I tried to translate it into words.

'He must have been on the steps ... Gennady. I thought I heard a pebble, a stone dislodged – I heard a noise – but then the man on the motorbike came and I forgot.'

'Gennady *shot* the biker who was trying to run you down? Actually shot him?'

'Yeah – he did.'

This shook even Myra's cool. 'Bloody hell,' she said, as she massaged the cards. 'Still, I suppose we shouldn't have been surprised that someone was after you. It's no secret you were nosing around and making enquiries about your papa.'

Maybe someone knew all along, had even known from the moment I arrived at the airport, knew almost before I knew myself. Maybe that other accident had been no accident at all; and the man on the motorbike that night and the dog in the road just an encounter designed very specially for me.

'So who's responsible?' said Myra.

'I don't know. Gennady said he made contact with my father,' and I told Myra what Gennady had told me. 'That explains him saying he was up to something, that someone needed his help. But then Gennady said that my father told *him*, Gennady, something interesting. Only he didn't say what it was.'

'Maddening not to tell you.'

Yes, but I couldn't explain to her what still possessed me: the uncomprehending terror when I thought it was Lennox on the bike. 'The horrible thing was, the really terrible thing, I thought it was Lennox. Because he was on a bike I just assumed – I couldn't see his face, you see, because of the helmet, the visor.'

'Enough of this.' She shuffled the cards again. 'Cut ...

cut again.' She dealt, then turned the cards over one by one, stared at the spread and frowned.

'The cards are ambiguous. But they're warning you of something. Yes – there's a very strong warning . . . Something – or someone. Let's think for a minute. Gennady? What do we know about him? Only what he's told you. Does it make sense – that he's trying to drum up support? Maybe it's all a fantasy. Or some kind of scam . . . But he knew you'd be at Angel Point. And he had a gun. On the other hand, anyone can have a gun. "Just another guy who thinks a gun in your hand means the world by the tail."'

'Gennady's smarter than that,' I said. 'I think Gennady's on the level – so far as this goes, anyway. It's all quite plausible. He could easily have heard Adam talking to me.'

Myra nodded. 'But I wish he'd told you what your father told him. Still . . . if it's true, I guess he'll tell us soon enough. And who sent you the message about Angel Point? You didn't take the call?'

'No, it was Adam. I told you.'

'Adam!'

'Yes. He said Lennox had phoned.'

'Well then, there are three possibilities, aren't there? Either Lennox did leave the message, but someone else knew about it and sent the biker along to deal with you. Or someone pretending to be Lennox left the message. Or – or there wasn't a message and Adam just made it up.'

Silence. A chilling little drop of poison trickled into my brain.

'We can easily ask him,' said Myra, 'see if he's absolutely sure. Ask Gennady, I mean.' Then she added, 'I never thought it was a good idea, staying at the Café. It kind of encouraged him.'

'But what's that got to do with –'

'I mean, how *do* we know there ever was a phone call?'

'Oh, Christ!'

'He *is* slightly off his trolley about you.' Myra looked at me grimly, as though it were my fault.

'But I hadn't seen him for *five years*.'

She went on looking at the spread of cards. I thought about what she'd just said.

'That doesn't make sense. If Adam's obsessed with me, like you say, the last thing he'd do would be . . .'

Myra took no notice. After a while she said, 'I think I feel like a trip to the Café.'

'Can you pick up my things?'

'I'll try to talk to Gennady.'

'He said he'd come back.'

'I can't wait – you get some sleep. If you feel bad in the morning we'll take you to the hospital.'

Unfortunately the kind of bad I felt wasn't the kind they dealt with in casualty.

When I woke my headache had all but gone, although the bruise was a painful spot on my skull. I could hear voices and sounds, and smell coffee. Myra was back. The sun shone. Things were normal again – almost.

I heard Emma call goodbye. The front door slammed. I pulled on the robe from last night.

'You were late?'

Myra looked dishevelled, and red-eyed with fatigue. Yet she seemed full of energy.

'How d'you feel today?' she asked.

'Okay. Just bring me the coffee.'

'I got some in specially. You know it plays havoc with your system. Kills you in the end.'

'Frankly, I don't care.' I took the cup she handed me. 'Did you bring my clothes?'

'Your other ones are clean, the ones you were wearing, the wet ones, I took them to the all night laundry.'

'My new shoes are ruined,' I said.

'Justine! Someone's tried to kill you, and you're worrying about your shoes? Come on!'

'Well, they were nice, they cost a lot of money.'

'Jesus!'

'Okay, okay, just tell me what happened.'

'Well, when I arrived at the Café Adam wasn't there.'

'Unusual!'

'Well, he wasn't. Gennady was in charge. Meant he was too busy to talk. It was a pain. I had to wait till it closed. I waited outside for Gennady. He locked up and we took off together. We went looking for Lennox, thought he might be down on the beach.'

'Why Lennox?' I asked.

Myra looked at me. 'Why d'you think! To find out about the call, of course. In the end we did find him. Said he didn't know anything about any call. Or rather – that's not right. He said he'd tried to call you, but Adam wouldn't take a message, and anyway, this was several days ago –'

'He could easily have got hold of me if he'd wanted to –'

'Oh, you know what he's like, he's always off somewhere up to his little schemes, or semi-underground – Anyway, what happened then was,' said Myra, 'Gennady was angry with him about something. They started to argue, and went off along the beach, but when they came back it was like everything was okay. I was furious with them for leaving me like that. Lennox said he was going down the tunnels, but he sent a message for you. A real one this time – I can vouch for it. You're to meet him this evening – I'll explain later on. There's more to tell you – listen to this.

'We went back to the Café. It was in darkness, but Adam must have returned, for the Alvis was parked on the quay. So Gennady pinched his car keys – he knew where Adam kept them, on a hook behind the bar – and we took off for Camden Bay in Adam's Alvis.

'Camden Bay?'

'Violet Frankenberg's flat, of course! The front door was boarded up, but Gennady went round to the back. The flats are built against a hill, you know, and at the back, her windows are only one floor from the ground. The police hadn't bothered much with the windows on that side, and Gennady got in by climbing first onto a low wall, then onto an adjacent balcony.

'So he said, anyway. I didn't actually see, I waited in the car. Quite a while. Even I was getting nervous. Suppose a police patrol came along. How'd I have explained why I was sitting there? Luckily they didn't. Anyway, when Gennady came back, he'd got what he wanted,' said Myra. 'He said maybe whoever ransacked the place didn't know what they were looking for. You said the place'd been turned upside-down – but anyway, in the end Gennady found a loose tile in the floor, and hidden underneath it was a little key.'

'Why didn't she send it back to me with her letter and the photo, then?'

'Gennady didn't know about any of that, of course,' said Myra. 'Who knows? The only thing he and I could think of was just that she simply forgot. Or that she thought she was going to see you and wouldn't send it through the post. It's here.'

She handed me a key with a round red disc attached to it. It looked like a locker key to me.

'What happens now?'

Chapter
Eighteen

It was dusk when I set out. I drove past the flying saucer building I'd seen from the hospital window, on and on to a far distant underground station, the end of the line. Its entrance was barricaded, and the whole area fenced off with corrugated iron.

I parked the Lada up a side road, as I'd been instructed, and climbed stiffly out. I was stiff not so much on account of my bruises, but because of the banknotes. I'd secured them in wads round my chest with an elaborate string harness which crossed my chest and shoulders and tied round my waist at the back.

Money in such quantities! My brokers had sent me the cheque, and I'd cashed it at the bank, brazening it out against the studiously blank face of the cashier. There's something suspect about so many bundles of notes. What legal transaction would ever be paid for like that?

The road followed the route of the underground tracks, although a wooden fence topped with barbed wire hid the track from view. I was looking for a gap where the wooden fence changed to heavy wire mesh. The mesh was coming away from the concrete post to which it had been attached, I'd been told. Through this gap I would be able to reach the embankment and climb down to the track.

At this time of evening cars passed frequently along the suburban road, and there were pedestrians too, some returning late from work, some setting out for an evening's enjoyment.

I walked at a purposeful pace, trying not to look suspicious. The wooden fence was ending, and I could see the concrete post.

Only, there was no gap. The wire mesh was now tightly nailed to the post from top to bottom. To climb through was impossible.

For one moment I felt almost relieved. Then came a wave of panic. That meant someone knew, didn't it, knew about the gap, knew that it would be used again, knew that I was coming. I was alone and exposed in an empty street. Someone might be watching and waiting for me now. Police hired houses, didn't they, to keep a watch, behind the blank black windows of one of these suburban semis they might be watching, ready to spring out and –

'Gotcha!'

With a yell, two boys on bikes shot out of an alleyway right beside me and tangled laughing against the lamp post. They didn't even notice me, and I hadn't noticed the alleyway. It seemed designed for flashers and suburban rape, but I was glad of it now. It was some sort of hiding place, and I turned into it without giving myself time to think.

The railway track changed direction at this point, and swerved away rightwards, and the alley, which ran diagonally from the road along which I'd walked, followed the track as the road had previously done. On the left side of the alleyway was a hedge, to the right the back gardens of a row of houses. I walked on firmly, yet unsure of where I was going or what I'd do when I got there.

After I'd been walking for about five minutes, the hedge ended, and I saw allotments on a triangle of land that spread along the top of the embankment. This slice of land was protected simply by a low fence. So far as getting onto the track was concerned, my problems were over.

It would have been easier to turn back. I could not

erase the image of the biker and his blind surge towards me. I knew it couldn't have been Lennox, and yet . . . He frightened me now.

This way down the embankment looked much easier than wriggling through the wire fence, but as soon as I'd got beyond the allotments, I found out I was wrong. Further down it was virtually impassable. I had to take enormous steps to get over giant rhubarb and cow parsley plants, and everywhere brambles dragged and whipped across my path, at times so tangled that I had to turn sideways and find another way forward. I trod down nettles and pushed through elderberry bushes. Whenever I paused in my own crashing through the undergrowth, I heard rustling sounds, and each time I froze with horror, thinking how close my foot might have come to a snake or a rat, but at last I got through the worst of it, although my legs were scratched and stinging, and I wished I'd worn trousers instead of shorts.

I walked back until the station came into view. It was further than I'd thought. I was twenty minutes late. Deep down I half-hoped he wouldn't have waited, wouldn't be there.

The embankment ended at the slope which led up to the platform. The glazed roof had fallen in and broken glass crunched under my feet. At the far end of the platform a stairway must once have led up to the exit.

The moon was coming up full. I stood still. From far away I heard the expressway traffic, washing like waves at the rim of the real world, but the breathless silence that had settled over the ghostly station was only intensified by that background sigh of noise from the world I had left so definitively behind me.

'Lennox!'

The silence sank softly back again. It was quite dark now. The light of the moon turned the scene livid.

'Lennox! Are you there!' I yelled. My voice died in the still air.

I peered up into the cobwebby shadows of the staircase.

A few dead leaves rustled, although there was no wind. I whirled round. Nothing there. The platform stretched back towards the undergrowth I'd left.

I turned and took a few paces. And then my heart hammered in my chest, for a figure stood by the covered stairway leading to the bridge. Slight, wearing dark glasses, in black, a headscarf.

I watched and waited, rooted to the spot. Yet I wasn't exactly frightened now.

'Lennox couldn't come. I came myself.'

I recognised the voice. Drops of icy sweat dripped down my spine. She pulled the chiffon scarf from her hair and removed her dark glasses.

Anna said, 'It's okay, I'm not a ghost.' Her voice and face were expressionless, just tinged with amused contempt. 'You're late,' she said, 'I'd almost given you up.'

'So you're the person Lennox wanted me to meet.'

She stood there.

'At least he said you wanted to see me.'

'We must go back into the Tunnels. Walk along the tunnel.'

'Is that safe?'

'No, not specially. Safer than being out here, that's all.'

'I meant the line, the electricity. Are you sure the current's been switched off?'

'Of course. Why would it be on? Come on.'

'All sorts of rumours were going around today. On the news. They say they're going to raid the Tunnels, close it down.'

'They're always saying that.' She climbed down onto the rails. I followed her reluctantly. However much reason reassured me that she was right, that the current was off, an enormous effort of will was required to place one's feet near the 'live' rail, marked out as it was with round, white ceramic fixtures every yard or so. I thought about the electric chair as I walked gingerly along, and stumbled a little from time to time. Anna paced on ahead, more sure-footed than I.

We made our way back past the jungle of weeds and the allotments up on our right. There was still another stretch of embankment, becoming steeper as we neared the tunnel's gaping mouth. Even in the darkness, it looked black and ready to swallow us up.

Anna walked a few yards into it, stopped and switched on a torch.

'Did you bring a torch?'

'No.'

'Bit stupid of you. I always noticed, though, you never were practical.'

'You hardly saw me – you don't know anything about me.'

'I know a lot about you. I lived with Charles for months, remember. And then you came back for about five minutes and left everything in complete and utter chaos.'

'Look –'

'Oh, let's get on, we've quite a way to go. We'll have plenty of time to argue when we've got where we're going to.'

'Where are we going to?'

'Station One. The one where we met is Station Zero.'

She switched off her torch suddenly. I gasped at the unnatural, total darkness.

'Look back,' she said, 'the last of the upper regions, now we descend into the nether world.' She laughed. Why was she mocking me? Maybe she hated me. I felt uneasy. Perhaps she – what? Had killed my father? Run away? I could refuse to go on. It wasn't too late.

I looked back. I could still just see the entrance to the tunnel, a pale blur.

No. I had to go on – whether for my father, for Lennox, for myself. I had to be brave.

Anna switched on her torch again. We walked further and further into the tunnel, which sloped downwards, gradually but steadily away from the light. Anna's torch cast rearing shadows over the sooty walls.

'Some of the tunnels have fallen in,' she told me, 'parts of the system you can't get to at all any more.'

We walked on, downwards. I wondered how long we would have to go on walking.

I tried to remember how long it was between stations. Two minutes on the train – half a mile – or a mile? That was already half an hour's walk at the pace we could go. And out in the suburbs the distances had always been longer.

At last we came to a station. The beam of the torch revealed a rubble-strewn platform. It was dark and deserted, and had that crypt-like smell of damp. Now I could definitely hear the scrabbling and squeaking of rats.

'Is this it?'

'Of course not. This one's uninhabitable.'

'How much further is it then?'

'Not much further.'

This non-answer annoyed me. 'Well, how long will it take to walk it? Ten minutes, an hour, three hours?'

'About half an hour,' she said.

That didn't sound so terrible, but the tunnel wound on and on. I was sure we'd been going for nearer an hour, and still there seemed no end in sight. My feet and legs hurt more and more as we picked our way forward. It was hot and airless.

'The ventilating system doesn't work properly any more.'

'Isn't that dangerous?' I said.

'I guess so.'

Just as I was beginning to feel that I simply couldn't

go on I became aware of sounds. Music. Anna stopped and switched off the torch again. 'See?' she said.

A faint orange glow showed up ahead. We walked the last part more easily – I did, at least – and as we reached the station, the voice of Tatiana, the Russian star, throbbed huskily from somewhere.

We had reached another station, a shelf suddenly widening out of the tunnel. This was lit, and inhabited, it had been cleared and swept, and rows of possessions – rolled-up sleeping bags, boxes and rucksacks – were placed in a neat line against the curved wall. The music seemed to be coming through one of the entrances from the next platform.

We climbed onto the platform. The light was soft, a smoky, fuzzy glow, and the forgotten yet familiar smell of paraffin told me that it came from oil lamps.

'Surely that's a fire hazard, if the ventilation –'

'Of course,' she said scornfully, 'everyone has to be extremely careful.'

We walked through to the adjacent platform. Some young men and women – I wasn't sure how many, somewhere between six and eight – were seated in a circle, round a paraffin stove. I could hear a sizzling sound, which mingled with their voices.

I was beginning to look around for Lennox. We took the exit stairs up to the landing where tunnels and corridors led off in several directions, and three escalators stretched up into the shadows at the top.

Anna knocked on a door marked 'Private'. When no one answered she tried it. It wasn't locked, so we went in.

It had obviously once been a little rest-room for the underground staff, and there was still a gas ring, a disconnected telephone and a first-aid cupboard. There was also a desk and three chairs. We sat down.

'We all use this room. I expect he'll be back soon. Would you like coffee?'

'I thought Lennox wanted to talk to me. I thought you

wanted to meet me. Isn't that why I'm here? I didn't come for coffee. What's it all about?'

'Okay, but I want some anyway.' She lit a small camping gaz stove, on which a kettle was standing. When it boiled she made instant coffee whitened with milk substitute, and we sat there holding our polystyrene cups.

'I knew there was something wrong,' I said, 'when they said you took drugs. I just knew you weren't into drugs.'

She smiled. 'But how would you have known – really – whether I used drugs or not? You didn't know me at all. You didn't try to get to know me. You showed not the slightest interest in me. I was just a convenience while Charles was alive, a relief there was someone to keep him company, maybe look after him. And after he died I was helpful as a caretaker. You hoped. You never thought what it must have been like for me to come home and find him dead like that.'

I was taken aback. 'That's not fair. What could I . . .'

'It's totally fair. I was terrified. You never thought how horrible it would be to stay there on my own. And also, I was fond of him. It upset me very much that he died.'

'But you said you wanted to stay on. I asked you. You didn't have to stay.'

'What choice did I have? It was rent free, not that you sullied your hands with any of that. You didn't even ask, did you? You just assumed the lawyer would take care of the sordid details.'

'Why did my father let you have it rent free?'

'Why d'you think?'

I stared at her. I was embarrassed, jealous even. Was she suggesting that they'd been lovers? Surely she must be.

'I've no idea,' I said.

'Even now you don't know the connection? You haven't discovered much, have you?'

'I didn't know there was a connection.'

'Well, there was.' She stopped.

I waited for her to continue, and when she didn't, I said, 'It's difficult to talk. You're right, I don't know you, I didn't bother. I'm sorry, it's all my fault. I never thought. I had too much on my mind.'

Still she was silent, but now I thought that she was holding back tears. I'd have put an arm round her, only her stiff way of sitting inhibited me. I was afraid of a rebuff. Eventually I said, 'Please tell me what it's all about.'

'You really don't know!' She laughed. 'Well, where shall I start?' She paused, sipped her coffee.

'My father died when I was little. My memories of him are few, and they're not very happy ones. There was something wrong with him. As a child, I couldn't understand, but – it was there. There was a smell, a smell I didn't like, a smell that wasn't quite like medicine. My mother looked after him. She was much younger – I didn't think of her as young, mind you, but I did think he was really, really old. I think she loved him. She never told me the whole story, but she was in trouble of some kind when they met. He was a journalist, he met her on an assignment, he was doing a story about migrant labour, she came from Turkey, you know, she hadn't got any papers or anything.

'Maybe he married her to give her the right to stay here, but however it was, I'm sure there was love as well. Even at the end, when he got worse and worse, she nursed him, she never gave up. I was the one who was left out. And he was a drunk, yes, but he never hit her or shouted. It was more he was maudlin, pathetic. Disgusting. He disgusted me. Not her, though, I really don't think so. But of course she must have been so depressed by the time he died.

'We lived down the coast. He fell off the cliff. We struggled along, the two of us – she was drinking, too, by then. It was awful. People like you,' said Anna bitterly, 'you don't know you're born. You've lived in privilege all your life, you don't know what it's like to have a horrible childhood, you didn't even appreciate Charles.'

I sat by the table, my head propped up in my hand. I stared at the surface of the table, old, scrubbed wood, and traced a line of the soft graining with my thumbnail.

'You've guessed who he was now, my father?'

'Colin Fox,' I said.

'Right first time – your parents had given up on my father by the time I was born, in fact I should think they'd given up on him years before that.

'Anyway, when I was sixteen my mother took a trip back home. Just left me. I was still at school. I hung around with some kids, quite a nice bunch, they were all doing okay at school, so was I as a matter of fact – well, I went to stay with one of them, her parents took me in, more or less. They were kind – I suppose they didn't know quite what to do – weeks, months went by and my mother didn't come back.

'It was bonfire night. We all went up to see the fire and the fireworks. On the way back I saw a man through the window of his house – oh, I can't explain – it was strange, and wonderful, magical –

'Anyway, I went and lived with him. The people I'd been staying with, my friend's parents, they were worried about me. But what could they do? Then my mother came back. Not for long. Said she was going home to Turkey for good. She seemed to have stopped drinking. I didn't want to go with her. She left me my father's papers. Said they meant a lot to him.

'After she'd gone, I left school and I just lived with Paul. Everything was all right at first. In fact it was wonderful. I suppose it was the sex. Transcendental. We lived in this private universe of intensity. I didn't mind that he'd stopped my education – I couldn't wait to leave school anyway.

'After a while, though, he began to beat me up. It wasn't

so bad at first, I thought of it as, well, he just wasn't himself. A different person. And afterwards he'd be so sweet and so sorry, and he always promised it'd never happen again. But it always did, and gradually things got worse and worse. I began to be frightened of him. Time went on and I grew more and more frightened. It was unbearable.'

She paused, frowned slightly. 'It was as if every little bit of my independence had to be smashed into the ground. I had to be an echo of him. I had to just be his ghost. He made me be – nothing. And then when I was nothing he didn't like it. I agreed with everything he said and he thought I was mocking him. But if I disagreed I was somehow destroying him.

'I was so afraid. For a long time the fear paralysed me. In the end, though, there came a point when I simply couldn't stand it any more. Or – well, I knew that if I didn't leave him, he'd kill me quite soon. And I had just enough life in me to not want that to happen. So I began to make a plan of how I'd get away. I gave him the slip and went back to the people who'd taken me in before.

'They were shocked, they were sorry, but they weren't as helpful as I'd expected them to be. They had troubles of their own by then. The only thing they could do to help was to put me in touch with Charles. They were much younger than him, of course, but I suppose they knew him through politics. Anyway, they knew he had a room to rent. I hadn't any money, so he took me on as a sort of housekeeper. Afterwards he got it to seem like he'd done it through the University, we were afraid that Paul would find out where I was. And then I really did become a student. Charles was terrific. He encouraged me.

'Charles was the only person who ever talked to me about my father – he was the only person who could have, I suppose. He told me a lot of things.' She looked at me, and I looked back at her.

'About my mother?' I said, 'I do know about all that.

But he never talked to me about it, you know.' It hurt, he'd talked to Anna, never to me. 'I suppose that would have been too difficult.'

I could have been Colin Fox's child myself – Anna and I could have been half-sisters. If it wasn't that I looked so like my father . . . But anyway, I'd have been much older.

She smiled, almost for the first time. 'Charles helped me, protected me, supported me. Made me change my name. Musgrove isn't Paul's name, it isn't my married name. Anna's not my name either – at least, well, it *is* my name, now. But it's not my real name, not my original name.

'I think Charles felt guilty about my father. As if it had been somehow partly his fault; as if he could have made him, I don't know, not destroy himself somehow.

'When I first came to live in Charles's house,' continued Anna, 'I was still recovering from Paul – scared I might see him whenever I went out, always afraid he was following me, that somehow he'd tracked me down. He was an obsessive type, you know. His jealousy became a disease. Destroyed everything around him and destroyed him too. I even changed my appearance, wore a wig and all that.'

I ran my fingernail along the wood. 'But you never wore nail varnish, did you.'

She looked at me.

'When I found what I thought was your body – the hand, it – she had varnished nails.'

Anna continued, 'Gradually I began to feel better as I didn't see Paul and it seemed as if I was safe. Safer, anyhow. Charles and I used to have a meal together in the evenings. Those were the times we talked about my father.

'Charles used to say what an adventurer he'd been, a daredevil who couldn't cope with ordinary life. They were in Germany together, and there was some crazy thing he'd done. They somehow met this guy – I can't remember all the details. He was an undercover Communist agent of some kind. Lithuanian. He'd fallen foul of some of his fellow countrymen who hated Stalin and all that. "It was very murky, you know," Charles said to me, "everyone and everything was in turmoil, trying to get out or get in, some fleeing to the West, some in the opposite direction, some hunting down the Nazis, others killing Communists."

'This man they met, he was an ideas man, Party intelligentsia, some kind of writer. But he hadn't any papers, and he was trapped. He told them he wanted to come to England to continue the good work. What an asset to the Party! Then, when things had quietened down, when he'd escaped the Fascists and the nationalists, he'd be able to go back to the Soviet Union and help the British comrades from there. They were so young, they wanted to do something special – so they agreed to help.

'They cooked up this crazy scheme. They were to get him false papers, and pass him off as a member of the British armed forces – or someone attached to the occupying army. They invented him. It wasn't as difficult as you might have expected, Charles said. And they managed it. Charles said it only dawned on him afterwards that my father must have had some pretty shady contacts, it must have been the black market that supplied the passport, the papers. But it worked.

'It didn't end there though. Something happened when they got back home. Charles never really explained. But anyway, the Lithuanian disappeared.

'Charles said my father tracked him down, though. He said he had something over him. He even hinted at blackmail.'

'There was blackmail,' I said. 'I know that.'

'Well, my father wasn't stupid – he hung on to the papers the Lithuanian had given him in the beginning – some pass he had. My father got him the new false papers, but he kept the man's other papers, though, the old ones. Kept them all those years.

'Not long before my father died we were burgled. Everything was turned upside-down – but nothing was stolen at all. Whoever it was didn't find the documents either – if that's what they were after. My dad kept them in the bank. When my mum went back to Turkey, she gave them to me.'

She paused and looked at me. 'It was such bad luck – an irony, if you like. At Charles's I was safe from Paul, but then they were after Charles, and they found out about me.'

'Who did?'

'Gennady said it wasn't safe for me. So I came down here. But I left one thing behind. That time you saw me in the University library –'

'I *did* see you then! I thought I was hallucinating.'

'I kept the papers in a special hiding place in the library. They weren't safe in Charles's house. I didn't even trust the bank. So I had this special place, in amongst some old pamphlets in a box. Old stuff – one in a million if anyone ever even looked at them. I suppose it was a risk, but – anyway, once I got down here it made me anxious. I felt it was safer to have them with me. So I went back up, just the once. And I had the bad luck to see you.'

'It was *good* luck, wasn't it? Better than seeing your husband, anyway. And what could I do to hurt you?'

'I didn't want you talking – I was afraid you'd talk.'

'Anyway, who was this man? The man your father blackmailed?'

Before she had time to answer the door was flung open.

Chapter
Nineteen

'You're here.' Lennox stood by the open door. No one said anything. I had a feeling he was waiting for Anna to leave, but she didn't. So he said, 'I'll – er – show you round.'

I followed him across the landing and along a corridor. Round a corner, steps led down to another set of platforms. 'Over two hundred and fifty people living down here, you know.'

We walked along one of the platforms, and climbed steps up to another landing. Lennox shone his torch up the silent escalators. Our feet sounded loudly on the metal as we trudged upwards.

'Have you got it?' he asked.

'Of course.'

At the top the abandoned ticket hall was strewn with rubble and plaster. The silence and emptiness contrasted sharply with the thronged and convivial platforms. Lennox pushed open a door marked 'Private'. 'This was a surveillance room,' he said. 'None of it works now, of course.'

There were television screens and an intercom mike, and tables fitted to the walls.

'This isn't going to last much longer. Sitting target, they know exactly where you are. I've come to the conclusion it'd be safer just to get lost in the city. I should have seen that from the start. Even travelling in convoys would be better, at least you can move on.'

There was a mattress in one corner, and a rucksack. No chairs, so I sat on the mattress and he perched on the table.

'Why did I have to come down here with the stuff?'

With one long finger he made a pattern in the dust on the table. I gazed at his heavy eyelids, his beautiful mouth, so feminine and languorous.

'Anna wanted to meet you, and she was scared to go up again.'

'But that's different. The money's separate from that.'

Silence.

'Well, why?' Having all that money tied round my body gave me a feeling of power. Yet that sense of power was laced with irony, for now of course he couldn't offer, and I couldn't ask for what I wanted so much, because it would be too crudely and obviously payment for services rendered. Paradoxically this freed me, I no longer felt tense and jittery, I was simply going to drown him in a torrent of banknotes as a selfless finale to unrequited love.

'What are you laughing about?' he said.

'I don't know. It's so ridiculous. I could have handed it over anywhere, at Myra's, at my father's house. I could have handed you a large brown envelope in the Café even.'

'No, you couldn't have done that,' he said.

'Maybe not.'

There was another awkward little silence. Then, 'before I forget,' he said, 'I want you to go and see Urban Foster.'

'Urban Foster?'

'He might be able to help – with your dad.'

'Urban? I don't think so. I asked him – so why do you say that?'

'Just go, that's all.'

There was a further silence. He seemed uneasy, even hostile, dying to get his hands on the cash, but not wanting to ask outright – too many scruples for a revolutionary.

'It's weird down here,' he said at length, 'not very *political*. Disappointing. The real tubies are okay, but there are so many crooks hiding out down here. You can buy anything. Absolutely anything. You'd be amazed. Semtex, heroin, diamonds – the biggest black market since . . .'

'You'll be able to go on a spending spree, then.' I undid the loose shirt I'd worn to cover it up. 'I tied the money round my body, I thought it was safer that way.'

He laughed. 'Incredible. You're covered in money.'

I stood with my back to him. 'You'll have to untie the knot.'

I could feel him picking at it. 'It's very tight.' He laughed, then as it still wouldn't give, gave a half-smothered exclamation of exasperation. 'Shit, I'll have to . . .' He pushed the string off my shoulders, his hands sliding over my skin. 'Can you . . .'

And then his voice changed. 'If you can just turn round a minute . . .' But his hands tightened on my shoulders – and I knew then – and he kissed the back of my neck.

I turned round.

'I've never made love to anyone dressed in money before.'

'It's a well-known aphrodisiac.'

But he wasn't smiling now. He took a knife from his pocket, opened it, and carefully cut the string at my waist, and as he took hold of me the banknotes started to slide and shift and he stumbled against the edge of the mattress and we lurched towards the floor in a snowstorm of printed paper, and as I unbuckled his belt and rubbed my face against his unshaven cheek I was conscious of absolute triumph and absolute terror.

It was a long time since I'd been with a man, and if he'd ever slept with a woman I didn't know it, but so strong was my need and so unlooked-for his capitulation that I forgot my fear as his half-smiling mask of detachment was displaced by a martyr's frown of pleasure, and as he held my head back by the hair to kiss me I imagined that all I wanted was for him to annihilate me, to kiss me till my mouth bled and fuck me till it burned. Only then it became more than that, and it was I who wanted to overwhelm him, to be for him whatever impossible thing it was he craved; and I became the willing creature of whether my fantasy or his I no longer knew; and as I unbuttoned his flies and felt his hard, smooth skin, it wasn't just that his had become the only body in the world, his prick the only prick in the world, it was that this was all there was in the world, and I wanted nothing more ever than that moment when I experienced the vulnerability of the invulnerable in his surrender.

Someone was shouting for Lennox. They were banging on the door. I didn't know where I was. Yes I did. I looked at my watch. We'd been here for hours. Lennox rolled over and opened his eyes. He stared at me blankly. He sprang to his feet.

'Oh Christ! What's the time?'

He was throwing on his clothes, the white T-shirt that had smelled of clean laundry. He bent, scrabbling for the notes, and stuffed them into a plastic bag. 'I was meant to meet Joe hours ago. Oh God, I'm sorry . . .'

I was still getting dressed when he flung open the door. Two young men stood there.

'Something's happened – crowds of people coming down the tunnel from Station Three. Rumours going around like wildfire – the live rail's going to be turned on; we'll all be trapped; they're sending the Specials down.'

'Have you seen Joe? I have to see him.' He rushed away, followed by the others.

I ran down the escalator in their wake, but by the time I reached the bottom he'd disappeared. I found my way back to the rest-room. Anna was still there.

'They've told you?' She looked at me. 'The platforms downstairs are jammed – someone's going to get crushed quite soon, it's getting out of hand. What happened to Lennox?'

'He had to see someone,' I said.

'If only we could get out up here. We'll have to try and make our way out by the tunnel before the stampede begins.'

'But the live rail –' I said.

'I expect that's just a rumour,' said Anna. 'They don't want a massacre, do they, the government I mean. Wouldn't look good. Mess up Kingdom's chances of getting the leadership. They want to scare everyone out and make arrests. We'll be all right so long as no one panics, that's the real danger – so we have to get down there quickly.'

We went out on to the landing, and started to push our way down the stairs, now thronged with agitated men and women, crushing against us, just like an old-time rush hour, except that everyone was so young. The closer we got to the platforms the harder it was to push through the jammed-up bodies. All the new arrivals were coming from the end opposite from the way we'd come in, so at least we were moving with rather than against the crowd, propelled along by the push push of those moving in from the tunnel, but we were trying to move faster than the rest, and they cursed and pushed and jabbed us with their elbows as we squeezed our way through.

We finally made it to the end of the platform, by the opening of the tunnel. Someone was shouting orders from the far end of the platform. The crowds only became more agitated.

We slipped down on to the track as unobtrusively as possible. We thought no one had noticed us, but a woman nearby cried, 'Be careful! Be careful! Don't go down – don't touch the live rail!'

We eased into the darkness. Anna's torch lit the way

ahead. The voices of the crowd we'd left behind us hummed like a swarm of bees. We scrambled away along the tunnel, scrabbling like rats, but we hadn't got far before the sound, instead of dying away, rose to a roar. Then there were screams of what sounded like 'Fire!'

We stopped and looked back. The tunnel opening seemed foggy. The light had increased. The noise wound up to a higher pitch. There was an acrid smell. My eyes began to water.

'Come *on*, it looks like smoke. We must be quick, they'll catch up with us.'

I started back, stumbling as I tried to run.

Anna caught hold of my arm. 'What are you doing? Are you crazy – they'll soon forget about the live rail, they'll come after us and crush us in here – or else we go back and get suffocated.'

'I must – what about Lennox? We can't leave him.'

'He can look after himself. We can't go back. We *can't*, Justine.'

She pulled me violently, wouldn't let go, and in the end I followed her. No one climbed down after us on to the track. We went forward again. We picked our way along with even greater difficulty than during the inward journey, because now we both kept well clear of the electric rail, just in case. We stumbled and hurried, and after a time we left the sounds of confusion and panic behind, and moved doggedly forward in silence, following the wavering light of Anna's torch.

At least we were on the way out, eventually we'd breathe fresh air again. We began to be walking notice-ably uphill. We forced ourselves on. I had a stitch, my legs and back ached worse than ever and I'd turned my ankle, but there was no hostility between us any more. We were in this together. Every so often, without speaking, we stopped by mutual agreement, for a short rest, then trudged on again.

At last we saw a gleam of light ahead. We staggered

onwards. It was still so far ahead, it tantalised and beckoned, but I felt we'd never get there. Until at last we did. We reached the end of the tunnel.

Day was breaking. The sky was turning radiant as the sun dissolved the cobwebby first light.

We stopped at the mouth of the tunnel and looked out over the rails, which curved round out of sight in the direction of the station. A yellow crane towered over them like some sort of horror movie monster.

Only it wasn't a crane. It was a police floodlight. 'It's a trap,' I muttered, 'get back out of sight.'

The tracks seemed deserted and empty. But I felt as if binoculars were trained on us from every direction.

'We have to go on – we can't stay here. I've got Colin's papers – they have to be safe.' Anna spoke quietly, but her voice echoed alarmingly. 'We have to try to get away. They'll be coming along behind us – we haven't any choice. We can't go back in.'

But perhaps there weren't any others. The fire might be a holocaust by now.

Bushes were growing at the entrance to the tunnel, and these gave us some cover. We eased round them. I scraped myself against the wall of the entrance. We crouched at the bottom of the embankment, still partly shielded by the shrubs. Nothing stirred. We started to crawl up the slope and along the top until we came to the allotments.

We heard voices and noises from below. Looking down we saw a column of police in riot gear assembling, trickling along the line from the direction of the station. I knew for certain then that of course there'd never been any intention to switch on the current – Kingdom wasn't about to electrocute the cream of his Special Squad.

We crouched still lower and watched. They were

taking up positions near the tunnel mouth – not going in.

I looked all round. If we wriggled a little further along we could roll under the wire and then we'd be in the alleyway, soon safely out of sight behind the hedge. But what if the streets were crawling with police? I moved forward and eventually reached a point from which I could peer into the alleyway: deserted. A wooden fence ran along the other side of the alley, and doors led to the gardens behind.

'Let's hide in someone's garden,' I whispered, 'until it's a reasonable time to be on the streets.'

'I'm desperate to pee.'

'Once we're in the alleyway, they can't see us from down there.'

'Okay. Now!'

We made it and stood up behind the hedge. We walked along and tried the first gate. It was locked. A dog started to bark furiously and we could hear it pounding and scraping its claws against the fence.

'Oh, Christ.'

'Don't panic.'

We avoided the next gate – still too close to the dog, but the third opened silently, and we slipped inside. We crouched down out of sight in the shelter of a shed and a big umbrella pine.

'Now I'm going to pee.'

We both did. Then we sat down with our backs against the shed.

'How long need we stay here?' I asked.

'For a while.'

There were steps along the alleyway and a man shouted, 'Come on – this way.' More steps. They died away. It grew quiet again. Very quiet. Time passed slowly, if at all. We seemed to be suspended in some nightmarish space, crouching among the snails and withered leaves.

'Lennox – I hope he's okay.' But I had no feeling about it now. I simply felt as if someone had peeled away a layer of skin and left me, exposed and shell-less; or as if someone had slit me open and gouged out my entrails, leaving just an empty husk. In another life he'd kissed me, but that didn't matter now.

'You never finished the story,' I said.

'Story! That's a funny way of putting it.'

'You know what I mean.'

'To you it's all just a story, isn't it?'

I thought about it. 'No,' I said, 'but ever since I got back things have just seemed . . . so like a dream.'

She sniffed and rubbed her nose. She was hostile again.

'Don't be angry,' I said. 'Story was a stupid word, but it's all so strange and there's so much I don't understand.' I hesitated. 'It's funny to think, isn't it, that my mother and your father had an affair.'

She looked at me. 'What are you talking about? Who said anything about affairs?'

Steps thudded past in the alleyway and we heard shouting and then the sound of horses' hooves drumming along the alleyway two feet from where we were sitting.

They must have started to pour out of the tunnel, the tubies, that is. I imagined it all too easily: those at the front walking out to find the cops waiting. A few just behind them could have scattered up the embankment, tried to make a run for it, others would try to push back into the tunnel, there'd be a panic, people would stumble and fall, they'd be crushed as others came on out into the arms of the Specials.

We crouched behind the shed. It had gone very quiet in the alleyway again, but now we began to hear yells and screams from the direction of the embankment. It sounded like a pitched battle was being fought down there.

So she told me the rest of her story. We talked and talked about it, and I forgot about Lennox for a while. When next I looked at my watch it was nine o'clock. We'd been there four hours. I was stiff and cold in the shadows.

Chapter
Twenty

'But how did Anna come back from the dead?' said Myra. 'You haven't explained that at all.'

'As soon as the cops said she was a junkie, I knew it couldn't be her.'

It had taken hours to drive back into the city: police and road blocks everywhere. When we finally got to Myra's Anna had gone to bed. Myra and I talked all day, listened to the radio, and drank coffee and herbal tea.

The early bulletins reported bombs. Later the newscaster mentioned a fire, only a small one, nothing to worry about. For sure they didn't want any listeners to think what the implications of a really big fire might be – the whole foundations of the city devoured by fire from beneath; but even as we listened, we could hear fire engines screaming past in the distance, and we thought of the flames reaching up through the pavements, belching from stations, leaping up air vents.

'The lines never reached out here,' said Myra uneasily. 'They were going to build one, but it never happened.' Later still they admitted there'd been casualties. Alex Kingdom came on the air. His grave, measured tones conveyed both his sorrow at the deaths and how necessary they'd been. He'd had to take a stand. The country would be safer from now on. The terrorists were under control at last.

'But I don't think they were terrorists down there.' I said wearily. 'They were just kids, hippies.' Then I remembered what Lennox had said. 'Most of them, anyway.'

'Marvellous publicity for him, though,' said Myra. 'A full-scale urban riot with himself as saviour of the city. He can even make out they started the fire deliberately. Of course he won't get any bombers, but it makes him look busy. Makes him look *brilliant*.'

'Is this all really just so he can be prime minister?'

It certainly looked like it. He was the man of the hour.

I hadn't slept, or only for half an hour or so, and I hadn't eaten either; the coffee was zizzing through my veins, and Lennox might be dead or arrested for all I knew, yet his body was still all over me, I could smell it on my hands, my lips felt raw, my jaw was stiff, my cunt hurt, there was a bruise on my thigh.

But life must go on, or so they say, and I was telling Myra what Anna had told me. I retold the story of her husband, of the parents of her school friend, and of how my father took her in.

'So Anna was living in my father's house. And then one day Gennady turns up. Anna said my father *loved* Gennady. He made him laugh, he talked to him about socialism, about the Soviet Union, it was wonderful. They got on like a house on fire. Of course, they often didn't agree, but Anna said it was so great the way Gennady cheered him up. Anna said Gennady made him feel the struggle wasn't over, that they'd only lost a battle, not the war.

'My father must have told Gennady something about Anna, told him who her father was, because Gennady starts to chat her up. I don't mean sex. One day she told him all about Colin, about the burglary, the documents, how he fell off the cliff. Possibly Gennady already knew another bit of the story – perhaps my father told him about their adventures in Germany, after the war. Anyway, I don't know how, but Gennady seems to have worked out who it was Colin had blackmailed. And he decided he'll do the same.

'Only this time, of course, it was for a different reason. Not just money – though that was part of it; mainly it was political. Some kind of support for Gennady's oppositional movement back in Russia. You see, the man's in the big time, he's become a politician.'

Myra frowned. 'But surely your father must have known this.'

'Apparently not. I know it seems odd, but he'd changed his appearance to some extent. And anyway, you know how it is, you see someone who reminds you of someone else. You think, oh, he's just like so-and-so who I knew years ago. You don't think, oh my god, he *is* so-and-so. Not necessarily. Not if you knew that person in a completely different context.

'Anyway, when Gennady told my father this, he was terribly angry. Anna said she was worried. She nearly telephoned me in the States. I wish she had . . .'

'Go on.'

'What happened was, my father offered to act as go-between. Insisted, in fact. Gennady didn't want him to at first. Only then I suppose it seemed like a good idea – from Gennady's point of view. How else would he get to the guy? But if my father appeared – as the spectre of blackmail, Colin's ghost, so to speak – then at least he'd get a hearing. That must have been what my father was talking about, when he went to see Jack Morris and Violet Frankenberg. At last he could do something, if not in this country at least for socialism in Russia. So he went to see him – he managed to get an interview. But that made him dangerous. He was the link with the past after all. So they got to him.'

'But why was he suddenly so dangerous?' objected Myra. 'If he was dangerous now, he was dangerous all those years. Why wasn't he murdered years ago, like Colin Fox?'

'Christ knows. I have no idea. A case of let sleeping dogs lie, I suppose. Or, well, he didn't know the secret, not the whole of it, anyway.

'After his death Anna was terrified; certain they must know who she was as well. She got hold of Gennady – he was in a state, too, as you can imagine, my father dying like that really rattled him. Added to which he felt guilty – hadn't he dropped the old man in the shit?

'Gennady agreed she wasn't safe – not in that house, on her own. Star told me that some fellow students saw her with a man in town somewhere. It must have been Gennady, I think. Anyway, he persuaded her to go down the Tunnels.'

'So what about the body? It wasn't hers? Was there a body?'

'That's the nasty part. It was Gennady's idea. He found some junkie, homeless, living on the streets, and he paid her to go and live there. Didn't have to pay her much, she was only too pleased. Anna said it bothered her, it seemed wrong to let her run the risk. And Anna was also worried she might let other street people in, break the place up. But she was very quiet, very passive.'

Myra objected again. 'She couldn't have impersonated Anna at College, though – oh, but it was the vacation, I suppose.'

'Yes – it couldn't have gone on indefinitely. It was just that Gennady thought that if the house was being watched or – anything like that – that Anna should *seem* to be there, to give Anna time to decide what to do. Anna said it was a piece of luck, the woman really looked quite like her. Except for her hair. Hence the wig. She had to persuade her to wear a wig. Her wig. The one she'd been wearing.'

Myra looked sceptical. 'How very convenient. So whoever it was Colin Fox had originally blackmailed got rid of your dad, and then killed the wrong woman. But why did he wait all those years?'

We decided the sleeping dogs theory must be the correct one. It was only when Gennady opened the whole thing up again and the man who'd been blackmailed – that shadowy figure – felt endangered once more, that he had to get rid of everyone who knew anything about his past. The stakes were higher than they'd ever been – and along came Gennady and threatened to let the genie out of the bottle.

It still didn't really add up.

'Why not do Gennady in?' said Myra, 'wouldn't that have been simpler? Why your father?'

'My father acted as go-between for that very reason.' I explained, 'so Gennady needn't blow his cover. He – whoever he is – the man who was blackmailed – knew that there was a Gennady, so to speak, but he didn't know it was actually Gennady. D'you see? He knew my father was acting for the Russian Opposition, but didn't know which particular Russian or Russians were involved.'

In one way it did add up. 'I knew there was something wrong with the house,' I said. 'Something different. Anna always looked after it. Then, when I came home the second time it was all so dusty and neglected . . .'

'So who's the mystery man?' Myra stared at me, squinting with curiosity. 'Justine – I believe you know. Go on, tell me. Who is it? You're holding something back. You are! You're hiding something from me.'

'I'm not sure – it's just an idea – and it doesn't really seem possible. Oh God. I'm *exhausted*.' I lay back in the cushions.

Myra sipped her tisane. 'You're frightened for Lennox, aren't you?'

'Of course.'

'Want to talk about it?'

'No.'

I hadn't time, even had I wanted to. 'There are things I have to do,' I said. 'Lennox asked me to see someone.

And then there's the locker key, I've remembered what it belongs to now.'

Then I remembered another thing. It came back to me unbidden, from the confusion of last night, something he'd said, at some point.

'Lennox said he'd come here later. Be sure you wait for him, Myra.'

The only thing was, would he be able to come? Or – But I didn't want to think of the alternatives.

The key with its red plastic disc was warm in my pocket as I drove to the centre of the city. The traffic was so awful that I left the Lada in an underground car park which cost an écu a second, and continued on foot. It had turned sultry. The air was still, the sky a whitish glare.

I'd phoned Urban Foster from the car park. This time he was only too anxious to meet me. He was fidgeting at the top of the steps that led up to the entrance of his black-glass office, and when he saw me he skipped down the steps, seized my arm and led me away from it at double quick time.

'What did that *bitch* tell you?'

'Bitch! Oh dear, what nasty language. Are you referring to Lennox, by any chance?'

'Lennox! Of course I'm referring to Lennox!'

'To think you fucked men all this time. And you with three children. That was a well-kept secret, wasn't it? Is your wife in the know? Poor Celia. I always liked her. Worth ten of you I always thought.'

He steered me into a dark little side alley. This was a far cry from the glamorous goldfish bowl of our previous rendezvous. 'No-one from the paper comes in here.'

It was a dismal little tapas bar, and most of the tables were empty. He ordered mineral water without consulting me, but I didn't care what we drank.

'How on earth did you meet Lennox?'

'I met him down on the beach –'

'Oh, so you go down to the beach for sex. You better be careful – you want to be an MP, don't you? They're going to love that when you go for selection.'

'Don't try to threaten me, Justine. I have some powerful friends.'

'I bet you have. And that's just what I wanted to talk about. Your powerful friends. Well, friend, actually. You wrote a biography of Alex Kingdom. You're a good journalist. You must have found out quite a lot about him. And yet your book is very very bland. And it leaves out so many things – and there are lies, that sentimental crap about his childhood, to begin with. Talk to me about Alex Kingdom – and what he did to persuade you.'

Urban's chubby face was sagging. 'What did Lennox tell you?'

'Lennox has a lot of stuff on Kingdom. So does –' but I stopped myself in time – much better not to mention Jack Morris and the Port campaign.

'Alex is clever at nosing out one's little weaknesses, one's – he intuitively knows what people really want. He knew I wanted to get into politics –'

'On his side? Oh, Urban, what would your parents have said?' I laughed, but I felt angry. 'You really mean you'd join the Coalition, just to get a little whiff of power.'

He fidgeted around in his seat. 'Well there isn't an opposition any more,' he muttered.

'Never mind about that. Your creepy little life plan is your business. I just want to know what you didn't put into the book. What else you knew.'

'Not a lot.' He was looking a bit pale now. 'Nothing really. It was just the terms on which he agreed to do it. Nothing controversial, no independent research, just what he told me, nothing else. And – well, everyone knows that some of his deals won't really stand up to close scrutiny, and there've been dodgy rumours from time to time, but –'

'But what?'

Urban bit his silicone implant lip. 'Well, he owns whole chunks of the media, doesn't he, along with everything else. Or did. He had to sell a lot, when he started to go places in politics. There could have been conflicts of interest. But the people he sold to – half of them are in his pocket. He's a big fish in a big pond, Justine. A *huge* fish. You don't want to be on the wrong side of him. I mean, getting to do his biography, that was a really big deal, you know. Lots of competition.'

'Well, congratulations, Urban. I'm so happy – for you.'

'Why don't you ask Lennox? Lennox knows too much for his own good. He recognised me, you know. He knew who I was, on the beach. That's the only reason he went with me, the little tart. To pick my brains.

'He knew more than I did. I was bloody glad I hadn't met him before I did the book. Might have thought twice about it.'

'You ought to have talked to my father. He knew all about Kingdom. In the end he knew,' I said.

It was a long walk to the National Library. My silk shirt was the best thing to have worn, but still it was too hot – it clung damply. The weather was what in Albion is called 'close'. A good word – the air was thick and heavy as claustrophobia. Yellow clouds hung over the city. It was like being indoors. The airless heat closed in.

I explained what I wanted to the librarian at the enquiries desk, and he directed me to the side room that housed the readers' individual lockers – a relatively new service for regular users, introduced not long before I went away.

The state I was in, I was more or less on automatic pilot, meant I was past feeling anything as I opened the locker door, but it was still with a sense of let-down that I saw there was nothing there except a few bits of paper. They were just a few old notes. I was about to shut it again, but thought I'd better make quite sure, so I felt around, and at the very back my fingers touched a little plastic box. I drew it out. It was a miniature dictaphone tape.

A tape. So then I had to buy one of those miniature machines to play it on.

By the time I got back to Myra's, a wind was starting to blow along the grassy wasteland between the houses, and moan between the towers and whip through the plaza. The yellow clouds were turning bruised and dark by the time Lennox came.

He looked taut and pale. His hair was still pulled tightly back, but his T-shirt was smudged and dirtied.

He washed, and Myra got him something to eat. 'Oh curry – thanks, Myra. You're brilliant.'

'It was touch and go,' he said. 'We had to find another way out. The fire itself wasn't so terrible, if everyone hadn't panicked, but of course they did. Me too. We were upstairs, but the smoke was coming up and the smell – there wasn't much for it to take hold of on the stairs, but you felt you were going to choke, the acrid taste, it burnt your throat – I was fucking terrified. Downstairs people were getting trampled on, crushing one another in the mêlée, after a while there was fighting. Some were in the tunnel – they could walk on, but others were coming in from behind, those on the platform tried to push them back or go back themselves. I'm not sure, I wasn't there, but some of them who managed to get up the stairs said those on the platforms *behind* the fire couldn't go either way, they were trapped. That was probably the safest thing to do, come up on to the landing. We thought there was no way out, but we went through a door which led to another passage and then we found an air shaft, just a few of us, and we managed to climb out. It didn't exactly have stairs, but it had these little iron footholds in the wall. We came up further along the line. Then we had to hide for hours till it was safe. After that, I found a bicycle in someone's garden, and rode around through the side streets back into the city. It felt horrible, leaving the rest of them. But what else could I do?'

All the time he talked, he was behaving like I didn't exist. I had the feeling something awful had happened, but when he'd finished eating, he finally looked at me, and said:

'Can you drive me somewhere? I have to go somewhere with a friend.'

'Of course,' I said very quietly. 'Yeah, I'll drive you. Wherever you want to go.'

Chapter
Twenty-One

A young man was leaning against the Lada. When he saw us he grinned.

'I've been waiting hours, Len. Thought you'd chickened out.'

Lennox frowned. 'This is Joe.'

Lennox and I had walked across the plaza in stony silence. Once, I'd just touched his arm, and he'd flinched, frozen.

'Drive west,' said Lennox.

The young man, who was carrying a canvas plumber's bag, got in the back. Lennox sat beside me, but he twisted round and talked exclusively to his companion.

If I looked sideways I could see the bruise on Lennox's neck where I'd bitten him. It was like that had never been. Wiped out of history.

To begin with I felt as if my insides were draining away and taking me down the plughole with them. Then I decided the only thing to do was be angry. So I started to hate him, and that felt a lot better.

'I like the way you drive, Jenny,' said Joe, leaning forward, 'boy that's driving, no messing, you're giving them hell. That's driving with *attitude*.'

Christ, who was this nerd? 'The name's Justine.'

'Uh-uh. Justine. Funny name. Haven't heard that name before.'

'The original Justine was the masochistic heroine of a pornographic novel.'

'Oh wow, really, is that so?'

'This is it.'

It was the building shaped like a flying saucer that I'd seen from my hospital room, and then passed – when was it, yesterday evening? It seemed like centuries ago. Close to, its dome was huge, and the rim hung out over the angled steel struts that held it up from the ground. These enclosed the core of the building. The lobby was brightly lit, but the place appeared to be deserted.

A sliproad had been constructed especially to get to it. I turned off. The expressway reared above us, as the approach road took us to an iron gateway, or grille.

Lennox got out. He seemed to be punching in the code on a security lock. The grille slid sideways. He returned to us waiting.

'Stay here in the car,' he said to me. 'We won't be long.'

'I think I'll come with you,' I said.

'You can't do that.'

'I don't see why not. I don't fancy waiting in this gruesome sliproad on my own.'

'Justine!'

'I'm coming.'

The two men exchanged looks. Then Lennox shrugged very very faintly. 'Okay.'

The main doors, made of steel, opened with a card that Lennox produced. He also spoke into an automatic intercom.

'Good job it's not one of those that recognises voices,' he muttered.

'How did you get hold of the card?' I said.

'How d'you think? My journalist friend.'

The entrance hall stretched upwards to a skylight far, far above. Joe the nerd was looking round in a somewhat awestruck way, but Lennox made straight for the lift. The lift was the size of a room, and furnished like one as well – carpet, mirrors, vases of flowers, two little gilt chairs, etcetera – and lifted us soundlessly. We hovered to a halt, the doors opened, and we stepped out into a vast circular space with windows all around stretching almost from floor to ceiling. The lift formed part of a core at the centre. Directly in front of us a kind of furnished oasis swam in the emptiness: two fat satin sofas, one emerald, one fuchsia, and some squiggly iron chairs, like the ones in the Café, were arranged around a low table, and behind the sofas stood glass cabinets displaying small pots and ornaments.

We walked forward. Dusk had turned the air beyond the windows indigo and in the room there were pools of shadow between the spotlights. The space gaped with silence, empty.

'Well . . . er – I'll – have a look around, shall I?' Joe said. And winked.

Lennox looked at him. 'Yes. Do that. Don't be long. I want to get out of here.'

Joe clattered down a spiral metal staircase to the floor below.

Lennox leant against a thick white column. His expression was one I'd seen before; the mask of almost stoical detachment he'd worn that first night in the Café. Now I knew him better, I knew that – tonight at least – he was not detached, but tense.

The silence seemed to expand and to suck us into its vacuum. We waited. I walked over to the window. He was over to my left. As the silence lengthened, the space between us seemed to grow as well.

I turned towards him. My anger dissolved. I felt sorry for him. But as I stepped forward to make an effort with him, a door I hadn't noticed – it was almost concealed in the wall beside the lift – opened. A man came through it.

The look on Adam's face as he took in who we were reminded me, as had Lennox's, of that first evening at the

Café. It was more than surprise, it was a look of horror, of panic – and yet cunning as well.

'What in – Jesus!' He put his hand to his forehead. 'Justine! What are you *doing* here? How did you . . .'

'What are *you* doing here?' I hated him for being there, a rage of loathing was welling up in me. I felt as if he'd come between Lennox and me, when only moments ago I'd been hating Lennox for his killing silence. Now it seemed like a kind of intimacy into which Adam had grossly intruded.

Lennox said, 'I've got some information for Mr Kingdom.'

'He's not here,' said Adam stupidly.

'But you are. So you must be one of his henchmen, one of his fixers. That must be where you get all your work permits and your import concessions and your prime site deals.'

'Prime site deals – you're joking!'

'I know why I'm here,' said Lennox. 'A friend of mine gave me an entry card. But who gave you an entry card if not Kingdom himself?'

'Let's talk this over.'

Lennox wandered round the sofa, and looked at the ornaments in one of the glass cabinets. 'It's a pity you turned up this evening, because we can't stay long and I'd like to talk to you.'

'Lennox, for fuck's sake – I don't know what you're talking about, I don't know what you're doing here. And Justine, Justine, I told you –'

'I want to know why *you're* here,' said Lennox. 'What's your connection with Kingdom? There must be one or you couldn't have got in here.'

'The same hardly applies to you.'

Joe could be heard calling Lennox's name.

'I'm leaving now anyway,' said Lennox.

'You can't just leave.'

'Stop me.'

'I will.'

He made for the door from which he'd come, but I grabbed him. 'You have to explain. We have to talk.'

'Not now,' said Lennox.

'You have to tell me, Adam.'

He looked at me. 'There's a lot of stuff on Alex floating around, it was all getting out of control –' he muttered. 'But please, *please* stay out of this, love. You don't understand.'

'We need to leave,' said Lennox.

'Please believe me, Justine, I was worried for you. The whole thing about Charles, it was just an accident, it really was –'

'Charles?' Lennox looked puzzled.

'My father? Adam!'

Adam stared at me, earnest, sincere, but his hands were locked together, the knuckles showing white. 'I just wanted to expand the business. I was into raising a big loan. One of Kingdom's outfits was going to finance it. I suppose he looked into my credentials, found out I knew you, had a link to your father, could plausibly get in touch with him. That was a while back. I don't think Kingdom was that worried, it was just a loose end he wanted covered. Maybe the idea was even to do a deal. He thought I'd make a good go-between, friend of Charles's daughter – I rang your father, went round – but it didn't work out like I'd expected. He wasn't friendly, told me to mind my own business. Got quite aggressive. I thought he was paranoid, to tell you the truth. Yes, he was a sick man, your father – he told me to get out. Shouted at me. We were in the hall. Then he went upstairs – I don't know why, he was shouting at me to go. But I followed him. That was when it all got out of hand. He took a swipe at me – stumbled, tripped – I dodged aside, he fell down the stairs . . .'

Adam's voice dribbled away.

'That's how it happened?'

'Yes, *Yes*. You don't believe me, do you? But it's true. *Please*, Justine, you must believe me.'

'How could you have come back to the house with me? That evening – when I came back.'

'I was so pleased to see you.'

'You weren't, you were shitting yourself. And yet you came . . . I suppose you had to.'

'It wasn't easy. Anyway, it was months later.'

'Months later! So by that time it didn't matter, you'd forgotten.'

'No. No. You *must* believe me.'

'Believe you! You'd have called an ambulance, the police, even. If it had really been an accident.'

Lennox was standing very still now, as though he were listening to some noise far away, but his foot was tapping an agitated beat on the floor. I heard Joe's footsteps on the stairs.

'All that to get some finance for the Café. I suppose that's why you're smarming round the Port campaign, too.'

'It was a mistake to oppose the Development. It'll be for the best in the end. Generate employment, wealth creation.'

'And what's the pay-off?'

It surprised me how little emotion he showed. His slack face looked congested, red, and when he raised his hand to push his hair off his face, I could see a circle of sweat under the arm of his silk shirt, but he just said dully, 'I'm to get prime site premises further along the Waterfront, a much better position. And another one in the city centre. It'll be wonderful, you'll see.'

'Oh, come *on*!' I said, 'pretending to be on Jack's side, creeping around, double crossing – you don't deserve the Café. You were always riding on the back of poor Khan. It's a mystery how you ever managed to carry on without him. Anyway, the Café's only the Café where it is now. You could never recreate it somewhere else.'

Lennox had been watching us. Now Joe was standing at the top of the stairs, but Lennox stayed him with a movement of his hand. He came and stood close to Adam.

'I always hated the way you treated Khan. She's right. It was his idea and you cleaned up.'

Adam looked sulky, but then he smiled and looked even more unpleasant. 'He *died*, Lennox. Remember? What was I supposed to do?'

Joe said, 'Come on, fellas, we need to get out of here.'

'Just because Khan was your first lover.' Now Adam was taunting Lennox. 'You got this big chip on your shoulder about me. My God, he really liked them young, didn't he? How old were you, fifteen?'

'We're going now. Okay?'

'We'll use the fire escape,' said Joe. 'That'll be safer. It's over here.' He looked hard at Adam. Then he said to Lennox, 'You go first, with the girl. I'll follow – just thought of one last thing I gotta do.'

Adam just stood there. It was beginning to dawn on him that something was up.

I was too angry to be frightened. Instead I thought of Adam in the Café. Adam concerned, Adam protective, Adam wanting to know what I was doing, Adam wanting to come with me, Adam in the next room, while I lay unsuspecting on his narrow bed. False from start to finish. I was so conceited, I thought he really cared for me. But he'd been working for Kingdom all along, he'd been minding me for the Boss.

'And what about Violet Frankenberg, Adam?'

'That wasn't me. I swear I never hurt anyone. Never –'

'But she phoned me at the Café. I'd given her the number. You took the call – you could have listened in. So you knew she had some information, the information you didn't find up at the house. You could have passed that on, and then someone else could have gone round and done the dirty work.'

Adam didn't say anything, he didn't even try to deny it.

'And then you – was it you rang me when I was with Star? I bet it was you. But how did you know I was there?'

'It was only a joke. It was only a joke, I tell you. Jade came back to the bar, she was jealous you'd gone off with Star. I suppose I was jealous too. So I got her to do it, that's all it was, it was a practical joke.'

'It wasn't a joke, Adam, because it was telling me something had happened to Violet. You knew something had happened to her.'

'I – I just wanted you to be careful. I hoped it'd put you off going over to her flat. I was frightened of what Kingdom might do if you got involved. I just wanted you to stay away from it all.'

'Open this fucking window, Lennox. Get out of here, I said,' shouted Joe.

Lennox pushed. The window was stuck, but he finally got the window to slide back. I could feel the waft of warm air as it met the air-conditioned chill.

Joe said, 'I think you better –'

'Where's your bag, Joe?'

'Shut up and get going.' He was hustling me towards the window now, but I pulled back.

'There's just one more thing.'

'Never mind that now,' said Lennox, 'let's just go.'

'But I do mind. I need to know. That message you said was from Lennox. That I was to go to Angel Point. The night I nearly got killed.'

'I never left a message,' said Lennox, listening in spite of his haste.

'He said you did.'

'I sure as hell never sent a message through Adam.'

Adam said nothing. He just stared at me slackly.

'Come on,' said Lennox, through gritted teeth. His voice was quieter than ever.

'You won't get far. I'll call the police.'

Joe laughed and shook his head. 'I don't think so, sport. Come on. Let's go down.'

'Adam,' I said, 'you have to come with us – don't you realise what this is all about?'

And I followed Lennox on to the metal stairway. I looked out at the spangled night city floating below us; it stretched far away, as insubstantial as a sequinned chiffon scarf. It made me giddy, and I had to concentrate so hard on getting down the thing alive I had no time to worry about Adam getting blown up. And anyway, I thought I heard their steps above. They were surely following us down.

The fire escape wound round the building. Down, down we went, nearer and nearer the ground. I followed Lennox, my eyes on his back.

The railings that encircled the building were floodlit, and the open, derelict space was deserted. We walked back round the building. Joe and Adam hadn't caught up with us yet. We hadn't far to go, but as we reached the gates, we saw Adam's car. Gennady was standing beside it.

Chapter
Twenty-Two

There was a weird uncertainty about our group as it oscillated towards him. 'Baz told me.' He was speaking to Lennox. 'He's shitting himself. He'll kill you, baby.'

'Let's get going,' was all Lennox said.

Joe caught up with us.

'Where's Adam?' I said, 'we can't leave him in there. Not if –'

'We gotta go, Judy,' and Joe's hand was heavy on my shoulder. 'The guy wanted to stay there, that's his problem.'

Gennady looked from one to the other. 'You left *Adam* in there? You're crazy or something?'

'This creep turned up. He wouldn't leave.' It was still Joe doing all the talking. 'And – er – he couldn't leave. Could he. Know what I mean.' He winked, and put his finger to the side of his nose.

Lennox had seemed gripped in a kind of icy speechlessness. But now he said, 'Let's just get out of here. Let's go. Now.'

'We take the Alvis,' said Gennady, 'less likely to be stopped, and much faster than the Lada.'

'We can't leave the Lada here, can we,' said Lennox. 'That takes them straight to Justine.'

The wind gusted under the expressway, and large, isolated spots of rain started to fall. The storm was about to break.

I unlocked the car and they all got in. Lennox sat next to me again. I was shaking, and had trouble getting the car in gear.

'Where are we going?' I said.

'Just drive. Get onto the motorway, I'll give you directions from there.'

I was about to reverse when Gennady shouted, 'My bike!' and we had to wait while he got it. Joe and Lennox were getting very tense. I drove round the slip road and filtered up into the traffic. The windows were down. A hot wind blew on our faces. When the rain came down fast, we shut the windows. They steamed up and soon the windscreen was like Niagara Falls as well. Visibility nil.

'Am I glad you're driving slower, Judy. I was shit scared – the way you drove, that stuff can be really unstable, I thought we'd blow up on the freeway.'

'Pity you didn't say so at the time. You didn't exactly ask me if I wanted to be your wheelman.'

Lennox was looking at me, but I stared ahead, trying to see through the torrents of rain that poured down the window.

'You have to tell me where we're going, I can't just drive on indefinitely in this.'

Lennox said, 'Just drive north until you get to the second service area. Someone's meeting us there.'

Gennady exploded.

'Are you crazy? You're mad – I thought we agreed –' He cursed in Russian. 'Your crazy plan – you ruin everything! Amateurs! This is for sure the way to get killed.'

So that was it, the row Myra told me they'd had on the beach.

'You knew the plan,' said Gennady, 'we had the dirt, we'd got Urban, we were going to blow Kingdom wide apart, we could use Anna's stuff, we even got Charles's tape – and now, what you doing? You're giving the guy so much credibility this way! Poor man – an attempt on his life! Okay – he wasn't there but he might have been. And now turns out *Adam*'s there! Someone's killed. Bloody terrorists again. General crackdown. Our story's finished.'

'It's not that big,' said Joe, 'he'll probably survive.'

Gennady laughed. 'Oh, great. So then you're in the shit. They even have witness! Is marvellous.'

'There's still the story.' Lennox stared straight ahead into the rain.

'Makes it better. More of a spectacle,' said Joe.

That was the moment the explosion came, as we swooped along the expressway. It seemed to shake the car – maybe it shook the road.

The others looked back. 'There she goes,' said Joe. 'Boy, that was a big one.'

They couldn't have seen much, through the rain. A flash, maybe. I tried to drive a bit faster, as if getting away from it would help.

'What's all this about Urban Foster?' I said. The question was meant for Lennox, but it was Gennady who answered.

'He had a lot of stuff on Kingdom, he had weird relationship with that guy. He got worried about this, thinks maybe he know too much. We know things as well, we've found out – well, it's Lennox and the Port people – whole lot of stuff, really bad for Kingdom; Forest Brothers, all that, corruption, much more. Your dad's stuff about the past. And Urban, he's so sensitive you know, he has personal problems . . .'

'He's a fucking closet,' muttered Lennox. 'He gave me the card, told me how to get in. He was really in bed with Kingdom, then he got scared. And I suppose you could say we blackmailed him too. He was to run the story. He said he would, anyway.'

'If his editor lets him,' said Gennady, 'and no way this'll help. Still, too late to change your mind now, baby.'

The rain was easing off, and I accelerated. We'd left

the suburbs behind, there was only the indistinct grayish blur of trees and bushes. The string of headlights slid towards us down the southbound carriageway, beading the darkness.

We reached the second service station, and I swung off the motorway and into the familiar banality of petrol pumps and self-serve coffee shops.

'We leave you here, yes?' said Gennady. 'We bring you here, now what you do is your crazy business. Just get the hell out of here.'

Lennox looked at me. 'Justine, I'm sorry,' he said.

My hand lifted itself from the steering wheel and gave him a ringing slap across the cheek. I'd never done that to anyone before, and it was extremely satisfying, another new experience to cherish, and, if possible, repeat.

The red mark faded from his cheek quite quickly.

'I asked for that,' he said.

The rain was still coming down hard, though less ferociously than before. Gennady and I just sat there. I began to shiver. After a while Gennady said, 'He knows he did the wrong thing, you know.'

'Does he?'

'Too bad you're stuck on him, though.'

'I'm not any more. I hope I never see him again. I just want coffee,' I said, 'and then I want to play the tape.'

He got out. When he returned with the coffees he brought out his little flask of brandy. We both took a swig.

'You know, Justine, I liked your dad. Liked him a lot, but all I manage is make problems for him. He never had realised who Kingdom is, you know, didn't recognise him, didn't know the whole story anyway.

'When I tell him – he's mad to go and see Kingdom, he thinks this is great opportunity. But I was wrong, too. We were wrong, the Russian Opposition. Kingdom could never help us. Could have given us money, sure, he would do that, but he could never get the political support I was hoping. That was always stupid idea of ours, of our people back home. I realise too late. If there's big scandal about Kingdom, his pals in the government just ditch him, of course. Yes, it's a scandal, and it's good if it comes out, but they'll do that any day, dump him, do what they have to do, never in a hundred years he's going to make them support socialist insurgents in Russia. So the whole exercise was complete waste of time. Worse than that. I put your father in danger. It's me, I'm responsible for that.'

'Oh, Gennady! He was a grown man. It was his choice.'

But I was so tired of these men and their politics, all their talk and then their crazy actions.

'I move the body, too, you know,' said Gennady. 'That time you come into the Café, the first time, remember. I know who you are. At once. Charles had photograph, and anyway you're looking like him. So when you go upstairs with Adam, I nip up there and listen outside the door. And afterwards I slip away – I have keys to the house, Charles gave me – bloody nearly kill myself getting her down to the ditch.'

'Why though? I don't understand.' I was bewildered – but then so much had been coming at me I couldn't take in anything more.

'I don't want police come nosing around. I don't want anyone finding out it's not Anna at all. Then I come back and Adam's doing his nut –'

'So what about this tape?' I said wearily.

'Yes – the tape, Charles got the tape. I give him this tiny machine, wonderful new machine I find in the Nippon Emporium, so small you can hide it behind a lapel. And Charles was clever, he somehow persuaded Kingdom to talk.'

I slipped the tape into the cassette recorder I'd bought. There was the usual hissing sound of silence as the tape began to unreel. Then Kingdom's voice came clearly, and that sneering laugh of his.

'I heard this already,' said Gennady. 'Charles play it to me right away. Then we edit it, get rid of Charles's voice, for obvious reasons.'

It was weird to hear Kingdom's voice, as though he were sitting beside us in the Lada. 'You ask what really happened. That's not a very philosophical question. Who is to define the real, and so on. And it's all so long ago.'

There was a another sibilant silence. I was afraid something had gone wrong with the tape, or that it hadn't been powerful enough to pick up his words, but then his voice came through again.

'I was born in Vilnius. My father was a clerk, a minor bureaucrat, one of the few, Lithuania being mostly an agricultural country, and he came from a family of peasants, but he was the son that made good, that got an education, so he became different. Petits bourgeois – some of them go to the right, some to the left. He went to the left. Became a Communist. My mother was German, one of the German minority. Well, things got rather rough, you know, and he went to Moscow. There, he must have fallen out of favour. Not an uncommon fate. So he was liquidated. Or died in a prison camp. I never found out what happened to him.

'After 1939 in Lithuania everyone was very frightened that the Soviets were coming. Any minute now. My mother was bitter and disillusioned, she didn't know what to do, her husband had left her, that's how it seemed, she was frightened of the Russian soldiers too, just like her neighbours, like everyone. She decided to go to Germany.

'Yes, when the Red Army was coming, she got out and she left me behind. I can never forgive her for that. Left me with an aunt, my father's sister. And yet I can understand it in a way.

'You have no idea how life was during those years. Shall

243

I tell you something? No one has ever really recovered from that period. Oh – we thought we had: the fifties, the boom. We're feeling better again, in the West at any rate. Things improve. Life's normal at last. In the East, however, all that poison is simply frozen. It's all there beneath the Stalinist permafrost waiting to burst open again. Not that I regret the passing of the glorious Soviet Union. No, no, don't get me wrong there. It's more a question of – how does it go – the famous lines by the poet Dryden?

> All, all of a piece throughout;
> Thy chase had a beast in view;
> Thy wars brought nothing about;
> Thy lovers were all untrue.
> Tis well an old age is out,
> And time to begin a new.

'Unfortunately the new has turned out to be just like the old, don't you agree? But perhaps that's what he meant to imply –

> The world was a fool, e'er since it begun,
> And since neither Janus, nor Chronos, nor I,
> Can hinder the crimes,
> Or mend the bad times,
> Tis better to laugh than to cry.'

'I do so agree, don't you? "'Tis better to laugh than to cry." An excellent motto.

'Anyway, those six, seven years of the war were almost unimaginable. You look back, and you think, how did I survive? But you did. And once you survived that, you know that you will survive everything. But everything. For ever. Believe me, my friend.

'Now, when the Red Army came, it wasn't the real

Communists they worked with. It was more a question of collaboration. And I wasn't keen on the Communists anyway. My father had always been a hard man to me. And anyway, he'd gone. I had no time for the glorious revolution and Lithuanian socialist republic. Fifteen years old, and already I was too much a realist for that. For me it was just a question of survival.

'Well, there was a strong Lithuanian resistance movement you know, maybe if I'd known anyone, that's what I would have joined, it was touch and go, I daresay. But I was no longer in Vilnius, I was on my aunt's farm. Not that there weren't patriots in the countryside too, but I didn't meet them at the critical moment. Instead, very soon, with the produce and so on, I found my way into the black market that was beginning. It was dangerous, of course, but I was very young, very innocent looking. And anyway, everything about life was dangerous. That made it exciting, in a way.

'The Russians were rounding people up and deporting them – to work for them, or to fight. Everyone hated them. They were an occupying army. No one ever accepted that Lithuania could become part of the Soviet Union. Men like my father, the few Communists that there had been, it was different then. Before the war, there was a sort of fascist régime, much milder than Hitler – of course you know all this, my friend – but I suppose you can't be surprised that the workers should oppose it, that's what the trades unions and the workers' parties and organisations, and the intellectuals are there for, after all, isn't it? It's their destiny to oppose. You know all about that. And men like my father – bright, intelligent, couldn't get on as far as he'd have liked – well, naturally that would appeal to him too, he bought the dream of socialism.

'Then in July 1941 the Germans took Vilnius. The Russians were in full retreat. It was the turn of the Germans to occupy. At first, people were pleased. Anything was better than the Slav pigs. For the Baltic peoples are not Slavs. They are a very ancient people. The language is quite close to Sanscrit, the most ancient Indo-European language.

'But the honeymoon with the Germans didn't last long, either. People collaborated, of course, a lot of people had some fun killing Jews, there were many who sided with the Nazis, who *became* Nazis, but the Resistance movement was also strong. There were more deportations, more round-ups, more conscription. People were sent to work in Germany.

'I merely adapted my black market activities to the new conditions. It's money that counts, you know. I learned that early on. Greed, hunger, the will to live, are all so much more important than your philosophies, or your high-sounding political words. I would not say I became a fascist. People of your sort throw such words around so easily, you know. Anyone or anything you don't like is 'fascist' or 'racist'. I hate exaggeration, the impreciseness of that.

'After a time, however, I had to go into hiding. Life was more and more difficult. They were closing in. By this time, Germany was really defeated already, although the war still went on. Now we began to fear the return of the Russians. We knew they'd be back. So men, women and children, everyone who could move began to flood into Germany itself. Sounds crazy, doesn't it – to rush like lemmings into that defeated country. But that's what happened.

'For young men like me – remember I was nineteen by now – it had become more dangerous than ever. We were too visible. The Germans had press gangs to round us up for forced labour in their factories. But we usually managed to keep just one step ahead. We wandered the countryside, kept to the little back roads in that lost German landscape for months.

'We lived from hand to mouth. It's amazing what you

can do if you have to! You live from day to day, thinking of nothing but the next piece of bread. That's as far as you think. And yet I never thought I would die. That never occurred to me. I knew I'd survive.

'Then came the bombings. I was not in Dresden you understand, although there were those who escaped even from that inferno, but there were rumours, people knew. We tried to move West, the Russians were behind us again, on our heels.

'I worked on a farm for a while. The woods were full of deserters, soldiers, refugees. I suppose I could have stayed in Lithuania, joined the Forest Brothers, the resistance. Sometimes I wished I had. But what for? Nationalism! National music, national dress, national religion. To die for one's country – that wasn't for me.

'Eventually, I was caught. By the Germans, that is. They rounded people up and made us go into the ruined cities and dig out the corpses. This was horrible work, back-breaking work. One time I remember I came to a foot sticking up out of the rubble. I dug some more. Now I could see part of the body. I pulled the foot then – and the leg came off. Just like that. Sometimes you would come on a shelter that had had rubble fall over it during a raid and when you opened it, they were all sitting there on their benches, dead as mutton. Just sitting there. Poisoned by fumes.

'We had a uniform of sorts. That made it difficult to escape. But I had one or two things up my sleeve. I bribed the German who was in charge of us with some brandy and cigarettes I had hidden away, and he gave me a pass. So I was free once more. I didn't dare get on a train, that would have been too dangerous. And I hadn't any money. So I just simply walked from city to city. The smoking ruins were everywhere. And one night I came to a city – didn't even know where it was – and I was picking my way through the craters and the – it was like the skeleton of a city, the walls with no roofs, with holes where the windows had been. It was a moonlit night. I might as well have been on the moon. I felt as if I was the last person in the world. The only person in the world. But do you know, I suddenly had this extraordinary feeling of exhilaration: because this loneliness made me the freest person in the world. I thought, "What does it matter what happens to me – or to anyone? What does it matter what I do? I can do anything. It makes no difference." That was a moment of such great freedom, the most important of my life, perhaps.

'Well, so the war was ending. For a time I worked on a farm. Now, as luck would have it, I was in the American zone. And in the American zone there was the most flourishing black market you have ever encountered in your life. *"Speculacija"*! That's what we called it. So I began to organise the produce from the farm in such a way as to be able to barter some of it in return for what the American soldiers could give us – chocolate, coffee, soap, pens, lighters. But above all, cigarettes. Cigarettes were the basic currency in the fantasy world that was postwar Germany. And after a while I began to act as go-between. For a few packs of cigarettes I could help those American GIs on their way to – whatever they wanted to ship home: fur coats, silverware, Meissen china, even grand pianos.

'Unfortunately, I then did something stupid and dangerous. I shot an American. This American must have been one of the few straight guys in the whole of the American zone. He was determined to put an end to the black market, he was going to pull the plug on the whole thing. Now that would have been just as uncomfortable for a lot of Americans, so I daresay it was quite convenient for them that he was out of the way. On the other hand, they could hardly turn a blind eye. People were dying every day, in their hundreds of thousands, but an American soldier, that was a bit different.

'So now I was in real trouble. And I decided the only thing to do was to somehow get into the British zone. We were quite near the dividing line, but I had no idea how to cross it. Time was short. I was sure I was about to be arrested.

'My black market contacts were no good to me now. They needed me where I was. I couldn't even tell them, they'd have killed me themselves when I became a liability.

'But then, by good luck, there was a visit to the farm. A contingent of British officers. Remember it? Of course you do. Our first meeting. I hung around and I heard you and Colin talking. You'd wandered away from the others and were smoking in a corner of the yard. You were so earnest, so sincere, saying how terrible the Americans were with all their black marketeering and profiteering. You remember? "Just businessmen in uniform," you said. And as you talked, I recognised that way of talking. It was the Communist way. I knew that from the way my father talked. An international language. I recognised it even in English. I'd picked up English by this time. Without languages you were lost, I can tell you. Made sense though. Why not? So I got talking with you.

'You remember, don't you – how I made out like I was a Communist too. I spun you a wonderful yarn. How the Americans had rumbled me, how anti-Communist they were. I really laid it on thick, didn't I?

'"But surely you can go back to Lithuania now? It's part of the Soviet Union. What's stopping you?" That's what you said. Oh God, it makes me laugh, even today. I had to think fast. "I'm on a mission," I said. "I've got to get to your country."'

'And you swallowed it! You swallowed it whole! Of course, you were only kids – well, the same age as me. Just think of it – the same age as me. But what had you seen? Nothing! Oh a little of the post-war Germany. That incredible fantasy world. But you were innocents. Or at least *you* were. Colin was a little different, wasn't he?

'You were alarmed at first, when I kind of suggested

you should help me get out, get into the British zone. But Colin was excited. He loved the whole idea.

'So we hatched our plan, didn't we? Soon I was sure that Colin was a bit of a kindred spirit – he said there'd be no problem getting me a pass. "The Military government's incredibly overstaffed," he told me, "we've got nothing to do but write letters, hand out permits, whole thing's a bloody farce."

'He was really the one, wasn't he, who smuggled me into the British zone? It was an enormous pity I had to leave my black market contacts, but in general the British zone was a much better proposition. The British liked the Balts. We were the "good" displaced persons. At least we weren't Slavs or Jews, after all. Mind you, the zone was run as if it were an outpost of the British Empire. The officers actually referred to "the natives". You must have hated them. But it was all so much easier there. The British weren't so careful in the DP camps, there wasn't so much screening. The Americans were tougher – although of course a lot of that was to get hold of Nazis and use them, not punish them at all, as I'm sure you know.

'There were plans for us Balts after the war, weren't there? How many hundreds of fascists were let into Britain?' He laughed. 'It was a joke, wasn't it? I needn't have bothered with you and Fox and all that cloak and dagger stuff at all. They let *everyone* in – collaborators, Nazis, they were only too pleased, they had plans for all of them.

'But for me, that was the problem. I didn't want to be part of their plans. I hadn't any information to give them, but neither did I want to be parachuted back into the Soviet Union by MI5 when they started the Third World War. I wanted to do it on my own. MI5 might have stuck me in some Lithuanian community in the provinces. I'd have lasted about five minutes. I'd soon have been found with a knife in my back up some dark alley.

'I began to think that Colin was into some little scam

of his own. He was what you used to call an adventurist, wasn't he? What he liked was the danger. He was one of those men who only live in wartime, don't you think, like so many of those Resistance types. Fell apart after it was all over.

'He had a good idea of what was going on, though. Unlike you, old man, if I may say so. He knew that not everything was so rosy in the good old USSR. He knew people got purged. And I think he thought that I was one of them maybe, a Communist, but an oppositionalist. And I kind of went along with that, dropped little hints. It was our unspoken secret. We protected you from it.

'Funny that. On the surface it was so clear – you the idealist, and Colin the cynic. But when I look back I don't think it was like that at all. You're no fool, are you? Maybe you were an innocent then, but later you knew the score. And you stayed in the Party to the end. You could bite on the bullet – can't make an omelette without breaking eggs, all that sort of thing, it was Colin who was the romantic. He realised communism wasn't all sweetness and light, and he couldn't take it.

'I never discovered exactly what Colin was up to, but he had first-class contacts. He got all the papers I needed. Didn't you ever wonder about that? Didn't it ever seem as if there was something that needed explaining?

'But there it was. I got away. A new identity. And then we were back in England together, all three of us. You were so good to me. I know it sounds awfully hollow, but I was grateful to you, you know. You helped me no end.

'But it was all so awkward. I couldn't go on pretending I was a Communist. Suppose they found out, someone at the Party headquarters, I mean. I had to carry on with the story about my secret mission, but it wasn't worked out, it just made people suspicious. And then I met Joyce. We all met Joyce. Don't be angry with me, please. Joyce was such a lovely girl. Full of hope, full of beauty, full of idealism . . . so prim, so serious, so sweet. It was a mistake, though, of course. A hostage to fortune. And so what with one thing and another, eventually I decided that there was no help for it – I just had to disappear.

'I changed my name again. No longer was I Vitas Valaitis; no longer was I even Francis Walker, the Englishman I'd become. Now I changed again. I rechristened myself Alex Kingdom. Now I was really on my own. Once more, it was a matter of survival. Naturally, I turned to what I had experience of: the black market. It wasn't so good in Britain, but I got by. And later I cleaned up on property. That was the big opportunity. Prime sites no one wanted. Whole high streets going for a song. Half-bombed houses in rundown areas that got gentrified fifteen years later. That's how I started.

'After a few years, things were beginning to look up. I was taking a law degree. I was already beginning to think of a career in politics. And then one fine day, who should turn up but Colin. It was as I said – he basically fell apart after the war. He was drinking, of course. He'd fallen out with the comrades – and here he was, turning up to blackmail me. How had he found out my new name? Or where I was living? Well, he was a newshound, even if he had become a drunken cynic. He was a freelance by now, keeping track of big business. He'd noticed my name, he'd followed me up, he realised that I'd come from nowhere, and then sooner or later he saw a photograph. Routine stuff, really. It was simply that he recognised my photo. Stupid of me. I shouldn't have let it happen. I'd changed my appearance to some extent, of course. But it didn't fool him.

'Now why did I let him blackmail me all those years? Maybe it was a lingering sense of gratitude. He'd got me out of Germany, after all. So I paid him off for a while. For a long while, actually. Too long. After all, as I say, he'd saved my bacon. I'm a man of honour, too, in my own way, you know. All those years, we were both helping him, you and I.

'You and Joyce. Did you know that Joyce had come to see me about it? She came to tell me I mustn't pay Colin off. She didn't understand. She didn't realise he'd found out all about my past in Lithuania. She'd known nothing about that, it goes without saying. But Colin knew the whole story.

'She was so upset, so tortured by it all. Wanting to hear it wasn't true, of course, that I hadn't done those things.

'Basically, though, she was right. It was a mistake to have paid him off for so long. I was beginning to go places politically, and he was a liability. What happened to him? I really can't remember. He got run over, fell off a cliff, something like that, sort of thing that'd happen to someone who's blind drunk all the time.

'After that, everything was fine. It was all going to plan. Until now. Until the Port group turned up. And now your Russian friend. Why have you come here to see me? Why are you doing this for him? What's in it for you, you'll only get hurt. Keep out of it, I beg you. Your community action friends are very well meaning, but they should steer clear of this other riff-raff.

'You see, it wasn't just that I'd killed a man in Germany – well, more than one, as it happens – or that I'd been a kind of collaborator in the war. Who cared about that! No one even knew any more, or so I thought. It wasn't just that I'd been a crooked business lawyer, although that could've put paid to my political career. It wasn't that Colin fell off a cliff – for who was ever going to pin that on me. It wasn't even the port development. No – I have to hand it to your friends – between them they found out something more. They discovered I'd financed Albion – well, I *created* Albion. Terrorism. Of course it's always there. But this was to be on an altogether larger scale. It was going to be –'

The tape clicked and stopped.

We sat in the car in silence.

Gennady said something in Russian again. He fidgeted around in his seat. 'It's no proof of anything,' he said. 'You recognise his voice? Yes – but – so what. Is never going to stand up – yes, maybe a journalist buy it. But it's hundred to one he can ever use the stuff. *Jesus Christ.*' And he banged his first against his head.

'There's the document,' I said, 'Anna's document.'

'I seen the bloody document. Is completely useless as well. No photograph – nothing. Who can prove this is anything to do with Kingdom? We're living in fantasy world here.'

'Why on earth did he say all that to my father? What could have possessed him? It doesn't make sense.'

'You know what I think, baby? When I heard it before, I thought like you say, this is crazy, for this man to spout out his life story this way. Course he doesn't know about the miniature recorder, but all the same, it's a strange thing to do. But now I listen again, I think, you know, he's *boasting*. He's so pleased. Like he said. He's invulnerable. He's got away with everything. *Everything.* Just think of it. He thinks nothing – but nothing – is ever going to get him. And there's poor Charles, whose wife really loved Kingdom and married Charles on the rebound, who backed the wrong horse, who's just a retired professor. He *loved* it. He thinks he's the hottest thing on earth. He thinks no one will ever catch up with him.'

'I don't expect they ever will.'

Chapter
Twenty-Three

I loved the Café in the early evening. That was the time for promising encounters, for a second wind and a first margarita. That was the time the guests were most at home, curled up on the sofas in intimate têtes-à-tête, or shouting and laughing in groups round the tables. That was the longed-for hour in the timeless time of the Café, when friends and lovers met, when plots were laid, and poses struck, and everyone expanded and relaxed, watching the larger spectacle of the city crowds through the windows, yet always part of the spectacle in the Lost Time Café.

Gennady stood by the till, and smiled as he watched the rooms. The Vietnamese pianist was about to play, flexing her fingers and setting off a first little ripple of notes, which slid like balls of silver mercury across a surface of laughter and talk.

Gennady was my manager. He went back to Russia, after what happened, but the underground movement sent him back to Kakania again. He said they felt he'd be most useful over here. Better than living a hunted life out in the backwoods of greater Russia, I reckoned. One day he would go back again, I knew, but for the moment the Café was his home, as it is for all exiles.

Myra billowed in. She'd started telling fortunes on the premises. She was a big draw – the Café was more crowded than ever. She used the balcony. Sometimes they queued on the stairs to consult her.

I needed to expand. Jack's group were organising a consortium, now that the port development land had been released to them. Yes, the community scheme was going ahead after all. They were starting to build social housing, workshops, small shops for artisans. There was nothing else the National Coalition could do, after all the dirt on Kingdom and Forest Brothers came out.

Forest Brothers – why did he call it that? Deep down in his heart he maybe wanted to believe he'd once been a partisan. Every man wants to have a glorious war record.

The truth was less glorious, even for me. Adam left me the Café in his will. I was to have had the Alvis too, but that was a write-off after the bomb, the bomb that killed Adam.

There was a moral dilemma there, wasn't there? I hadn't really tried to make Adam leave the building. Hadn't really stood up to that dickhead Joe. And nor had Lennox – Lennox saw that Adam'd be the fatal witness. So he and I had let it happen. I think Joe knocked him out – or worse – before he left. For Adam's death was rather a mystery. The bomb did extensive damage to Kingdom's flying saucer building, yet the floor on which Adam's body was found was relatively unscathed. They did a post mortem, found he had a fractured skull, due to a fall perhaps, as he'd tried to escape . . .

'Lucky for you he's brown bread,' said Gennady heartlessly, 'is better for you that way. He was going quietly round the bend, you know that, don't you? He had crazy ideas about you.'

So there was a moral dilemma. But what could I do? I couldn't – I just couldn't – say no to the Café. Gennady was right, too, that Adam was on some downward spiral of his own, his obsession with me, being mixed up with Kingdom . . . And after all, he would have let me die, he sent me out to Angel Point. The way he acted didn't make sense. He must have been round the bend.

I remember once my Uncle Henry expounding the difference between a cad and a bounder. One was more upper-class. I forget which. It made my father furious – what public school rubbish, he said. These days the distinction would have to be between a prat and a nerd, or a dickhead and a creep. Or a shit. Was Adam a shit or a creep? I'm not quite sure. Or was he just a man without a centre, who drifted with the tide?

Even if he was a creep or a shit or a madman, I don't know that he deserved to die. I don't know if I had the right to benefit either.

I got what I wanted, though. Or part of it. I might have seemed like a victim, or passive, or not in control of things, but that wouldn't be true. Not really.

So far as the media was concerned, the bomb was a mystery. No one was ever charged, although Joe was picked up not long afterwards in the course of a botched-up bank raid. At first word went round it was the Irish; next they thought it was the Russians; later an Albion splinter group issued a communiqué, and said they'd planted the bomb. Later still everyone lost interest – and by that time there were different bombs in other places to think about anyway.

Gennady and I persuaded Urban Foster to write the story on Kingdom's shady deals. Indeed, Urban didn't take much persuasion. He must have calculated that the moment had come to bite the hand that had fed him. The media had a field day.

Rumours had been circulating for months, and once the *Daily Post* decided to run them, the whole pack savaged Kingdom. His rivals in the government joined in, he was forced to resign, there was a public inquiry, a full-scale police investigation, prosecutions loomed; it turned out to involve so many people, the banks, the government, everyone.

So Roland Rodgers, the plump and Brussels-nurtured *bon vivant* became the next Prime Minister.

Meanwhile, in all the hubbub, Kingdom slipped away, helped, no doubt, by influential friends. From time to time there's a sighting – in Australia, in the Bahamas, even, ironically, in Central Europe.

Baz got his radio station going – though he can never have seen the money I gave Lennox. It isn't even a pirate station any more, he has a studio, he's part of a network, it's a big programme for minorities.

As for Lennox – well, Lennox just disappeared. I sometimes wonder how he'd feel if he knew I'd taken on the Café, and recreated it just as it had been when Khan was there.

Anna and I walked right out to Angel Point one day. It was high tide. Suddenly Anna pulled something from her bag and with a violent gesture, hurled it into the sea. 'That stupid document,' she said. 'The only point of hanging on to it was if we wanted something out of *him*. I don't know why I kept it for so long. Fear, I suppose – that he might come after me anyway, and I'd have nothing to bargain with, and he wouldn't believe I didn't have it.'

It might be washed back up on to the beach again. Someone might find it, but it wouldn't matter now, and anyway, as Gennady said, it could never have proved that Alex Kingdom had once been Vitas Valaitas. Now that my father and Colin are dead, there's no one who knows that for sure.

In any case, who knows but Vitas Valaitas has a new lease of life, and is playing the black market again, in Vilnius, or Riga, or maybe in Moscow itself.

The police did one thing right. They nailed Anna's husband, Paul. They proved it was he who'd killed the woman he thought was Anna. He got six years on a plea of manslaughter. They said he'd been under stress; he was upset because Anna had left him. His story was that someone had sent him the keys to my father's house through the post, and the address, that he'd been tipped off that that's where Anna was living. Kingdom again, I suppose – as everything began to unravel, or at least as he started to feel endangered, and yet was so close to his final goal, he began to overplay his hand and imagine he could do anything with impunity.

Paul learned at the trial, of course, that he'd killed the wrong woman, so he knows now that Anna's still around. He'll be out of prison in a couple of years, and none of us has worked out what to do.

I did one thing right, too. I held a memorial service for my father. Helped by Jack, I organised a meeting, a celebration of his life. It was a great occasion. His friends spoke. We sang both verses of the Internationale. Everyone came back to the Café afterwards.

Star went to work with Wilma, filming the last of the Amazon tribes. That was better for me, too. She reminded me too much of Lennox. I'm really a loner. A voyeur. I like the spectacle, the flirting, the dance on the surface, it's all that love and obsession that drags you down.

Work was the thing. The Café took up all my time. I had so much to learn, and I loved it. There was hardly any energy left over for meeting someone new. I see Jade, we have something going, but it's on a strictly casual basis so far as I'm concerned.

Yes, the Lost Time Café was my great love now.

Epilogue

        I leant on my corner of the bar, as usual, and admired myself in the mirror I'd just bought. It was a Millenial Art piece, and I'd hung it on the wall opposite the bar in the main room.

I looked just like a boy now. I was wearing a new black velvet jacket, and my head was almost shaved.

I was mixing a couple of daiquiris when the Café door swung open and hissed to. I didn't look round. I was busy with the ice.

Someone came and stood close across the bar from me.

'Justine.' That voice! It was so casual and intimate, as if he'd seen me yesterday. 'It's me. I've come back.'

It was the great impostor himself. He looked just the same, the same as ever.

'Justine – don't look so upset. I thought you'd be pleased to see me.'

Other books by Elizabeth Wilson

THE SPHINX IN THE CITY

'Cities, like dreams, are made of desires and fears'
– *Italo Calvino*

Elizabeth Wilson's elegant, provocative and scholarly study uses fiction, essays, film and art, as well as history and sociology, to look at some of the world's greatest cities – London, Paris, Moscow, New York, Chicago, Lusaka and São Paulo – and presents a powerful critique of utopian planning, anti-urbanism, postmodernism and traditional architecture. For women the city offers freedom, including sexual freedom, but also new dangers. Planners and reformers have repeatedly attempted to regulate women – and the working class and ethnic minorities – by means of grandiose, utopian plans, nearly destroying the richness of urban culture. City centres have become uninhabited business districts, the countryside suburbanised. There is danger without pleasure, consumerism without choice, safety without stimulation. What is urgently needed is a new vision of city life.

ADORNED IN DREAMS
Fashion and Modernity

Fashionable dress and the beautification of the self are often perceived as a form of behaviour, and within feminism as an expression of women's oppression. In this fascinating and provocative book, Elizabeth Wilson argues that to see fashion exclusively in these ways is to ignore the richness – and paradox – of its many cultural and political meanings. From fashion's rise in early capitalist society to its role in post-modernist culture; from fashion as the exclusive preserve of the rich to dress as a means of self-expression for the majority and of counter-cultural solidarity for minorities, she views it through a variety of lenses – aesthetics, social theory, psychology – in order 'to see what it has to say about the dreams and aspirations of a given epoch'.

Beautifully illustrated, and daring and multi-faceted in its perspective, *Adorned in Dreams* rehabilitates fashion as an exciting aspect of popular culture. It goes beyond the politics of gender and class to reflect the complexity, vitality and allure of fashion itself.